THE BUNNY AND T[...]

A dozen hidden eggs later, Bun became bored. He jumped up the slope and over the top of it while I worked. About thirty minutes later, I realized his absence was too long. It wasn't like Bun to go off without me for great lengths of time.

Returning to the spot where he'd taken off, I glanced at the moss where he might have left tracks when he returned. The soft moss showed nothing, so I looked closer and was startled when Bun flew from the brush on the slope. He tried to stop when he hit the paved path, but skidded to the other side of the trail and ended up tangled in a shrub.

Whatever Bun found upset him enough to send him rushing through the woods to find me. Certain I wouldn't be thrilled with whatever it was, I knew in my gut that I'd downright dislike it. "Tell me what's happened."

"I can't. I have to show you. Come on, follow me into the woods."

In the clearing, wildflowers grew in patches and green grass popped up around them. A mowed grassy oval lay just ahead and dipped somewhat. Before I could take another step, Bun warned, *"Continue carefully, very carefully."*

A mound of cloth lay in the center of the oval. I cupped a hand above my eyebrows to block the glare of the sun for a better view. When I realized it wasn't simply fabric, I gasped out loud, took a step back, and tripped over Bun. I hit the ground hard, spilling the contents of my bucket. Brightly colored eggs rolled away as I gawked at the body of Della Meeny . . .

Books by J.M. Griffin

LEFT FUR DEAD

WHO'S DEAD, DOC?

HOP 'TIL YOU DROP

Published by Kensington Publishing Corp.

Hop 'Til You Drop

J. M. GRIFFIN

KENSINGTON
PUBLISHING CORP.

www.kensingtonbooks.com

Chapter 1

Rabbits hopped about in their oversized playpen. Only one rabbit remained in her hutch, the one who would soon deliver a slew of kits. Bun, my housemate rabbit and sleuth partner, had joined the others while I finished chores. About to add water to each water bin, our in-house veterinarian, Jessica, called me to Petra's cage. The rabbit's sweet nature, long-haired fur coat, and beautiful coloring always drew a fan club of kids whenever she went to parties. We'd taught Petra tricks, but now that she was pregnant, the children's party days were behind her.

"Petra's doing very well. She should deliver her kits within the next week or two."

"You don't think she'll have any difficulty, do you?" I reached into the cage and smoothed Petra's coat. A social rabbit with soft, luxurious fur, she seemed to enjoy the attention.

Jess secured the cage door after I hooked a veggie-wrapped pocket of fruit onto the wire inside. "I'll be right here just in case. Not to worry, Jules."

We walked the aisles, added the same type of pockets to each rabbit cage, and filled water bins. As we moved along, I said, "I've been invited to participate as a volunteer, of course, in Windermere's Easter celebration. The council has decided to hold a Hop 'Til You Drop event and egg hunt." I stepped closer to Jess and whispered, "I'm wondering if I should take Bun."

"You have to. He'll be devastated if you don't. You know how sociable Bun is."

"I suppose you're right. He's great company, too."

"What will your job consist of?"

"Hiding eggs for the kids to find. We'll place them along the trail at Perkins Park. It's such a marvelous location for this sort of event. It seems several volunteers, besides me, will handle that part of the program."

"Then Bun won't get underfoot, and he'll enjoy the freedom of scampering around while you are busy with the eggs."

I thought about it for a minute. "He would have a good time. I guess I will take him." I leaned against a beam near the end of an aisle. "He needs exercise as much as I do."

Jess rolled her eyes. "I have patients to see. I'll check in with you later. Jason and Molly will be here today. I'm not sure what time, though."

I watched as she went off to her clinic. My helpers, Molly and Jason, were the only workers I had now that Peter, a college student, had moved on. Molly, enrolled in classes at the local college, taught spinning and weaving classes in my yarn shop classroom. I wasn't sure how much longer Jason would work for me before I'd have to seek out a new employee. So far, I'd had great luck in finding kids who enjoyed working with the rabbits.

Once the rabbits returned to their hutches and munched their snacks, I folded the pen and tucked it away while Bun yammered on about the upcoming egg hunt and festivities.

"You are taking me along, aren't you? I can most certainly assist in finding the best places to tuck Easter eggs. Places easy enough for the kids to find. I am going, right?"

"Of course. Where would I be without your help?" It wasn't as if I couldn't find places to put the eggs, but I knew he needed reassurance. I was concerned that he'd find some mischief to get into while we were there.

After entering the house, I fed Bun and made a snack to eat out on the porch. The air was fragrant with the scent of spring and smelled glorious. Flowers bloomed and the trees had blossomed in the yard. The sight and smell of such sweetness was heavenly.

I considered the risks of having Bun along on the egg-hiding end of the hop. I never used a collar or leash on Bun. He was smart enough to stay within a reasonable distance from me and not wander too far away. Of course, he'd get bored if he wasn't put to work, so his self-proclaimed skills to seek places to hide the eggs could work in my favor.

It would have been difficult to leave him home while I volunteered at the park. His feelings would be hurt, and I'd never hear the end of it. You see, Bun and I are best buds. We solve mysteries together, hang out all the time, and best of all, I know he always has my best interests at heart, just as I have his.

Bun had come to the farm by way of an animal rescue team that worked in and around Windermere. A woman and her family had abused Bun because they couldn't accept the fact that he communicated by way of telepathy. Determined and insisting he was the spawn of Satan, they made Bun's life dreadful and a misery. To this day, Bun finds violence and anger appalling. He'd tried for some time to convince me he was able to communicate, and eventually I realized he was able to talk to me without the ability to speak out loud. We've relished every moment of his communication skill ever since, other than when he nags me, that is.

His problem, the same one I admit to, is that he likes a good mystery. We both favor a genuine whodunit that needs solving, as long as we don't end up being done in by the killer. We've come close to it on occasion, but being survivors, Bun and I take care of ourselves and each other.

I'd eaten the last of the nuts and fruit mix and peeked into Bun's room and heard his sweet, tiny snore. His dreamer's wiggly whiskers meant he'd been asleep for a while. I left him to it and set off for the yarn shop connected to the barn.

New yarns were ready to sort and price. The display racks had lots of empty spaces to fill. The sale Molly had recommended succeeded in getting rid of our overstock, and only a few skeins of sale yarn were left. I set a large box on the counter, tore it open, and before I could empty it onto the countertop, brightly colored skeins of yarn popped out and spread across the counter, then tumbled to the floor. I scooped up one armful after another, certain Molly was scheduled to arrive any moment.

The phone rang as I stuffed hanks of yarn into the box.

I fumbled with loose skeins to answer the call. I sighed, picked up the phone, and said, "Jules Bridge."

"Jules, this is Alvin Peterson. I wanted to speak to you concerning the Easter egg Hop 'Til You Drop event."

Alvin sounded rather uptight. Whether that was his usual behavior, I didn't know. I spoke in a soft tone before I became uptight, too. "What can I do for you?"

"Della Meeny will be in charge of the scoop and stash station, where you're assigned to work. She mentioned you've worked events with a puppeteer and mentioned I should ask you for more information. Do you think the puppeteer would entertain at our event?"

"I'm certain she would if her schedule is open. Why don't you give me your phone number and I'll have her call you. Her name is Bailey Kimball."

"That would be very helpful, thank you."

I quickly jotted his number on a notepad and promised either Bailey or I would be in touch.

Wasting no time, I called Bailey. I repeated Alvin's invite and offered his information. I listened to her chatter excitedly over how thrilled she was. She was right to feel this way, since it offered us an opportunity to expand our business contacts. That alone was better than any advertisement we could generate.

The call ended as Molly parked in front of the shop. Aware of the mess I'd been in the middle of before the call came in, I hurried to get the yarn in order. Molly's grin widened when she saw the colorful piles of yarn.

"Having fun?" Molly asked.

I heaved a sigh, gave her a grin in return, and explained what happened.

"You should know by now that skeins of yarn are always squashed into the boxes for shipping. Though, I wish it wasn't. It always seems to explode from the boxes when I open them. Give me a minute and I'll help you with that." She hung up her coat, stuck her handbag under the counter, and began by asking for the invoice.

"I know you haven't handled this in some time. Before we display the yarn, let's do an inventory of what the boxes contain."

To help her by unpacking the yarn before Molly's arrival, I had forgotten the importance of an inventory. Lately, I'd been too busy with mystery-solving and rabbit care to pay attention to this end of the business. Ashamed by my lack of attention to the shop, I leaned against the counter and said, "I've neglected the shop and you. I'm sorry."

Her eyes wide, a look of surprise crossed her features. "Don't be silly, Jules. I don't feel neglected in the least. As a matter of fact, I'm happy you have enough confidence in my abilities to let me handle the shop the way I do. You even give me a free hand in running the classes, which has increased my confidence. It's been helpful in my classes at college, too. I've learned some marketing skills while working here by seeing how you and Jessica each operate your businesses. I thank you for that."

Relieved and pleased to think Molly could hold her own and did it very well reassured me that I needn't hover over her shoulder. "Super. Let's get this job done."

In an hour or so, we finished the inventory and displayed the various yarns and hanks of wool for spinning. Pricing as we went left me impressed with Molly's way of working to create an atmosphere geared to shoppers. The shop had been in the red before my former employee came on the scene. When Molly took over, the business began to pay for itself and make a profit. I had lucked out when Molly said she wanted to run the shop and earn a college degree in fiber arts.

About to leave, I saw Bailey arrive and watched her rush toward the shop. Her excitement evident, Bailey could barely stand still. "I'm on my way to Perkins Park. Alvin will meet me there to go over a few things. Would you like to come along?"

I hesitated until Molly said, "Go on, I'll handle things here. Is Bun in the house?"

"He's napping. Could you check on him while I'm gone?"

She nodded, and I left with Bailey.

On the drive to Perkins Park, we talked nonstop. The construction of tents and canopies was well underway. A flatbed tractor trailer, loaded with tables and whatnot, had backed up to one tent, while another, smaller truck waited in line. Signposts were being erected. Activity abounded, leaving an impression of ants on a mound.

A medium-height, thin man, stared at Bailey's van and raised his hand for us to stop. He stepped to Bailey's side window and asked, "Are you Miss Kimball?"

She nodded.

"I'm Alvin Peterson. Nice to meet you." Alvin waved us to the left side of a tent. "You can park over there, at the eggcellent creation station. We'll talk inside."

"Okay." Bailey parked where he indicated. Before we left the van, she murmured, "They've got a good marketer. The names of the various tents draw attention and the grounds are huge. It's a perfect spot for this affair."

I gawked at all that went on and agreed. "I'm assigned to the scoop and stash station not far from here." I pointed to the canopied spot. All the canopies and tents were draped with what appeared to be sheets of white plastic that had huge Easter eggs printed on them. Children would find the colors fascinating. I wondered what else the committee had arranged for the attendees.

Inside the eggcellent tent, Alvin guided us to a table at the far end, out of the way of workers. Alvin waited until we were seated and asked if we wanted a beverage. Surprised when a young man stepped forward with a tray of drinks, I chose water while Bailey took lemonade. Alvin sipped his drink and, if I wasn't mistaken, it contained whiskey; the smell had wafted into my nostrils when a light breeze wended its way past.

"This is quite an undertaking, Mr. Peterson," I remarked.

"It is. We've never had this particular type of event. I'm pleased you could be with us this year. I'm sure the farm keeps you rather busy. You'll be bringing your rabbit, won't you?"

"I sure will. Bun loves the kids."

"Wonderful." His interest turned toward Bailey. "I'm unfamiliar with your puppets, but have heard lots of great stories about them. Tell me. What could you bring to our event in the way of a theme that would fit in?"

Quick as a wink, Bailey explained what she would do in the way of an Easter Bunny puppet show. Surprised to hear she had bunny puppets, I considered a show we could put together that would include a rabbit theme in the future. We might be able to increase our party reservations if we worked a theme at times. Hmm.

Questions and answers flew back and forth between Alvin and Bailey. I leaned back in the chair, sipped water, and wished I had a sandwich to go with it.

Satisfied with the results of their mutual interviews, since each of them had truly interviewed the other, I walked away when the time came to discuss payment for Bailey's act and various particulars.

"I'm going to walk the trail. Call my cell phone when you're finished," I said to Bailey.

She gave me a nod and I left them alone. The path was closer to the stash station than the eggcellent one was. I took the path thickly bordered by trees and bushes. Everything was loaded with buds and leaves. From the look of the growth, it wouldn't take long for everything to bloom fully. With ample places to hide Easter eggs for kids to find, I noted obvious spots.

My excitement grew as I went along the path and was ready to return to the parking lot when I heard a rustle of leaves. Stopped in my tracks, I peered into the trees and climbed onto an embankment that led toward the forest beyond. Trees opened on a clearing with metal benches placed at various angles for people to relax and take a break from their trek. Park custodians had set out huge wooden tubs filled with flowering plants and ivy from the greenhouses in another part of the Perkins acreage.

I sat for a few minutes, allowing the sun to warm my face. As the breeze sang through the trees, I closed my eyes and relaxed. I don't know how long I sat enjoying nature, when a harsh voice interrupted my quietude.

"What are you doing here? The park isn't open today. You're trespassing."

Startled, I opened my eyes and gaped at a short, stocky woman with frizzy gray hair that poked outward from under her hat. It looked as if the hair had received a few extra volts of electricity. I wondered if I'd entered the realm of fairies and mythical creatures.

The woman's bulbous nose, wickedly puckish lips, and mean glare from the muddiest brown eyes I'd ever seen, sat in a once round face that held flabby jowls. Her arms were short, as were her legs, and her fingers were a might stubby. While she wasn't a dwarf, she didn't seem too far from it. Again, I feared I was in the land of the fey, except I don't believe in fairies.

I leaped from the bench and said, "I'm so sorry, I was waiting for my friend to call and let me know she was ready to leave her meeting with Alvin something-or-other." Yeah, I was rattled.

Her gaze narrowed as she said, "Then I guess you'd better be off to meet your friend."

In my haste to leave, I stumbled a few times while leaving the wooded land to find the path once again. I broke into a full-on run and headed toward the parking lot, where Bailey probably awaited me.

A minute or so later, I saw the park grounds and noticed Bailey standing near the path's entrance.

With a wave of her hand she walked toward me. We met halfway and before I could say a word, she began to ramble on over the possibilities this event could provide for the two of us. Since it was a subject I had wanted to discuss with her, I tucked my recent episode away without mentioning it and entered the conversation as she drew a breath. We seemed to agree when it came down to entertaining.

Our ride home included a stop in Windermere for a sandwich and discussion of the hop.

"I wondered why the committee hadn't invited me. Thanks for the recommendation, Jules."

"When I received a call from someone named Della Meeny, I mentioned your name to her. Della gave your name to Alvin. I'm glad you were invited. This could work out well for both of us."

We ate lunch and talked over the value of our participation. I set my glass on the table and asked, "Would you be interested in doing a rabbit-themed puppet show as one of our gigs? I know you offer two shows when we work at a party together. The hop might initiate more party reservations for us. What do you think?"

"We're on the same wavelength today. I had the same thought while speaking with Alvin. We could come up with something, I'm sure. By the way, did you realize Alvin had whiskey of some sort in his glass of soda?"

I snickered. "The smell hit me right away when the breeze came through the tent and picked up the scent. Alvin must be quite a tippler to be drinking so early in the day."

"You're right, but each to his own is my motto."

"Mine, too." I glanced at the time and said I had to return home.

Bailey dropped me off at the end of the drive to the house. I wanted to walk the long road in. Birds chirped and flew across the fields bordering the drive as my attention turned to the woman who had approached me in the park's clearing. Who was she? Why was she so rude and what was *she* doing there?

Chapter 2

Ecstatic that I'd returned home, Bun hopped around my ankles until he was out of breath.

"I think I need more exercise. I'm winded from all that jumping around. Whew. I'd never win in a hop 'til you drop contest. What took you so long? I thought you might have become involved in an adventure without my guidance."

"I know better than to do that." I should be so lucky, but then cut the thought short. Bun was invaluable to our investigations. I looked down at his handsome black and white face and smoothed the fur on his head and ears.

"I had the weirdest thing happen to me while I waited for Bailey to finish her discussion with Alvin Peterson."

"Ooh, it sounds mysterious. Tell me, tell me."

His glee brought a smile to my lips. Bun was as excited about the hop as I was. It would be an adventure for us, somehow or other, especially after what took place earlier today.

I quickly explained my experience at the park and described the woman.

"You aren't making this up, are you?"

I crossed my heart and said, "No word of a lie. She startled me so badly that I flew off the bench and rushed into the woods after she told me to leave. She was weird." I went on to explain how rude and obnoxious her behavior was.

"We're not too far from being weird ourselves, Jules. I'm a telepathic talking rabbit, and you even talk back to me. How's that for weird?"

Bun's lips pulled up a bit and his nostrils wiggled a tad, which I took as a sign of humor on his part. *"So, how did you handle the situation?"*

"For one thing, I nearly jumped out of my skin when I opened my eyes and saw her. She was aggressive and seemed quite fearsome, too. I think the fact that she took me by surprise caused my reaction."

"See? You need to take me with you everywhere so I can protect you from the likes of the oddballs you run into all the time."

While Bun often accompanied me, I couldn't always bring him along when I had errands to run, though I didn't mention it. "Did you have a snack this afternoon?"

"Molly gave me a fruit and veg pod when the other rabbits had theirs. I ate in the barn, then went outside to run myself ragged. You know how much I enjoy the outdoors."

"Yes, I do."

"I think Molly is coming through the breezeway. I can tell by the softness of her footsteps."

I met her at the door and asked if everything was okay. She assured me all was well as she entered the kitchen. "I just had a call from Mrs. Carver. She'd like to bring a friend to class this evening. We've had one cancellation for this class. I don't mind if Mrs. Carver's friend would like to come, but I can't promise her a regular seat if she wants to spin. What do you think I should do?"

"Just what you said. If Meredith's friend wants to join an ongoing class, we can order another spinning wheel. Just let her know she's filling an empty spot in tonight's class."

Relief flooded Molly's face. "I hoped you'd say that. I wanted to be sure, is all."

"Thanks for checking with me first. I wouldn't want to find the woman is interested and then say there isn't a place in the class for her. If you think you can handle an additional student, then tell Meredith to bring her along and explain the situation."

"Okay, I'll be leaving for a while, but I will be back before class time." Molly started toward the door and then turned back. "Jason has finished for the day, the rabbits went outside for their exercise, then were fed and watered. Everyone is back in their hutches."

"Terrific. Later, I'll put away the order that surely arrived while I was gone. Thanks, Molly."

"Oh, not to worry, Jason and I handled that, too."

Grateful for their thoughtfulness, I walked alongside Molly through the breezeway with Bun at our heels. In the barn, I found everything in order. When we went into the shop, I realized Molly had created a wonderful display of the new yarn. The hanks of wool to spin lay curled into rounds that reminded me of colorful bird nests.

"These are beautiful and also inviting to the touch. Good work."

"I couldn't help myself. The wool is so soft and pliable, I just had to make coiled rounds from them. When I stepped back to view them, it seemed I'd had the right idea."

She gathered her handbag and promised to return before the students arrived.

"She's a very special human, don't you think?"

"Why, yes, I do. We're fortunate to have Molly and Jason on our staff. They take great care of you and the bunnies, and rightfully so. Now, I have to go figure out what to make for supper tonight. I think Jessica is staying, so it won't be just sandwiches."

"Jess doesn't mind sandwiches. I heard her say so just this morning."

"Really? Then maybe soup will be on the menu, too."

The door behind me opened and Jessica asked, "Talking to Bun again?"

"Of course, he's always ready to listen." I gave her a wink and asked if soup and sandwiches would be good enough for supper.

"Sure, I'm not fussy. How did you and Bailey get along with Alvin Peterson?"

"He's an interesting fellow. We discussed a bunch of topics before he honed in on Bailey. While they chatted, I walked the path and ended up in one of the forest clearings. The park custodians have added tubs of flowering plants and cleaned the benches for people to rest. I noticed there was a slew of wildflowers growing along the edge of the clearing. I was so relaxed, I almost fell asleep."

"Some of those flowers might be poisonous. I know

there's a huge patch of lilies of the valley that grow near the bottom of the hill. I stay far away from them. Now, tell Jess about the grouch who scared the wits out of you."

I stared down at Bun, raised an eyebrow, and then asked Jess, "What time do you want supper? Today is your long day, isn't it?"

With a nod, Jess said, "Around four-thirty or five o'clock should be fine. That way, I'll be ready for my first evening appointment at six-fifteen."

I listened to the grandfather clock strike three. "Okay, I'll get started, then." The day had flown and for the life of me, I had no idea where it had gone. With soup and sandwiches for supper, I could take time to write out ideas for themed events Bailey and I might attempt. If we worked out a coordinated angle, we could offer ideas for children's parties.

"Jess sure is busy lately. She looks tired." He toddled off while I considered Jessica's state of being. I hadn't noticed she was tired, though we didn't see much of each other like we did before she opened the clinic. I'd have to ask and see what I could do to lighten her load.

My notes made for Bailey to consider, I stirred the soup and finished setting the table. Jess strode into the house and checked the contents of the kettle before she plunked into a chair. "Is that vegetable soup and chicken salad for supper?"

"It is, along with a loaf of crusty *boule* bread." I set the container of chicken salad on the table and then ladled soup into our bowls while Jess poured glasses of ice water.

Sliced bread, piled with delicious chicken salad, was tasty. We ate until there was nothing left. Never one to miss a meal if I could help it, I leaned back, chewed my last mouthful, and took a long look at Jessica.

The light shadows under her eyes showed something was going on that she hadn't mentioned. I wondered why.

"You look a little tired. Are you okay? What can I do to help you out?"

"I'm overbooked and haven't had a minute to change my schedule. I'm exhausted. We both know that's not healthy. I need a helper at least a few hours a day, but it seems I don't have enough time to address that either."

"Would you mind a piece of advice?"

"Go ahead. I could use some."

"First, change the appointments. That will give you extra time to address patient file notes before the next patient arrives. If you don't, this will only get worse."

Jess rubbed her hands over her face, massaged her temples, and said, "I should have done that a month ago. Instead, I put it off, thinking I'd get to it, but didn't."

"You've assisted me so often, the least I can do is help you figure out a solution. You can't go on like this. Have you thought of getting a vet student to work for or with you?"

"I had considered it. I'm starting to earn decent money, but can't afford to add a vet or a student right now. Remember how I said almost the exact thing to you because you were so tired and overworked when you started with the rabbits? Your answer then was the same as mine is now." With a sigh, she leaned her elbows on the table and cupped her chin in her hand.

"Have you spoken to your mother about the need for a receptionist? You have mentioned she's adept at office work, and now that she's retired from her job, she might want to give you a hand."

"My mother volunteered to do that, but I thought I could handle it, so I put her off. Maybe I should ask her. If you realize I'm exhausted, she will, too." Jess pushed her chair back and then said, "I think I'll call her tonight. Thanks, Jules."

As Jess began to clear the table, I motioned her away and said she should make that phone call. Once she left the kitchen, Bun popped his head out of his room and said, *"Well done. I told you she was tired, didn't I? Good thing I noticed, huh?"*

"Thanks, and yes, you have an eye for what I don't always see." I had to agree and tried not to let him see me roll my eyes toward the heavens at being reminded of his abilities.

The dishwasher ran while I checked and settled the rabbits and then went over the list of ideas for upcoming entertainment engagements. I sat on the stool in the shop with Bun wandering the room at his leisure. The fireplace warmed the room, and Bun plunked down on the rug in front of it. He sprawled with his front legs stretched forward, and his hind legs straight out behind him. It was comical to see him that way and I snickered.

Suddenly, I heard him say, *"I'm very comfortable. Thank you."* His manner a tad snooty, I almost laughed aloud, but knew better. Bun tended to become insulted by things humans wouldn't.

"It looks that way from here. I wish I could stretch out on that rug."

He responded with a tiny snort that I let pass and scribbled on the notepad. Molly flew into the room as the clock struck six. I stared at her as she threw her jacket onto the hook in a way I could never manage. Her handbag landed on the countertop, and she began to set the room up for everyone on her schedule.

I shoved the pad aside and asked what she wanted me to do. She gave me instructions while we finished organizing the spinning wheels. Students entered the shop. They always sat in the same seats, which amazed me because I couldn't figure out how they knew which spinning wheel was theirs. Maybe it didn't matter, since all the wheels were the same brand and style.

Molly greeted each one of them by name as they came through the door. She leaned toward me and whispered, "Thanks for helping me."

I nodded. Bun crossed the room once everyone was seated and said, *"That's a large group of students."*

I picked him off the floor and tucked him under my arm. "I'll leave you to it, Molly."

"Wait a minute. I have a question for you."

"Okay."

"Let me get them started. Then I'll be right with you."

Meredith arrived with her friend in tow. I greeted them both and welcomed the newcomer.

Meredith, always a ray of sunshine, petted Bun's head and asked how I was.

"I'm fine, thanks."

"I heard you're going to help with the Hop 'Til You Drop event. I'm on that committee. It's going to be a great day."

"I'll be at the scoop and stash station. Several of us will hide the Easter eggs for the kiddies to find."

Her expression changed. I couldn't tell whether I thought that was good or bad. Her voice cool, she said, "Yes . . . uh, Della Meeny is handling that particular part of things." She turned her back to the class and whispered, "Watch your back, Juliette."

Before I could respond, Meredith walked to her seat and offered an apology for keeping everyone waiting. I waited for Molly and set Bun on the floor. "Stay with me," I whispered.

His ears twitched as he hunkered down next to my ankle. Molly worked her way from one student to another, watching as they started their projects, and then she beckoned to us.

At the counter, she withdrew a binder that held pages upon pages of the types of supplies used in spinning and weaving. She opened the book to a particular bookmarked page and pointed out two items she wanted for the shop.

One was a smaller version of the spinning wheel like those already in use. The other item was a weaving loom. Neither piece was cheap, not even close to it, but the quality was outstanding. I knew the owner of the company that sold them. Handmade from the best wood possible, they were worth the cost.

I said, "Let me see what I can do."

Her head bobbed up and down. I left her to teach, tore the top sheet of notes off a paper pad, and went into the house with Bun.

"What does she want you to buy this time? I saw you study the page she pointed out. Whatever she wants must cost a lot, huh?"

In the kitchen, I took out the bank statements that had arrived two days ago. I hadn't opened the envelopes and did so now. I scanned the accounts and realized I had more than enough funds to pay for what Molly wanted.

There was no doubt the potential income outweighed the cost.

Molly tended to be frugal when shop spending came into play. If she asked for something, it was because she knew it would pay for itself in the end. I'd let her know I'd place the order before she left for the night, and said to Bun, "We can make this purchase. I wouldn't buy something cheaper from another vendor when I know Stephen Morton makes his products by hand and doesn't scrimp on materials."

As I answered the phone, Bun went into the living room and nestled in front of the gas fireplace.

Della Meeny was on the line. Her voice as harsh as a rocky mountain slope, I tried to envision what the woman looked like, but couldn't.

"I take it you're all set for this weekend?"

"Yes, of course. I said as much to Alvin today."

"He doesn't always tell me stuff, so I wanted to check with you. Will the rabbit be there?"

"He most certainly will, unless there's a problem."

"No, no, that'll be fine. I guess your friend Bailey will be entertaining the rug rats?"

Unimpressed by her name for the kids, I agreed that Bailey would be there and that children adored her puppet shows.

"Huh, well, it'll keep them out of our hair. I'll see you bright and early on Saturday. Don't be late."

The line went dead before I could utter a sound. I put the phone in its charger and joined Bun in the living room.

"Who was that?"

"Della Meeny. I think she's an unhappy person. Maybe even a meanie of sorts."

"Would that be what humans call a play on words?"

"I suppose so. Della doesn't sound like a warm, friendly type of person, that's for sure. Her voice seemed familiar, but I can't place it. I'm going to check on the rabbits once more for water and such before they're settled for the night. Are you coming along?"

"Most certainly."

In the barn, I walked the aisles with Bun next to me. I kept thinking of Della Meeny's attitude. She didn't give me the impression of a person who enjoyed her job, so why become involved in this town-sponsored affair? I shrugged and filled water bins.

I'd reached Petra's hutch and petted her gently while softly murmuring to her. She hadn't presented her kits, though Jessica and I thought she would do so at any time.

I withdrew my hand from her luscious fur and closed the hutch door, making sure to flip the latch in place. Walkabout Willy wasn't the only rabbit in this bunch to figure out how to escape the confines of a hutch.

After I let Molly know about the purchase she had requested, Bun and I returned to the house for the night. I'd gotten comfortable on the sofa and started to doze when the phone rang.

"So much for resting."

"I know." I answered the phone on the third ring.

"Jules, did you get a call from that Meeny woman?" Bailey asked.

"I did." Annoyed by Della's attitude, the same way I had been, she said, "She sounds like a real gem. She even gave me the third degree over what I would use to entertain the kids. Then insisted it be age-appropriate. After that, she ranted on about how Alvin never tells her any-thing. As if that's my fault. Good grief. Have you ever met her in person?"

Okay, so Della had managed to get under Bailey's skin, which took some doing. I took a deep breath and said, "I've never met her, but she does have a way of putting people on the defensive. Don't worry, if Alvin liked what you presented, then you're all set. He makes the final decisions. Maybe there's a power struggle going on in their department. If there is, I want no part of it."

"I knew you'd be the voice of reason. Thanks for calming me down. Della was so rude on the phone. I can only imagine what she's like face-to-face. Thank good-ness I'm not working under her supervision. I wish you weren't."

"All I have to do is hide eggs beforehand. I'll also help other volunteers sign in the families and hand out the bas-kets when the event begins. That's it. Are you all set for your show?"

"My bunny puppets are all prettied up. They haven't been used in a few years and needed refreshing. I think the show will make the audience happy."

"Sounds great to me. I'll try to catch it if I finish in time."

"That would be nice. Let's get together soon to discuss the possibilities of working out our themes for parties."

I agreed and ended the call.

Bun heaved a small sigh and asked, *"Bailey's not happy with the meanie, huh?"*

"Della certainly has a lousy disposition. It must be awful to live that way."

"If she always acts bossy, she might not think she's rude, but outspoken instead."

"Mm, she certainly doesn't sound like a very pleasant person. I'm surprised her boss doesn't reprimand her. Though, maybe no one has complained."

"We'll see what she's like on Saturday. I'm off to bed."

I nodded and watched him hop away.

Now wide awake, I took my laptop from the desk and got comfy on the sofa again. The website for the spinning wheel and weaver popped up on my list on the internet. I browsed various categories before I made a purchase.

I shut down the site and Googled Della Meeny's name. I caught my breath while reading up on her. Della had served three months in jail for a misdemeanor, then additional time for misbehavior in the courtroom. The article stated she'd insulted Judge Moore. He'd ordered Della removed from the courtroom. When she refused to apologize for her behavior, Judge Moore had extended her sentence and added one month of community service. Yikes, Della Meeny was a criminal. Well, maybe not that bad, but she certainly had ticked off Judge Moore, who was an easygoing fellow. Could that be the reason Meredith had told me to watch my back? Hmm.

Chapter 3

The remainder of the week passed without incident or Petra's kits being born. Worried by it, I mentioned as much to Jessica.

"They will arrive when they're ready. I might have miscalculated the delivery date. After all, this is only my second delivery. Petra's going to be fine, and she will let us know when she's ready to give us those tiny sweeties."

"You're right, of course. Did you speak to your mother about working with you?"

"I did, and she will. Isn't that wonderful? I look forward to it; she has a great way with animals and people, too. That must be where I got my ability." She glanced at her watch and said, "You'd better get going, if you want to arrive at Perkins Park early. Della Meeny won't be happy if you're late."

I slipped on a cardigan and buttoned it up. "You know Della?"

"No, I've only heard the gossip."

"I looked her up on the computer. She spent a brief time in jail because she aggravated Judge Moore."

"That takes some doing. He's a nice person and has empathy."

"I thought so, too. Got to run, I'll see you later."

We arrived early. Bun stayed in the car while I went into the information center for directions to the scoop and stash station. The clerk handed me a map with the spot marked with an X.

I turned to leave and stumbled into a person standing behind me. We both reached out to right each other. "I apologize, I didn't realize you were there. I'm Jules Bridge, from Fur Bridge Farm."

"Nice to meet you. My name is Stacey Farnsworth. I own The Eatery, a soup and sandwich deli in Windermere. Are you a volunteer this weekend?"

"Yes, are you?"

"I'm supposed to show up at a place named the egg-cellent creation station. Do you know where it is?"

"I've been there, but I don't know the way from here. I'm heading over to the scoop and stash station and needed directions."

She stepped close and murmured, "Della Meeny is running that portion of the hop. Watch out for her."

Surprised to hear that advice from a stranger, I said, "So I'm told. Thanks, I've got to go."

"I'll see you around." Stacey stepped up to the counter.

I got into the car and started the engine.

"Did you get lost in there?"

"No, I ran into someone who started a conversation. Sorry to make you wait, Bun." I read the map and set off toward our station.

"I'm anxious to get this job underway. It should be fun. I can find wondrous places for you to put the eggs."

I swear that if Bun had hands instead of paws, he'd have clapped them together as if to dust them off, thus being satisfied with his part in the job.

We made tracks from our parking spot across the grounds to the place where a bunch of stations stood. Gigantic tarpaulins pitched on poles that resembled a big circus tarp, sat covered with printed Easter egg sheets of plastic. Wind blew across the wide expanse, ruffling the short tarp skirt.

Pausing to read the signs as we went, the eggcellent creation station wasn't too far off to our right. I stopped and wondered why I hadn't remembered this. Bailey and I had met Alvin here. Filled with volunteers painting wooden eggs in brilliant colors, Bun scooted toward it, leaving me to follow. Everyone laughed and joked as they worked. Sets of huge drying racks sat stacked on a platform at the far end of the rectangular tent. Loaded with eggs that had reached the dried and distribute stage, the colors were brilliant, even from this distance.

Fascinated by the amount of work it took to produce the hop, I wandered from table to table, admiring the artistic abilities of those who made painting seem easy. I had no such talent and stood in awe of the teams dedicated to their job. Each table held plastic bins of unpainted wooden eggs awaiting the magic brushstrokes that made them beautiful.

Bun had gone off to who knew where and then popped

up next to me as I lifted a table cover in search of him under the table. Startled at his appearance, I ruffled his fur and admonished him softly for leaving my side.

"Do you always talk to your rabbit?" an artisan asked as I plucked Bun off the floor and tucked him in the crook of my arm.

I nodded and said to her, "I talk to all of them. I'm Juliette Bridge of Fur Bridge Farm."

"You own the rabbit haven on the outskirts of town, right?"

"A bit further out than that, but yes, that's my farm."

"My sister spoke of your rabbit program and the kids' parties you bring them to. You educate people about these creatures, too, don't you?"

"That's right. Rabbits are wonderful animals." I glanced at my watch and said I had to get to the scoop and stash station.

"Good luck with that." The young woman smirked as I walked away.

Wondering if she'd meant the job itself or the woman in charge of the station, I didn't dawdle or stop to watch any of the other artists. Instead, I peeked at the painted eggs on the racks.

Bun hopped out of my arms and said, *"I want to look at those, down there."*

I let him do so and admired a few more eggs. I glanced around and saw Bun near the far end of the racks, his ears standing straight up in listening mode. The sound of harsh voices could be heard, but not what was said. I knew that with Bun's super hearing, he'd have much to share when we were alone.

"Psst, psst, come over here," I whispered to him.

He raced over to me, jumped into my arms, and we left the tent before being seen by those who were not happy about something or other.

"Want to know what that was all about?"

"Not right now, we'll talk about it later. We'll be late if I don't hurry up. Now, stay with me and don't wander off, okay?"

With a sigh and a beleaguered look, Bun said, *"All right. You do take the fun out of things at times."*

"I could say the same of you, my furry friend." We'd stepped inside our station and found buckets upon buckets of painted eggs crowded on tabletops. This wouldn't be an hour or so job. It would be more like the entire afternoon—good thing I'd brought Bun snacks and water.

Several other people arrived. They studied the bins of eggs and remarked on them. Bun and I stayed put.

"Looks like nobody is here to tell us what to do or where to do it."

"Mmm."

"You'd think with all these eggs to be hidden, that our boss would be present to get us started."

Bun no sooner finished his sentence, when the same mean-spirited woman who had kicked me out of the woods, while Bailey had met with Alvin Peterson, crossed the space between our station and the eggcellent one. She stomped her way to us, looking angrier with each step taken. I looked at the other volunteers and said, "Our boss is here."

"That's the woman who made you leave the other day, right? I sense your tension rising."

I took a minute to slip the sling from around my waist and positioned it over my shoulder and torso. I leaned

down and Bun snuggled inside. When I stood up, I faced
the woman who was now under the tent's canopy. She
gave each person a glaring study, then gave us our orders.

"The buckets of eggs are over there," she said, and
pointed to them. "I'm Della Meeny. I'm in charge of this
portion of the event. If you can't fulfill your promise to
hide all the eggs we have here and those in the eggcellent
station, you can leave. I don't need slackers. I need workers."

"She's worse than a drill sergeant."

I patted his body through the fabric, then walked over
to a table and grabbed a bucket. The volunteers offered
each other raised brow expressions and followed my
lead. Then I returned to the entrance where Della handed
out maps.

"Stick to your sections. Each one of you has a number
on your identification pin, which is the area where you'll
hide your eggs. When these are hidden, return for more
and continue until there aren't any left to hide. Do you all
understand?"

We nodded in unison before one of the volunteers,
number six, stepped forward and remarked, "How did
you get this job, anyway?"

"That's none of your business. What you need to do is
stop talking and get going."

Appalled by Della's rudeness, I, too, wondered why
she was involved in this event. Her personality didn't fit
with the whole "have fun" atmosphere the council en-
deavored to portray.

Unwilling to receive a scathing comment, I kept my
mouth shut, left the tent and Della Meeny behind, and
sought the peace and tranquility of Tucker Trail.

Bun wanted out of the sling. I held the opening wide to allow him space to jump out. *"She's a treasure, don't you think?"*

His sarcasm evident, I nodded. "I've never seen such a miserable person, that's for sure. Let's get on with our job and leave Della to hers, shall we?"

"She argued with a man in the eggcellent tent. Angry about a young woman who had canceled at the last moment, Della wanted one of his volunteers. He refused and she said he'd be sorry for having done that."

"That was the reason she looked so fearsome when she walked from that tent to ours. I wondered why she had such a stormy look about her."

Bun sniffed the air and said, *"She gave me the heebie-jeebies."* Then he searched the moss-laden parts of the path marked on our assigned location of the map.

A dozen hidden eggs later, Bun became bored. He jumped up the slope and over the top of it while I worked. About thirty minutes later, I realized his absence was too long. It wasn't like Bun to go off without me for great lengths of time.

Returning to the spot where he'd taken off, I glanced at the moss where he might have left tracks when he returned. The soft moss showed nothing, so I looked closer and was startled when Bun flew from the brush on the slope. He tried to stop when he hit the paved path, but skidded to the other side of the trail and ended up tangled in a shrub.

In a frantic state, Bun struggled to disengage himself and talk to me at the same time. His words sounded like gibberish. His eyes were wide and bulging when he eventually freed himself and hopped about as though he'd gone mad. I kneeled on the ground and spoke softly to him. As usual, the calm tone of my voice brought him to his senses, and he sat in front of me.

Whatever Bun found upset him enough to send him rushing through the woods to find me. Certain I wouldn't be thrilled with whatever it was, I knew in my gut that I'd downright dislike it. "Tell me what's happened."

"I can't. I have to show you. Come on, follow me into the woods."

Hesitating when Bun made such a demand is tantamount to refusing to believe anything is wrong. Bun isn't happy when that happens, and the fallout of such actions on my part, in turn, brings dissension. That's when I noticed his foot tapping against the pavement.

"You must come with me right now. Right now, I say."

Realizing the futility of refusal, I agreed to follow him off the path and into the brush. We climbed a short slope, trekked through a section of pine trees, then past oaks and maples, to end up at the edge of a clearing. While Bun didn't rant, he'd talked nonstop about what was ahead as though giving me a tour of the woodland. Goosebumps rose on my arms with every step I took.

In the clearing, wildflowers grew in patches and green grass popped up around them. A mowed grassy oval lay just ahead and dipped somewhat. Before I could take another step, Bun warned, *"Continue carefully, very carefully."*

A mound of cloth lay in the center of the oval. I cupped a hand above my eyebrows to block the glare of the sun for a better view. When I realized it wasn't simply fabric. I gasped out loud, took a step back, and tripped over Bun. I hit the ground hard, spilling the contents of my bucket. Brightly colored eggs rolled away as I gawked at the body of Della Meeny.

Surrounded with Easter eggs, Della's chest was laden with stems of lily of the valley blossoms. The garish eggs held no resemblance to the lovely painted ones done by the volunteers. Instead, they were awful, like the woman herself. Unsure of how long Bun and I sat like two blocks of stone, I finally turned to Bun and asked, "Was she like this when you found her?"

His ears flopped up and down, as his whiskers swayed in the wind. I reached out, smoothed his fur, and said, "This is worse than I had imagined. I'll call the sheriff."

"Don't you want a closer look? We might find some evidence that will lead Sheriff Carver to the killer."

I knew Bun would hound me to investigate, like he always did in this type of instance. He'd been whining about boredom lately, too. I took a deep breath, pulled my phone from my pocket, and called the police department. I reported what I saw and gave directions to our location. Told to stay put until the police arrived, I agreed and hung up.

"They'll be here shortly."

"Okay, then let's make the most of our time before that happens." Bun set off down the knoll. Dragging my feet, I was in no hurry to view Della in this situation or any other.

Bun stopped and turned his head toward me. *"Are you going to take all day, or what?"*

"I'm coming, all right?"

We drew a few steps closer to the body when a movement caught my eye. I swung toward it and knew my jaw had dropped, leaving my mouth wide open. A tall, two-legged, white rabbit fled into the woods, a sight I never thought I'd see.

"What's wrong?"

"Did you see that rabbit?"

"What rabbit?" Bun swung his head toward the direction I pointed and then said, *"I don't see any rabbit."*

"He must have been almost six feet tall," I insisted.

"Are you feeling all right? Rabbits don't grow that large."

"Maybe it was a person in a rabbit costume."

"That is downright insulting. Rabbits don't dress up as humans, so why do humans think they should dress up to look like us? Disgusting, it's absolutely disgusting."

Okay, so I had cranked Bun up like an overwound clock, and I would now pay the price for it. "We'd better get over to her. I think the police are about to descend upon us any minute. I think they're coming through the woods."

Bun's ears perked upright. Then he sniffed and flicked his whiskers a bit. *"Indeed, Sheriff Carver is complaining about the briar patch he'd stumbled into."*

Bun, amused by the sheriff's misfortune, since the sheriff wasn't a favorite of his, started to hop closer to Della.

"I'm going to snap a couple of pictures with my phone. Keep an eye out for the sheriff."

"Sure will, but get going. We have to pick up your eggs, or they'll become part of the crime scene."

Darn, he was right. I went to Della, took pictures, then I scrambled about for the eggs and flung them into my basket. I looked for the basket that had held the eggs that surrounded Della. With no sign of a basket, other than mine, there was a lack of scuffle or drag marks to indicate what had happened to the woman. Our eggs gathered, Bun and I made for the knoll and stood at the top when police officers, the sheriff, and a rescue crew burst from the woods.

Sheriff Carver demanded, "How did you end up here, of all places?"

"Bun and I needed a rest from hiding eggs and came here. That's when we found the body."

"It's far from the trail, but then you do know this place well. You and the rabbit come here often, don't you?"

"Every chance we get. Della Meeny is over there." I turned and pointed to her body and waited until the scene hit home for Carver and the rest.

They gawked, almost as long as I had. With odd facial expressions, they waited for direction from the sheriff. Bun sat at my feet and said, *"You should tell him about the human disguised as a rabbit."*

I stared down at him, but he ignored me. I knew Bun wasn't sure of what I saw, but then, I wasn't either. We stepped aside as the entire crew of cops and rescuers went down the slope into the clearing. They waited until Sheriff Carver finished his cursory examination of Della's body without actually touching her.

Over his shoulder, Carver yelled, "What do you think the eggs signify?"

I approached him as he stepped away to let the rescue team do their job. When we met, I explained the scoop and stash station and what the nice eggs stood for. They would be found, turned in, and donated to the elderly in the nursing home and children at the hospital. I had no idea what the ugly eggs meant unless it referred to Della herself.

"They would give these ugly eggs to kids and needy people?" Carver asked.

I dipped my hand into my basket and held up one of

the beautifully painted eggs for Jack to see. "No, these will be donated, not those. I don't know where the ugly ones came from."

Jack stared at the egg I held out, and then murmured, "I wonder why someone would do this to her? Any ideas?"

"To say Della was a warm and fuzzy person would be the greatest overstatement of all time. She was a harridan, a mean woman, without a positive bone in her body, and rude to everyone she came across. I don't know what those eggs represent, but my guess would be somebody had a serious enough grudge to kill her and use them for purposes that only she and the culprit would understand."

One of the rescuers motioned Jack over to where he stood. Before he walked away, Jack said I could leave and that if he had further questions, he'd be in touch. I nodded, grabbed Bun, and helped him into the sling. We left as quickly as possible.

"You didn't tell him about the human in disguise."

"Nope, and I hope I don't have to. Now hang on, I'm going to make quick work of getting through these woods and onto the path. We still have eggs to hide."

While Bun complained of being jostled by my increased pace, we made tracks to get back to work.

Chapter 4

Once we hit the trail again, I let Bun loose. "Stay with me. Do not wander off. I mean it, Bun."

"No need to speak so sternly. I already planned to stick around."

"Then find the next hiding spot so I can get these eggs off my hands."

We worked in silence for a while. The basket nearly empty, I kept on going. My mind, in marathon mode, held thoughts that crowded my brain until I stopped short and drew a deep breath. I plucked the last egg from my basket and dropped it where Bun tapped his foot.

"Thanks, Bun. Let's return to the station now."

"Great, I'm hungry and tired. I've had way too much excitement for one day. Do you think we should investigate the murder?"

"I'd rather not. Petra will soon give birth, and the farm

is busy right now, as is the shop. Why do you want to get involved in Della's demise?"

"That rabbit disguised person has caught my attention. I know you probably think I'm silly to feel insulted by it, and maybe I am, but no one should be murdered and then left in such a way. There's also an underlying reason for those ugly eggs. Consider the meaning, and I will, too. Then we'll compare thoughts, okay?"

As much as I wanted to refrain from involvement, Bun and I were on the same wavelength. Giving thought to the ugly eggs, I wondered the same thing, and the rabbit costume also had significance. What that was would be anybody's guess. Asking around a bit wouldn't hurt, as long as we didn't interfere with Jack's investigation. It became tiresome when he ranted on and on about leaving police work to those trained for it.

We backtracked to the scoop and stash station and found chaos. All the workers talked at once, and no one understood another. I waited off to the side to understand what the problem was. One member of the group had sidled up to us and stood next to me. The tag on his shirt had number four printed on it and the name Denton Clarke.

Denton's blue eyes held a twinkle that matched his diamond earring. His brown hair cropped short and the bridge of his nose a tad sunburned, he smiled when I glanced at him. He sidled closer and murmured, "The help is about to revolt."

"Why?"

"Our trusty leader has mysteriously disappeared, and no one is smart enough to get the rest of the eggs from that back table to finish the job."

"Then, let's lead the way."

"I thought the same thing." Denton waved his hand and beckoned a few others to join us. They gave him a thumbs-up and we met at the far end of the tent.

I set my empty bucket aside and took one from those ready to go. I started walking away with Denton and his friends right behind. The remaining group had quieted and stared in surprise when we walked by.

A woman with a shock of rich auburn hair asked, "Where are you going with those eggs?"

Denton hesitated as I turned and said, "To finish the job, of course. We aren't children who need direction. We're adults who know what we're supposed to do."

The woman looked at the ground for a second or two and then said to the others, "She's right. Just because Della is absent doesn't mean we shouldn't complete what we've started. Come on. Let's get to work."

I glanced over my shoulder as the stragglers took one or two of the remaining buckets of eggs and hurried to follow us. Once we entered Tucker Trail, each worker set off toward their appointed section.

"You were great and didn't let on that Della was dead. These folks might run into a cop or two on their routes, though. I'm surprised they haven't already."

Alone, we could easily converse. I looked over my shoulder to make certain we didn't have company, and said, "I wondered why the volunteers were so upset when we got there, but couldn't think of a way to ask without seeming as though I knew something they didn't."

"One of them knew something, a guy at the outer edge of the group. He seemed to study those involved in the uproar. He might be the one who caused it."

"You're so astute and have admirable attention to detail, Bun. Did you happen to catch what had them in such a tizzy?"

"I couldn't grasp too much because they were all yammering at the same time, but it became clear that Della's absence was the cause of confusion. One of them might have had a reason to get rid of her, you know."

"True. Let's hide these eggs and then see if Sheriff Carver is still on the grounds. I want a word with him."

"He isn't going to listen to you. I can feel it in my lucky foot."

"Maybe he won't, but he will want to speak to those in our group, as well as to the other groups involved in the hop. The more he knows, the easier his job becomes."

Bun left the sling and took to the lower part of the slope where he discovered easy-to-find spots for me to tuck eggs. I encouraged him on and, within an hour, we were on our way back to the tent. He hopped alongside me and laid out the how and why of our solving the mystery. I rolled my eyes a few times and was glad he didn't see me do so.

"You've got this all planned out."

"You and I are a great team, especially when it comes to finding answers the police can't. Our contacts are growing, and there's no good reason why we shouldn't tap into them to solve this mystery. I know you're itching to find out who killed Della. Even a miserable sort deserves justice."

No doubt Bun could reason with the best of them. If he was a human, I swear he'd have taken debate teams by storm. He was right: Della's killer should be caught, but I wasn't sure it ought to be us who did the job.

One or two members of our group were in the tent.

Sandwiches and beverages had magically been set out for us with enough to go around. Pleased to think the council had shown their appreciation by feeding us, I found that I was hungry. After I'd tended to Bun's lunch, I dug into the selection of food and beverages with fervor. I smiled at Bun as he feasted and then indulged in a second sandwich.

Ice cold tea with fresh slices of lemon satisfied my thirst, and I suddenly realized how warm the day had become. Denton strode into the tent, settled across from me, and then asked, "Does your rabbit go everywhere with you?"

"Almost. Why?"

"He's very sociable. I'm surprised by it."

"Rabbits are social animals; they like to be spoken to and are energetic. I own Fur Bridge Farm and have about fifteen or so rabbits now. There were more, but they have new homes."

He remarked, "No offense, but I would never have taken you for a farmer."

"None taken. What do you do for a living?"

"I work at Windermere College. I'm a marketing professor."

I summed him up and then said, "No offense, but I'd never have taken you for a scholar, let alone a marketing professor."

Denton leaned back in his chair and grinned. "Touché."

"How did you come to be involved with the hop?"

"I was asked to handle the marketing. It's a terrific family-related event. Once I got going on the marketing end of things, I found I wanted to know more and do more. How about you?"

I explained that since I had rabbits and the hop was

centered around Easter and the egg hunt, that when I was asked to give a hand, I couldn't refuse. I finished by saying, "It's good marketing on my part and a community service, too."

I rose as Bun sat back on his haunches and then crouched as rabbits do. "I've got to get back to the farm. Maybe I'll see you tomorrow when things gear up and children take to the trail in search of eggs."

"Sure, I look forward to it. I'm leaving now, too; I'll walk you out."

My curiosity took over as I agreed to his offer. I bundled Bun's dishes into the carryall, let him climb into the sling, and set off. I'd only gone a few steps when I heard Sheriff Carver call my name. I turned and saw him stride from the trail onto the park grounds.

He raised a hand and beckoned me to join him. I looked at Denton, who found this of interest.

"Are you in trouble with the sheriff?"

"Why do you ask?"

"I saw the cops inspecting the trail earlier and wondered what had happened. Do you know?"

I leaned toward him and whispered, "Della was murdered." When I stepped back, I noticed his face had filled with a shocked expression.

"You sure do know how to break bad news, Jules." Bun's voice dripped with sarcasm.

"Sorry, I have to go." I walked away with the carryall over one shoulder and Bun in the sling hanging off the other.

Carver and I met up halfway between the tent and the trail. He glanced past me and asked, "Is he a member of the stash team?"

I followed his look and returned Denton's wave before

he walked away. "He is and he's also the council's marketing guru. To top that off, he's a marketing professor at the college."

Jack's brows hiked up a notch. "I see you've found out who is who and all that. I'm not foolish enough to tell you not to interfere with my investigation. I'll only say you should watch yourself. One of the stash crew might be the killer."

"Why jump to that conclusion?"

"One of them approached me on the trail earlier, stating he'd heard an argument between Della Meeny and someone else before you all got started. Do you know about that?"

"Now that you mention it, Bun and I were in the egg-cellent tent admiring the eggs when I heard two people arguing. I couldn't make out what was said, but their tones of voice were enough to know it was a disagreement."

"Not telling him all of it, huh? It's always good to hold some information back."

"Is that it? You don't have any idea at all what it was about?"

With a shake of my head, I added, "When Della came toward the stash tent, she appeared angry. While she was a mean sort, she never let on that she had argued with someone. Her instructions were short and to the point. She also made unnecessary rude remarks to the workers before we left."

"Like what?"

"She could put someone down in a heartbeat. She never encouraged the workers, and all but said we were a lazy bunch. She gave orders like a she was in the military, demanding we get busy."

"I've heard she didn't have a great personality. If you can get closer to the group to find out about them, I'd appreciate it. I have a list of those who worked at this station today and will interview as many as possible before they leave. You'll be involved in the events tomorrow?"

"Yes, we're all scheduled to participate."

"Are you gonna tell him about the human rabbit?"

"I'll see you then, Juliette. Don't take chances. There's a killer on the loose and once he, or she, has committed murder, it becomes easier to kill again."

"Gee, that makes me feel so warm and fuzzy, Jack. Don't you think I know that by now?" Without waiting for a response, I strode off.

I murmured to Bun, "I had no intention of telling him about the rabbit."

"I doubt he'd have taken you seriously, anyway. Save that tidbit for later when he's overrun with possible suspects. It will narrow his list."

On the drive home, Bun dozed until we reached the countryside. I took a right and passed under the overhead sign, then parked in front of the barn as Jessica came out to greet us.

"How did it go? Are the eggs all set for tomorrow?"

"Sure are. The kiddies should have a great time."

"Anything else happen? You seem . . . uh, like something might be wrong."

I weighed how much to tell her when Bun piped up with, *"You might as well tell her the whole thing. She'll hear it on the news, anyway."*

We got out of the car. I leaned against the fender. "Bun and I found Della Meeny's body."

With a quick intake of breath, Jessica said, "You have the worst luck of anyone I know. Honestly, you do. I can't imagine coming across a dead person once, let alone as many times as you have. What happened?"

"Let's go inside. I could use a cup of tea and a change of clothes. My feet are killing me from all the walking we did."

"Okay, while you change, I'll make the tea. Get going."

We went our separate ways. I showered quickly and then dressed in sweatpants and a jersey. When I arrived in the kitchen, Jess had set out cookies and a pot of tea to share. Bun had gone to his room to rest. I peeked in on him and saw him sprawled across his pillow.

"Tell me," Jess ordered as she poured tea into our mugs.

I gave her a rundown of what the day had been like until discovering Della, but omitted Bun had found her first.

"She was dead when you arrived in the clearing?"

"Very dead. It was a weird scene, too." I went on to explain the eggs, the flowers on her chest, and ended with the human rabbit.

Astonished, Jess gasped. "How crazy is that?"

"Exactly what I thought. I have no idea what the eggs around Della mean, nor the flowers, but there has to be a reason in the mind of the killer." I took out my phone and showed the pictures to Jess, who shuddered when she saw them.

"Does the sheriff know you have these?"

"No, he doesn't. I want it to stay that way, too."

She sat back in her chair and gave me a long look. "Don't even tell me that you plan to investigate this murder."

"Kinda."

Her hand slapped the table hard enough to make the teapot lid rattle.

"Haven't you taken enough risks to last you a lifetime, Jules? Geesh, I can't believe you would get involved in yet another mystery."

Startled by her reaction to the idea of my nosing about, I said, "I'll be helping the sheriff."

"Did he ask for your assistance?"

"Not in so many words. Jack mentioned I should let him know if I find anything amiss with any of the workers that I've become acquainted with."

Slumped in her chair, Jessica sighed. "As long as he's aware that you will be poking your nose where it doesn't belong. I guess the rest of us will do what we can to help you." She leaned forward and propped her elbows on the table, holding her tea mug in both hands. "Have you ever thought you might be better off as an investigator than trying to balance snooping and rabbit farming?"

From the other room, I heard, *"Didn't I mention that? We're fine the way we are, Jules. Besides, you'd miss the rabbits."*

"I would miss the rabbits and I earn more money with the farm than I would as an investigator. On top of that, Jack would have a fit." I chuckled over what his reaction would be, as did Jess.

"That's for sure. Jack would more likely become outraged to think you'd poke your nose into every case he has."

Chapter 5

The table cleared, Jess, Bun, and I went into the barn and began the late-day chores. We freshened the hutches and cages, then fed and watered all the rabbits. I checked on Petra to see how she was doing and Jess met me at the cage.

She reached in to pet the rabbit. "She's well. Her kits should arrive soon. I rechecked the dates and found I had misjudged the time frame for her delivery. As with all births, the kits will arrive when they are ready to make their debut."

"She seems comfortable enough."

"We'll keep an eye on her, though. I don't think she'll have difficulties, but one never knows for sure."

We scrubbed up at the sink and turned in unison when Molly burst through the door.

Her eyes wide and her face shocked, she blurted, "Have you heard that Della Meeny is dead?"

Jess nodded. "And that Jules and Bun found her?"

"Oh my goodness, you did not. How awful for you, Jules."

"How did you find out about Della?"

"When I called my marketing instructor to get the schedule for a paper that's due soon, he told me."

"Your instructor is Professor Clarke?"

With a nod, Molly said, "He's super. He's got such a great personality, too. Under his direction, marketing seems easy. Professor Clarke handled publicity for the hop."

"He did mention that. I'd never have thought he was a professor."

She snickered. "Denton looks too young to be one, don't you agree?"

I nodded and the three of us entered the shop. Neat as a pin, the spinning and weaving sections for the upcoming class were prepared and ready for the students. Twice a month, Molly offered a free class for ongoing students to work on projects they wanted to finish. Since they paid dearly for their classes, Molly insisted on giving them a freebie.

The one provision for attendance was they only use the time to complete a project, or for extra help. That had been a smart move on her part. The word had spread and we now had a waiting list for future class openings. At this rate, we would need to reorganize the room to create additional space.

"As always, you're ready for class. Looks great, Molly."

Jessica added, "You might consider changing things around a bit to accommodate more students."

Molly gave the room a long look and turned to me. "You'd have to approve the idea and order equipment. I was worried about asking, since you've already spent a lot on the shop lately."

She had such a hopeful expression, I said, "This end of the business is very self-sufficient. Early on, we were in the red, but your predecessor got things underway and since you've taken over, it has paid off. My only worry is that your studies will fall by the wayside as you become more involved here."

"My focus is somewhat split, but still, my classes fit in with the creativity here. I've got it covered; you needn't be concerned. My mother has offered to give me a hand now and then if I become overwhelmed."

"I'll think it over. If you come up with a better floor plan than what we now have, then it might be doable. I don't want this to become too much for you, Molly."

While Molly nodded, Jessica said, "Jules is right. Your education comes first and this job does offer you the opportunity to practice what you're learning. I think it's splendid." She patted Molly on the shoulder. "As Jules said, the expansion idea needs some thought."

Not to be excluded from sharing an opinion, Bun nudged my ankle. *"She's a smart one, that Molly. Give her what she wants. She can do it. I feel it in my lucky foot. Besides, you'll make more money and might not have to do so many children's parties. They are very exhausting for us rabbits, you know."*

I stared down at him, then scooped him off the floor. "I'm walking to the lake. Does anyone want to come along?"

Both women shook their heads and Jess said, "Take Bun, he'll enjoy the fresh air."

His nostrils quivered as did his whiskers. *"As if I didn't already have enough of that today."*

"I have my phone with me, should I be needed. See you two later."

Taking our usual route, Bun and I headed for Lake Plantain. We'd reached the gated lane and swerved toward the beach. Waves gently lapped the shore, and while it was getting late in the day, the sand was still warm when we sat down.

"Do you know how we're going to solve Della's murder?"

"A good place to start would be to engage those who worked as volunteers. Jack is questioning those at the eggcellent station. Our group is supposed to show up tomorrow, which will be a great chance to get a feel for who had a serious enough grudge against Della to kill her."

"We might have a tough time sorting out who would be that dangerous. Della wasn't liked by many and didn't even like herself. You know, Jules, you have to be happy with yourself to be happy with anyone else. Just look at us: We like ourselves, don't we?"

"We do." Bun's outlook often made me smile, but he made sense.

"Sheriff Carver will need our assistance more than ever. He's come to rely on our expertise in getting close to those who might be villains. People don't talk to cops like they talk to us. We're trustworthy and they know it. Cops, on the other hand . . . well, they have to live by the law."

I looked at Bun. "We live by the law."

His whiskers jittered and his lips pulled back a bit, showing his front teeth. As a kind of smile, it was odd, but then, I couldn't imagine how else a rabbit would smile.

"On one side or the other, I'd say."

Considering we illegally entered homes and sneaked around a lot, I could see what Bun meant. I rose from the beach, brushed sand off my pants, and said it was time to go. Unlike other instances when we'd been here, this one was quite pleasant, with our solitude unbroken.

On the way home, a police cruiser approached. Undoubtedly, I had been too confident over the solitude thing. We watched the car roll to a stop. Sheriff Carver summoned us to get in.

I heaved a sigh, took Bun in my arms, and got into the passenger seat. "Were you looking for us?"

"I stopped by the farm and was told you were here. Nice place for contemplation."

"It was." I wasn't snarky, but Carver thought I was.

"You know, Juliette, I do have a murder on my hands and you are key to solving it. You could be less rude."

"Geesh, I wasn't rude. I just meant it was nice to be here alone and have a chance to think."

"Let's move on, then." Jack parked the cruiser in front of the barn.

"Yes, let's." I led the way indoors.

His campaign hat on the table, Jack said, "Tomorrow, I want you to speak with as many of the volunteers at your station as you can. Use your rabbit to start a conversation and whatever it is that encourages people to tell you their secrets and whatnot. People talk to you, they like the rabbit, and you get more information than I ever could."

"Sure, I can do that. I'm surprised you won't have undercover people hanging about listening to all that's said."

He glanced away and then cleared his throat.

I gasped. "You will, won't you? It would have been nice if you'd said so. Would anyone on the stash team be one of your people?"

"Unfortunately, not. If I'd thought for one second there would be a murder, I would have had half my officers volunteer for everything and anything."

His chagrin apparent, I understood how frustrating it could be. I also knew Jack was capable of sleuthing with the best of us, including Bun. While he didn't have superpowers, like Bun's, Jack read people better than anyone I knew.

"I'll do my best to gather information for you if you promise to keep me posted on what you find out, too. I don't like walking around not knowing who the players are, okay?"

"Fair enough." Jack put his hat on and walked out the door.

I wandered out to the shop, peeked into the room, and noticed a few students had stayed longer than expected. Each hard at work, they used as much of Molly's knowledge as they could glean from her. Patient as ever, Molly guided each of them in turn. She glanced up, smiled at me, and turned back to answer the question Meredith had posed.

The evening sky darkened. I'd missed dinner and hadn't seen Jessica leave. Bun and I went into the barn. I closed the door behind us and took stock of the rabbits. I double-checked Petra, who was calmly settled in her hutch.

Walkabout Willy had begun to gnaw on his hutch. Rabbits do like to gnaw, but with Willy, it was a way to escape. He enjoyed going off on his own, even though he returned. I made a mental note to take care of the hutch portion he had a taste for. It just wouldn't do for him to get loose and wander off if the barn door was open.

The rabbits had all they needed for the night, though I would make the rounds once again before going to bed. Bun and I set off for the house and some dinner.

I heated a bowl of leftover soup and made a grilled cheese sandwich to go with it. Bun had alfalfa bits of hay mixed with fruit and veggies bundled up in greens. The pocket of food wasn't large, but enough to hold Bun over until the morning. He munched, as did I until the phone rang.

"Hello."

"Hi, Juliette. I have a question."

I recognized Denton Clarke's voice. "How can I help?"

"My niece Tilly will be turning four next month. I'm sure she would enjoy having you and your rabbits, along with the puppeteer, at her party. I've already spoken to my sister and she approves of the idea. What does your schedule look like?"

He gave me the date and I checked my calendar to see if it would work. "I can do that date, but I'll have to contact Bailey to make sure she can. I'll get back to you when I know. How's that?"

"Perfect. I know Tilly will be excited over having you all there."

"Thanks for considering us."

He gave me his cell phone number and said, "Call me back."

When the call ended, I dialed Bailey's number. She answered on the second ring.

"Hey, Bailey. It's Jules. I just heard from Denton Clarke, one of the volunteers from today. He's asked if we could entertain at his niece's birthday party next month." I gave her the date and then explained who Denton was.

"That sounds great. I've got that day available, too. How old is the child?"

"She's going to be four."

"Okay, that gives me something to work with for the age level of the program. Thanks for the call. I'm delighted to be asked."

"Me, too. I'll call Denton and let him know we're all set. Thanks, Bailey."

After she hung up I called Denton.

He answered right away. "You're both available, aren't you?"

"We are. If you give me your sister's information, I can contact her for details."

I jotted down Belinda's information and thanked Denton before hanging up.

"Was that an invitation to do another party?"

"It was. Once I speak with Belinda, I should have a better idea of what to expect."

"I suppose I can put up with more kids yelling and screaming while they run around unattended. I get a lot of information by listening to the women gossip and that can come in handy, don't you think?"

"With your excellent hearing and my being busy with the kids and rabbits, it's a perfect setup." I leaned down and rubbed his ears. "You are invaluable to me."

He gave a tiny sigh. *"I know. We're lucky I'm so adept at sleuthing."*

My conversation with Belinda went well. We outlined plans and she invited me to visit her home prior to the date for a look at the yard where Bailey and I would set up.

I'd just hung up when Bailey called. Sharing the information from Belinda, a squeal of excitement crossed the line.

"This might be the start of a great partnership. Very exciting, at least for me. How far away is Belinda's home from your farm?" Bailey asked.

"She's on the north side of Windermere, about five miles from here. You can ride with me if you want. We'll figure out a day to go look at the yard."

"That's fine. I wanted to offer my help for tomorrow's hop. Alvin called and said he changed the time of my show to the afternoon. I can give you a hand in the morning if you need it."

"Wonderful, I can use all the help I can get now that Della won't be around. While I'm not in charge, I know what needs doing and hopefully, everyone will take part. They didn't seem too organized this afternoon. They were shocked by Della's disappearance, I guess."

"I'm sure they were. I heard Della's dead. Too bad. I'm sure the police will get to the bottom of that."

"I believe an investigation is underway to determine what happened to her. Sheriff Carver isn't saying much as yet." Unwilling to discuss what Jack had said or done up to now, I changed the subject. "What time will you be available tomorrow?"

"I'll be at the station bright and early. See you then."

I put the phone in the charger and went to the shop. Students were on their way out the door when I stepped into the room. Only Meredith Carver remained. I listened as she spoke with Molly and smiled when she turned to me before leaving.

"You certainly had a busy day today, Jules. I imagine you were shocked to find Della dead and all." With a visible shiver, she continued. "I suppose you'll help Jack with his investigation?"

"He's asked me to keep my ears open for mention of what he might use to move the case forward." Unwilling to say more, since I knew Jack rarely spoke to his wife about work matters, I figured she'd gleaned that much from him before he refused to discuss it further.

She nodded. "Yes, it's a real shame that Della is gone. She was quite knowledgeable about everything that went on in the council. While she wasn't a sweet person, she knew how to organize."

Molly agreed. "She certainly did."

Meredith walked to the door. With her hand on the doorknob, she said, "I'm sure the council will be lost without her. If you have any questions about her background, let me know. Jack is deaf to my tidbits of information. He thinks they're only gossip, but they are facts."

"I'll keep that in mind. I know I can always count on you to point me in the right direction, Meredith."

She left with a smile on her face, certain that I would call on her should I need some pearls of wisdom that only she could give me where Della was concerned.

Molly gave me a grin and said, "That was pretty smooth."

"I know, huh? Meredith has been helpful before and she might be again this time around. How did things go tonight?"

"It seemed to go well. The students got what they needed and have promised to spread the word of future classes to their friends. By the way, I'll be at the hop tomorrow. If there's anything I can do to help, just ask."

"I will, thanks. Now go home, I'll clear things up in here. You've had a long day."

"If you insist."

I pointed to the door. Molly laughed, then grabbed her jacket and handbag and skedaddled.

"You sure know how to get people to help. They're practically falling over themselves to be part of our investigation. Jessica is the only one who hasn't offered, but then, I suppose someone has to remain behind while we hunt for a killer."

"Exactly. It isn't as though Jess doesn't want to help. She has a different outlook on our sleuthing. Why don't you turn in for the night? I'll organize this room and be in later."

"I'd rather stay here. Somebody might try to come in to harm you. You know how valuable I can be when you're in trouble."

Indeed, I did. Bun had come to my rescue a few times in the past. With what energy I had left, I straightened the room and then gave the rabbits a last look to make sure all was well as the grandfather clock struck ten.

Chapter 6

Breakfast for the rabbits served, I had all the chores finished early and then I headed for the shower. After blow-drying my hair and getting dressed, I dabbed a touch of lipstick to my lips. With a swish of mascara to my eyelashes, I was ready to leave. Bun waited at the bedroom door.

"Are you finally ready?"

"As I'll ever be. Let's go." In the kitchen, I grabbed a slice of toast from the toaster when it popped. I slathered it with butter before opening the door for Bun to go out first.

Jessica waited by my car. Surprised to see her, I said, "What are you doing here today?"

"I decided you could use some help since Della won't be at the hop."

"Great, get in, I want to be early. The programs end

around three o'clock. The rabbits will be fine until we get back, I'm sure. Besides, Jason offered to pop in for a while to check on them."

We arrived at the park by eight-thirty. With the event organized from the start, attendants guided drivers to parking spaces. Volunteers had a separate section. I put the window down and got directions on where to go.

"They are organized."

"The whole event should run like clockwork—if no one else gets murdered, that is."

Jess frowned and then asked, "Will you be on the path or at the station?"

"I'm not sure yet. I might be on the path to make sure no one has any problems. Some of us were assigned to various parts of the park."

"It sure looks like a lot has been done to make the day a success. I'd be happy to work the path if you want to stay on the grounds. That way, you'll know everything will run smoothly."

"Before I agree to that, let's see what the group is doing when we get to the station. Alvin is beckoning to us, so maybe there's been a change of plans."

When we reached Alvin, I noticed he held a clipboard and pen. Businesslike, he listed Jessica's name as a volunteer and then turned to me.

"Since Della is no longer with us, I'd like you to handle the station and volunteers. I have a radio for you to stay in touch should there be a problem. I'm short one person for Tucker Trail, so if you don't mind being a trail monitor, Jessica, I'll give you a radio, too."

He reached out to the table next to him and plucked two handheld radios from their chargers. After he'd checked the channel, he handed them to us and went over a few instructions for the trail monitors and gave their names. When he outlined my duties, I began to think this would be a very long day.

We walked toward the scoop and stash station. I mumbled that I didn't know why I was chosen to be in charge.

"You know you wouldn't have it any other way."

Jess piped up with, "Because you're good at it, that's why. Enjoy the challenge of keeping track of humans instead of rabbits."

"Nice of you to say, but I find rabbits much easier to deal with, and they're nicer than humans."

"No question there. You have a way about you that draws people in. They start talking and tell you much more than they had planned on. Consider it a gift, Jules."

"She sure knows us well. Between us, we have what it takes to handle all sorts of situations. People do take you into their confidence because they sense you're trustworthy."

"We can only wait to see how the day goes and what the other volunteers think of Alvin's decision. From here, I can see all but one worker has shown up. They appear restless to get on with their duties, too."

We arrived at the table with smiles on our faces, except for Bun, of course. I introduced Jessica and let each person introduce themselves, while I mentally associated each face to their name, even though they wore name tags. It was a trick I had learned in college.

The redhead, Felicia Brandt, stepped forward and said, "I'll handle the group from here on out."

I glanced at several volunteers to see their looks of surprise and something else. I couldn't tell what the something else was, so I spoke up.

"Alvin has decided that he would like me to handle the

station. If you want to be in charge of the trail monitors, Felicia, that will make the job easier."

Belligerent, Felicia didn't like the idea at all. "Why would I want to go into those bug-infested woods once again, when I can do this job instead?"

I figured she wanted the entire job or none at all. Trepidation, mixed with a healthy dose of stubbornness, nearly consumed me as I considered whether to take a stand or give in. Taking a stand won out.

"Because that's not what Alvin has requested." I glanced at my watch and handed lists of alphabetical names to the workers who would remain at the station. Felicia wasn't one of them.

Her face flushed and her eyes snapped with anger when I reached her. I said, "You need to make a decision. You can shoulder the responsibility of being in charge of the monitors, or you can work at one of the tables under another leader."

"Fine, I'll monitor the monitors." She flounced off, beckoning those who were assigned that task to join her. Jessica leaned in and whispered, "Gee, thanks. I'm now being bossed around by Attila the Hun."

I snickered and turned to Denton, Mary Lou Trout, and Charlie Cardiff, and pointed. "You three take the last table over there. The people with last names that start with the corresponding letters posted on the sign will come to you for a pass to pin onto their shirts." I moved to the next three volunteers and repeated the instructions for the second table. I finally followed my team to the first table. As I'd thought before, this day had started as one to remember. God, help me.

Families rushed forward and were sent to designated tables to get their pass. Each child received a basket before scooting off to Tucker Trail. Impressed with the volunteers, I gave them a thumbs up. Stragglers, with kids in tow, arrived as a bunch of egg hunters entered the trail. Eagerly, they grabbed their baskets and ran to catch up before all the eggs were found.

I'd just taken a seat when Stacey Farnsworth showed up with two other volunteers. They hauled wagons of coolers filled with drinks and food. Happy to know we'd be well taken care of, I thanked her. She waved as she left us to it. Denton and Joey Connell handed out cold beverages. I slugged down a bottle of lemonade, while others did the same. The day had warmed and the sun beat down on us.

Rather than sit in the heat, which was unusual for this time of year in New Hampshire, I suggested we move to the shade of the tent.

Wiping beads of sweat from his brow, Denton said, "Great idea. We can watch for the little eggsters to return from there."

Everyone pitched in and carried chairs and then brought tables to the edge of the tent. Relaxed in the shade, I put food and water out for Bun. He'd been suspiciously silent all morning, causing me to wonder if he was feeling well, or if he merely absorbed all he heard. While he had his snack, I listened to the others chat.

With his feet propped on a table, Frank Poland asked, "Who was questioned by Sheriff Carver?" He glanced at each volunteer, his grayish-blue eyes sharp and attentive.

The others mumbled that Carver had briefly spoken to them. All except for Rob Brayton, an arrogant, seemingly entitled, and resentful student from the local college. He'd refrained from entering any conversations, but did what he'd been assigned.

Curious, I asked, "How about you, Rob? Did the sheriff speak to you?"

Frank perked up and stared at Rob, an intense expression on his face.

His brows arched, Rob asked, "Why do you ask?"

"Just wondering. I was the one who found Della. It was quite an unpleasant and nerve-racking experience."

"I'm sure it was," he remarked with a smirk.

"Do you find her death funny?"

"Of course not, but she's no great loss, either."

Bun bumped my ankle with his nose. *"Tread carefully."*

"You knew her, then?"

Rob studied the entrance of Tucker trail for a moment or two before he looked at me, his green eyes void of emotion. "I'd run across her once or twice. We weren't friends."

Before I could ask any other questions, he dipped his wavy brown-haired head toward the trail. "Ah, the return of eggsters."

Parents carried youngsters or held their hands, and balanced overflowing buckets of colorful eggs as they strode toward our tables. Each volunteer returned to their assigned stations to count and note the amount of eggs collected. The children, though tired, remained excited and often clapped their hands or squealed with joy when they received the count of how many eggs they had found. Parents took a signed slip before they left. The announced winner would hand in the slip and receive their prize at the end of the event.

Our conversations continued between the onslaught of returning eggsters. A man stepped up to the table, a little girl's hand clasped in his. I looked at her and then up at the man, who just happened to be a cop I knew. Wondering if he was undercover, since Carver had mentioned some of his men would be, I didn't let on I knew him, but counted the eggs and handed him a slip. How I hadn't noticed him when he'd signed in earlier in the day was beyond me. I wished him and the child good luck and watched as they walked away.

"Do you know that guy?" Denton asked.

"No, do you?"

"He seems familiar, but I can't recall from where."

I smiled. "Some people have those kinds of faces."

"You're probably right."

"That was a close one. You did well, Jules."

Excusing myself from the table, I left Denton and Erin Britman to handle the next few eggsters. I poured more water into Bun's bowl and whispered, "Stay alert."

"I will."

I heard the shuffle of feet behind me. I stood up and saw Frank Poland not three feet away.

"I've heard that talking to your rabbits is good for them. Is that why you talk to yours?"

"Of course. They're sociable critters and grow comfortable with you, and react when spoken to."

His grin grew wide. "Do you think they understand?"

"It doesn't matter. Like other animals, they respond to the tone of voice, rather than what's said."

"I guess you'd know more about that than I would. As a kid, all I ever had was a goldfish."

I chuckled and returned to the table as a swarm of eggsters arrived. Surprised when Molly walked up and offered to help, I gladly accepted. She nodded at Denton, greeted Erin, and then waved to the other volunteers at their tables. It was then that I realized the value Molly could add to the investigation of Della's death. The young woman was familiar with the others and could give me backgrounds on them all. Elated by the thought, I heard Denton's laughter.

"What?" I asked.

"I heard that sigh. It's evident you had no idea how many participants there would be for this event alone."

"You're right. I didn't have a clue." I stared past the new arrivals to see Felicia Brandt exiting the trail in the company of someone dressed in a rabbit costume. Her hands waving, I could tell Felicia wasn't happy and wondered if that was her constant state of being. When she and the human rabbit parted ways, I noticed Jessica lagging a few feet behind. When Jess saw me, she hurried forward and ignored Felicia as she passed by her.

On alert for fear of what might have happened on the trail, I took in the entire group of volunteers who'd been monitoring the hunters as they approached. They appeared to be in good humor. I asked Denton to hand out food and beverages to them. He gave me a nod and went toward the coolers.

Jessica heard me and mentioned refreshments were available inside the tent when the others arrived. The monitors walked into the shade the tent provided and hurried over to Denton. I had watched and then turned to Jess.

"You should get some food before it disappears."

"I will, but give me some time at the end of the day, will you? I have lots to share." With that, Jess sauntered forward, declaring her need of a cold drink and a sandwich. Some of the others chuckled, while others made room for her to sit with them. Jessica was popular with all the volunteers—uh, well, maybe not all. Felicia glared at her, a frown on her face that caused her beauty to disappear completely. Another unhappy soul. The thought had popped into my mind and reminded me that I'd wondered the same about Della.

"She's got some serious issues, doesn't she?"

I picked Bun off the ground and petted him to let him know I agreed.

"Dear Felicia will need some watching, or should I say monitoring?"

I turned to the table volunteers and asked, "Have all the egg hunters returned?"

Chapter 7

Each group had checked off the hunters' names as they returned to have their eggs counted. With all but one name accounted for, I took a deep breath and let it out slowly.

"If you want to go on your way, I'll look for the straggler. I appreciate your hard work today. Enjoy the rest of the afternoon."

Molly and Jessica approached me as I packed up Bun's things and donned his sling. When I leaned down, Bun snuggled inside, got comfortable, and then poked his head out. Ready to get onto the trail, I set our supplies aside. About to begin the search, I found several volunteers standing around.

"What are you waiting for?"

Rob was the first to speak up. "In light of Della's recent demise, we think you shouldn't do this alone. We'll split up into twos and help you find this person. What's his name, anyway?" His stance was relaxed, his body lean, yet his muscles flexed when his arms moved as he pointed to Erin Britman, who anxiously teamed up with him.

I ran a finger down the list of names and paused at the only one without a check mark next to it. "Gerard Coldren—he had one child with him." I looked up, the searchers were ready, and I handed Denton my radio.

"Get in touch with Sheriff Carver. Make sure he knows we're searching for a straggler. Tell him we don't think there's any need to worry. Jessica still has her radio, so you can let us know what Carver says."

"I'll do that right now." Denton walked to the far end of the tent, talking a mile a minute, as the rest of us took off for the trail.

Jessica and Molly remained with me, the others partnered up, and we all agreed to meet back at the trail's entrance in an hour. My nerves were frantic like Mexican jumping beans. They didn't seem to realize there was nothing to be concerned about, or did they know more than my brain was willing to accept?

"There's no sense in letting anxiety rule you, Jules. This man and his daughter probably returned but didn't bother to check in with us. Try to relax."

Reasoning was one of Bun's attributes. When I became the least bit frazzled, Bun would calm my tattered nerves. I did the same for him.

"Maybe this man and his child just didn't check in," I said hopefully.

Molly took to the idea. "I thought of that, too."

Jessica rained on our hopes when she added her two cents' worth. "I watched the hunters and kids like a hawk. They passed me as they left this trail, and I don't remember seeing a name badge with that name on it. Sorry."

"Let's spread out and call to Mr. Coldren. Maybe he's had an accident or something. There are a few treacherous points in this park once you're off the path. He could have left the designated route, right?" My hands clenched in fists at my sides, I prayed that was the case and that the man and child were okay.

Jessica's radio crackled as Jack Carver's voice came through. "Officers are heading your way, Juliette. Call me if you can."

The three of us glanced at one another. I pulled my phone from my pocket and touched Jack's name with my finger. His phone rang once before I heard his voice.

"What do you think you're doing?" Carver growled.

"Making sure no one strayed from the path and lost their way, that's what."

"You don't think there's a body waiting to be found, then?"

"Why would you even consider that?"

"Because you're involved."

In no mood for a lecture that I hadn't earned, I said, "Oh. I think I hear your officers coming. Adam is calling my name. Gotta go, Jack. I'm sure Adam will keep you posted."

Six policemen came around the path's curve and slowed when they saw us.

"I just spoke to Jack. What does he want you to do?" I asked.

Adam shrugged and said, "He'd like you three escorted to the tent where you'll wait for us to find this missing person."

For the second time today, I stood my ground. "Well, that's not going to happen. We don't even know if this guy and his daughter are here. He never checked in at the end of the hunt. Our search is merely a precaution. Besides, we're wasting time and the other searchers will return to the start of the trail very soon. If you plan to help, then for goodness' sake, do it. Leave the path and search the valleys. There are two of them." I pointed up the hillside and then turned away.

"Whoa, you sure gave him an earful. You must be pretty upset."

"Jess, check in with Denton. Maybe this guy has wandered back to the tent."

While Jess contacted him, Molly and I looked over both sides of the path where it dipped. Molly climbed the knolls as we came upon them. Nothing found, no matter how hard we searched. A heavier dose of anxiety set in.

We'd made it halfway through the trail and wended our way along a winding portion of the path when one of the searchers ran toward us. His expression was filled with fear as he halted in front of us, his chest heaving. The man was out of breath and his words halting.

Edmund Fortin finally hauled in a deep breath and said, "We found him. His daughter is with him. They're both alive. Gerald has a broken leg and can't walk. His daughter was afraid to leave him."

I heaved a sigh of relief and called Sheriff Carver. Once he heard the specifics, I knew he would notify the medical personnel and contact Adam. We went with Edmund and joined the rest of the team at Gerald Coldren's location.

We slid down the steep embankment where Gerald lay. Jessica gave him a quick once-over and then concentrated on his broken leg. His yelp of pain was followed by epithets no child should hear. I covered her ears with my hands as Jessica kneeled back.

"It appears there's more than one fracture, but I can't tell for sure. This man needs to go to the hospital. Did Jack say when the rescue team will arrive?"

"No, he didn't."

Jess turned her gaze to Gerald and asked, "How did you come to be here?"

"I was protecting my daughter from a couple of bully boys who tried to take her eggs. As they grabbed her basket, I turned to see a tall guy in a rabbit suit, who then shoved me. I lost my balance, fell off the edge of the trail, and ended up here after I bounced off that boulder. I heard my leg snap. Emily slid down the hillside to be with me, and the rabbit took off without a backward glance."

I looked down at Emily.

"So the kids took your eggs and basket? Did you recognize them?"

She couldn't have been more than four or five years old—at least that was my best guess. Emily stared at the ground and whispered, "They took every one of them. They were pretty eggs. I don't know the boys, but they were mean to me." When she looked up, two enormous tears had rolled down her cheeks.

I knelt in front of her and promised she would get more pretty eggs and a new basket.

"Thank you." She reached out and touched Bun's soft nose and smoothed the fur on his face as he stared at her from the sling opening. "Is this your rabbit?"

"He is my friend. We're besties." The word I'd heard so many of the birthday guests use tickled me to no end. It must have been the right one, for Emily smiled.

"I'll wait until you come to the tent where there will be a basket of eggs ready and waiting for you."

By now, the police officers and rescue crew had arrived. They shooed us away from Gerald and Emily. Knowing they were in good hands, Edmund and the three of us women climbed the embankment to the trail and began our trek to the tent.

With his hand on my shoulder, Edmund remarked, "That was very generous of you. Where will you get the eggs? We hid all that we had."

Bun added, *"I think it was, too. I was generous enough to allow Emily to touch my face. Bullies are so mean. Margery was a bully, but you took care of her. I doubt she'll ever try to harm me again."*

"Bullies shouldn't be allowed to get away with those actions. I'll do my best to find out who they were. Gerald could have died from that fall. As for the eggs, the eggcellent station has extras to donate. I'm sure they won't mind giving some to Emily."

I left the others behind when we arrived at the tent and went to the eggcellent station. Large trays still held beautifully painted eggs that were a feast for my eyes. Stan Fin, the man in charge of the station, was the only soul left. He stared at me as I gasped in awe over the sight of the eggs.

"Are you looking for something special, Juliette?"

I quickly explained what happened to Emily and asked if I could replace the ones stolen from her.

"Poor kid. Go ahead, take what you think she'll like. Did you report this to the event chairman?"

"I plan to. I wanted to take care of this first." I reached for two more eggs and set them in the basket he had handed me.

"Make sure you tell him. He'll want to know so this doesn't happen again if we hold another hop next year."

I thanked Stan and returned to my station. Molly had found a bag of assembled bows with streaming ribbons attached under Della's stand. She rushed forward, brandishing a colorful bunch. In a flash, she'd fastened the glorious array to the basket's handle. We stepped back to admire our work.

"Looks perfect to me."

Molly grinned and agreed.

An hour later, Molly left with Jessica in tow, while I remained behind with Bun. All the volunteers were involved in other activities that were coming to an end. Sheriff Carver stepped into the shady tent, wiped perspiration from his brow, and set his hat on a table before he took a seat.

"You did well today. My people were impressed."

"Really? I nearly bit Adam's head off. I'm sure he mentioned that."

He snickered and nodded. "He did. It was my fault; he was only following orders."

"Yeah, well, I don't like being ordered around. You should know that by now, Jack."

He tipped his chin toward the rescuers as they exited the trail and remarked, "It's about time."

The team rolled Gerald, strapped onto the gurney, into the ambulance as we watched.

Adam escorted Emily to the tent. I handed her the basket that brought a squeal of delight from her.

"I can have this all to myself?"

"You sure can. You're very brave, Emily."

"I have to go now. Thank you and your rabbit, too." She stepped close and touched Bun's ears and nose, then hurried to the ambulance. Adam lifted her in and closed the double doors.

I heard a tiny sigh.

"She likes me a lot."

"Seems your rabbit has a fan club."

"You know, Jack, he is a wonderful rabbit. It's too bad you refuse to see that. I have to get home. I've missed out on the other functions today, but this job was important."

"I'll walk you to your car."

"No need. I'll stop to see Bailey, if she's still here."

Jack remarked, "Try to stay out of trouble, won't you?"

I rolled my eyes and walked away.

Crowds had thinned and the parking lots were almost empty. With a brief detour to speak with Alvin, I related Gerald's incident and assured him that the injuries weren't life-threatening. I omitted the fact that I had seen a human costumed as a rabbit like the one at Della's crime scene. If Sheriff Carver wanted to share that information with Alvin, then he could.

By the time I reached Bailey's section of the grounds, she'd taken down the stage and started the process of packing up the puppets.

I let Bun out of the sling and waggled my index finger

at him. He knew this meant he had to stay close. After all, I'd had enough excitement for the day and I didn't need him to wander off to create more. When his left ear tipped forward, I took it as a sign that he understood.

"Need a hand?"

"Yeah, can you open the back doors of the van for me and help me load up?"

"Sure thing."

I left Bun behind, trotted to the van, and opened the doors wide. It didn't take long before we'd fit everything into the vehicle. "Thanks, Jules. I appreciate the help."

"How did the show go?"

"The kids were wild and crazy until I started, then they became calm and engrossed in what was happening. It always amazes me that kids nowadays, most with access to the internet and mind-boggling video games and such, can still be entertained by puppets. It says something about live entertainment, doesn't it?"

"That's how I feel when they respond to the rabbits at parties and public functions. Not everything in life should be internet related. It's good for kids to have the option of real live animals, such as mine, and to be part of your interactive puppet shows. I like them, too."

"You do?"

"Do you?"

"Of course. It's great to see what scripts you come up with. You charm the kids, bring laughter and joy into their lives that doesn't include violence of any sort. It's rather refreshing."

I waited until she closed the van doors before I shared my day. As I got into the story, her look of astonishment became quite obvious. By the time I'd finished, she'd leaned against the vehicle, her arms crossed, and a look of disgust on her face.

"People never cease to amaze, do they?"

"That's for sure. I wish I had been able to get my hands on those bullies. I'd have turned them over to Jack Carver and let him scare the bejeepers out of them. My other thought was how their parents could allow the little beasties to do such a thing."

"If you can, share your thoughts with Alvin when the council meets to discuss the event. The first time is always the most difficult, since no one knows what might happen."

"I already did. I'd better get back to the farm."

"Oh, wait. I've had a couple of requests for us to entertain at upcoming birthday parties. I'll email you the info so you can check your calendar. Mora Lindsey stopped by between shows to ask if we were available in June to entertain at the summer camp for the elderly folks. I said you'd be in touch with her. I hope you don't mind."

"Not at all. I'll reach out and see what date and theme Mora has in mind. I'll be in touch." I scooped Bun into my arms and walked toward my car.

"At least one of you had a terrific day. All we got were difficulties."

"I think we managed to figure out who's nice and who isn't, who might have had a grudge against Della, and who might not. It's a place for us to start, anyway."

"Of course, you're right. I think I'm just overwhelmed by all that took place today." Bun pawed the sling I had tossed onto the seat and crumpled the material for comfort.

I drove through town, picked up fast food at a drive-through burger joint, and sped back to the farm. Bun wasn't the only one overwhelmed, so was I, even though there was rabbit work to do. I sighed and parked the car in front of the barn next to Sheriff Carver's. He leaned against the fender of his vehicle, looking around as if he had nothing better to do.

Chapter 8

Without a word of greeting between us, he dipped his hat covered head toward me and accompanied me into the house. Bun hopped onto the rug in front of the sink to listen. To hear what? It might have been to get the latest and greatest news. I wanted to know if he'd found any leads on Della's death, but then, I was anxious to dive into the burger and fries in the bag I'd dropped on the table. I still had to care for the rabbits.

Jack opened his mouth as the phone rang. Jessica's name and number scrolled across the screen. I answered the call and listened as she said that she and Molly had prepared supper for the rabbits. All I had to do was dole it out. About to hang up, I paused when she asked, "Did you hear that Sheriff Carver has a suspect in custody for Della's murder?"

"Is that so? I didn't know that."

"He's there, isn't he?"

"Yes, thanks for taking care of the rabbits. I'll be in touch."

A snort came across the line before our call ended.

"Would you like coffee or iced tea? How about a sandwich?" I asked as Jack took a seat at the kitchen table.

"Coffee would be great. It's been a long day."

I agreed and set the coffeepot to brew for two. "It sure has and it isn't over yet. What's your mind, Jack?" I pulled the meal from the bag and started to eat.

"I have a suspect at the station that I'll be questioning shortly. He might not be Della's killer, especially since the lab report isn't in yet, so we aren't certain how she died. I think he might know what took place that day, or at least knows why she was killed."

In between bites, I placed a milk pitcher and a sugar bowl on the table, along with a few napkins. Jack watched every move I made while he snatched a couple of fries. It was as though he was trying to read my body language. Cops learn that skill early in their training, and besides Adam, the sheriff was the only other officer I'd ever seen who could pick thoughts off a person. I knew this because both men had done as much to me, which I found disconcerting.

The coffee ready, I filled two mugs and brought them to the table, before settling in for what could prove to be an enlightening conversation, or time wasted while being questioned about Della's murder, again. I sipped my coffee. Jack blew on his and then took a swig that scalded his tongue. I held back a smirk.

"What does your suspect have to do with me?"

"Nothing, yet. I wondered if you'd come to the station to look the guy over and give me your opinion of him."

"Tonight?"

"Yeah, sorry, I know you've had an incredibly busy day and still have work to do, but it would help if you could do this for me. I don't have anything solid to charge him with and can't lock him up. He's waiting in the inter-rogation room."

The interrogation room was more like a box because it was square and encased in bulletproof glass panels on three sides. The fourth side was a solid wall that sported a two-way mirror where victims or witnesses could see the person being held. If identified as the guilty party, charges were filed and the culprit locked up. Otherwise, they'd be set free. I ruffled my curly hair with my fingers and considered a refusal. What if the guy was the killer, or knew who was? What then?

"You might as well give in and say you'll do it. Our help is needed. You realize that, don't you?"

"I suppose I can run down to the station after I feed the rabbits. You can give me a hand to make the work time shorter. That way, we can get to headquarters quicker so you can do your job." I never expected Jack to agree to my suggestion, but he did.

"I don't have to handle the rabbits, do I?"

His tone filled with disgust, Bun said, *"Oh, for good-ness' sake, doesn't the man know anything about feeding animals?"*

"Uh, no. Didn't you have a pet to care for when you were a kid?"

"Nope. My mother was allergic to animals—at least that's the story I got whenever I asked for a pet."

Instead of feeling sorry for his lack of a pet, I stood up and beckoned him into the barn. The fridge was stacked with neatly secured bundles of food. I set them on two trays and handed one of them to Jack, who looked bewildered.

"I'll show you how to hang one in a cage and you can handle it from there, okay?"

"Are you sure you trust him? He doesn't look eager to take on the job."

I glanced down, put a bundle in a bowl on the floor mat for Bun, and left him to it. Jack stood at the first cage staring at PR, short for Peter Rabbit, who waited for supper. His lovely brown fur coat was soft and shiny, his nose wiggled, and his whiskers jittered in anticipation.

I opened the small trap door next to the spot where I always hung bundles to show Jack how it worked. I hurriedly snapped the trap door closed. "Be sure the trap doors make that snapping sound, so you'll know it's secure."

Jack nodded and stepped to the next cage. He handled it so well, I left him and moved on. "I'll be in the next aisle."

Expecting him to fumble the job, I was pleasantly surprised when he said he'd run out of bundles. I took Petra's food to her cage and gave Jack the last few bunches left on my tray. Petra was fed a special diet during her pregnancy. I reached in, smoothed her long fur coat, spoke softly to her, and hung her meal lower than usual.

"Why is her food different than the others'?"

"She's pregnant. Jess thought it wise to set up a special diet for her. She should bring her kits into the world fairly soon."

Jack moved away from the cage, washed his hands in the sink, as did I, and asked, "Can we go now?"

"What is with him, anyway? It's not as if we're filthy, bug-infested critters."

I waited for Jack to leave. As he drove off, I said, "I have no idea why he reacts to you and the others that way. He doesn't seem to have a problem with dogs. Are you ready to go? I need your expertise."

"Of course, wild horses couldn't keep me away."

It didn't take long to get to the station, nor did we have to wait on the bench in the foyer. Jack escorted us into the room that overlooked all that happened during interrogation.

I caught my breath when I saw who faced the mirror. Rob Brayton relaxed in the chair, his hands resting lightly on the table. While his face was expressionless, his green eyes appeared intense. If the way Rob acted during our earlier conversation was any indication of how he fielded questions, Sheriff Carver's patience would be sorely pressed.

Carver shuffled papers from within a folder in front of him. "I understand you knew Della Meeny. How friendly were you?"

"Not friends, at all. I knew her by sight and from our interview for the volunteer position."

"So you knew her enough to speak to, then?"

Rob shrugged. "I guess."

His answer likely annoyed Jack, but he kept his cool.

Watching seemed a waste of my time, though while I observed Rob, the memory of Della's dead body returned. Mentally, I reviewed all I'd heard, seen, and smelled. The wind that rustled leftover fall leaves on the ground, crisp and shriveled from the weather. The potent, yet sweet, smell from lily of the valley flowers atop Della's chest. All was as clear to me as if I now stood at her side. I remembered how the tall figure in a rabbit costume, hurrying up an embankment across the small valley, had caught my attention.

I shook my head, cleared my mind, and searched my memory for any tiny bits that I might have disregarded at the time. Our eyes tend to play tricks on us when we least expect them to. The human rabbit had startled me, and I'd been taken aback by the sight of him. The tall rabbit, covered from head to toe, left no inkling of who might be wearing the disguise.

To accuse Rob of anything would be unfair, and I refused to do so. If, in the future, evidence came to light that implicated him, then so be it. I wouldn't take on the responsibility of claiming he was the person who had killed Della.

I took a deep breath, then exhaled slowly, and murmured, "Is there anything you remember about Della's scene that would make you believe Rob is her killer?"

"Not a thing, how about you?"

"Nothing. If Rob knows something about Della's death, he certainly won't share it with Jack, or anyone else."

A knock on the door of the interrogation room was interesting. A well-dressed man, who looked like he might be a high-priced and very sharp attorney, waited for Jack to open the door. Adam stood beside the man, his focus on him and no one else.

Jack let them in and I heard the man introduce himself as Rob's attorney. Ralph London knew his way around the law. His professionalism, attire, and sharp-eyed attitude said so. He shook hands with Jack and asked if Rob had been Mirandized.

Carver glanced at Rob. Still idle at the table, Rob shook his head.

Jack turned to back Ralph. "This young man is here for a friendly conversation, nothing more. I'm investigating the death of Della Meeny and plan to question everyone I can find who might have known her. Your client was a volunteer at the event held on the Perkins Park grounds. He knew Della. I'm trying to get a well-rounded picture of her, her life, and her associates."

"He hasn't been read his rights or charged, then?"

"No, he hasn't."

Ralph looked at Rob and asked, "Is there anything you want to say?"

Rob straightened in his chair, stared at the sheriff, and said, "It's time to leave."

The two men walked from the room without another word. Sheriff Carver watched them go and then looked at the mirror. I was at the door when I heard Jack say, "Don't leave yet; they are still here."

I stopped to wait until he said I could make my exit.

"Criminy, that sure was interesting. Why would Rob need a lawyer? Do you think he's been in trouble with the law in the past? He's arrogant, too."

"I think his arrogance is an act, but I don't know him very well and can't be sure. You're right, it was interesting. Unfortunately, Jack didn't get very far before the attorney arrived. Hmm."

The door opened and Jack stepped inside the room. "Well?"

"I don't think he's the rabbit, or the killer, but he's hiding something. I don't know what, but something. You could check with Denton Clarke. He might shed some light on Rob and what he's been up to."

"That occurred to me as well. Thanks for coming in, Juliette."

"If I remember any details from the day we found Della, I'll let you know."

"Before you go, did you speak with the volunteers during the event?"

"We had some downtime that I used to bring up Della's death. Rob's attitude wasn't much different than how he reacted to your questions. When I mentioned having found Della's body, he smirked and made a rude comment. That's when I asked if he found her unfortunate demise funny. He said no, but that she was no great loss. The kids and parents started to return, which ended any opportunity to find out more."

"Keep your ears open. You never know where you'll hear a tidbit or two that will lead to clues we've overlooked." Jack rubbed his eyes, tucked the file folder under his arm, and escorted Bun and me to my car.

As we left the station's parking lot, Bun sat up straight in the passenger's seat.

"We should have mentioned Felicia Brandt. She has an attitude the size of Texas. I bet she knows a lot more than she lets on. Being bossy and such means she likes to be in charge all the time. I thought you two would come to blows today."

"For a moment there, so did I. Good golly, I'm tired. We've had a busy day."

Our arrival at the farm was perfect timing. I wanted to

check on Petra and entered the barn before heading to the house. Petra was in full labor when I reached her hutch. I called Jess to tell her. She said she was on her way and would meet me in the barn.

Uninterested in the goings-on, Bun went straight to his room. I stared after him as he hopped through the breezeway, relieved to not have him underfoot during the delivery of Petra's kits.

Jess arrived and flipped on all the inside light switches. The motion-sensor lights outside illuminated the yard. Jess stood at Petra's hutch and took stock of the situation. As Petra's breath came quicker than usual, she nestled in a pile of hay lined with bits of fur she'd pulled from her coat. She had no difficulties as the kits arrived. We stood by, watched the delivery, and wondered how many kits Petra would bring into the world. One after another, eight tiny babies were born. Seeing there weren't any problems, we left after the last baby was clean and packed in with the others. All were alive and well with Petra in full mother mode.

We went into the house, poured glasses of wine, and toasted the births of the sweet little bunnies. After we'd gabbed about them, Jess asked how my afternoon had ended. She and Molly left the grounds before I did.

I attempted to explain the remainder of the day, but when I mentioned Felicia and her attitude, Jessica interrupted me. "That woman needs a serious attitude adjustment. She was barely civil to the egg hunters, their parents, and the staff. I could have gladly wrung her neck a couple of times."

"Really?"

"She started in on how miserable Della was, that she barked orders like a drill sergeant, and then harped about having been overlooked for Della's position after the woman was found dead. She insisted she had the experience needed to run your part of the operation, though she never mentioned you by name."

"What else did she have to say? Anything of use to Sheriff Carver?"

She paused a moment and then snapped her fingers. "Felicia and that guy—um, what's his name? I can't remember it—they had a whispered disagreement. I couldn't hear what was said, but when Felicia raised her voice, he shushed her and drew her down the path a ways. I don't think they argued about the event, though. Felicia had her back to me but kept glancing over her shoulder at me. It was odd."

"Anything else?"

"He was tall but not taller than Felicia. She's quite the Amazon, if you ask me. Maybe that's why she's so pushy. She seems more aggressive if she's standing above you, right?"

"True, but get back to the man."

"Uh, okay." Jess squeezed her eyes closed and concentrated. I grinned and then stopped when her eyes popped open again.

"It was Frank something-or-other. She had called him by name when he came along the trail."

"Frank Poland. Hmm, I was thinking more like Rob Brayton, but he doesn't appear to care for her at all. Interesting. I'll let Jack know; he can figure them out. You should get going. I know I'm exhausted, so you must be, too."

"You didn't finish telling me about your visit to the police station."

I rolled my eyes, encapsulated the story, and asked if Molly had ever mentioned Rob or any of the others.

"Not to me, but you should ask her about them. She's probably in classes with a few of them. I'll bet gossip spreads fast on that campus."

"Great idea. I'll check her schedule and when she comes to work, I'll broach the subject. Thanks, Jess."

Together, we looked in on Petra and the newborns. Finding all well and quiet, I did a head count, found all eight kits asleep with their mother, who kept an eye on us.

Chapter 9

I tried to sleep later than usual, but Bun would have none of that and stood in the doorway of my bedroom yammering on about extreme hunger and his ultimate starvation. Neither of those subjects applied to him, but I let him ramble for a few minutes until I couldn't stand it any longer.

"There are two things that will never happen while all you rabbits live here. First, you'll never go hungry. And second, you'll never starve. Are we clear on that?" I remarked from where I sat with my legs dangling off the edge of my bed, scratching my head, and ruffling my wild mass of hair that needed a trim as badly as I needed a manicure.

Jessica, Molly, and I seriously needed a girls' spa day. One where we could relax, have fun, and enjoy some pampering. I'd mention it when we had a chance to talk. In the meantime, chores awaited my attention.

After I'd dressed in work clothes, fed Bun, and slugged down a quick cup of coffee, I went into the barn. My first stop was Petra's cage. The kits and their mother were fine. I counted heads and found all eight of them had snuggled into Petra's long fur coat. The rest of the rabbits had awakened and I didn't waste time in getting their food ready. Once I'd fed them, I emptied, washed, and refilled their water containers. With fewer rabbits than I'd had last year, the workload took less time than usual. Emptying the final fecal tray into the hopper, I sanitized it, and was on my way to return it to Walkabout Willy's hutch, when Jessica arrived.

I glanced over my shoulder when she entered the barn. "What are you doing here, it's Sunday."

"I have stuff to do in the clinic, but I wanted to see Petra and her little ones."

"They had a good night and all was quiet." I continued down the aisle as Jess visited Petra.

With the rabbits set for a while, I organized the play area for them. While the rabbits would get their exercise, I could clean the hutches, replace the hay they needed, and look for damages. Rabbits, like dogs, aren't particular about what they chew. I strive to keep that in mind, and look over the hutches and wire portions of each cage daily.

Jess, finished admiring and cooing at the kits, said she'd give me a hand. There was only one cage needing repair. Walkabout Willy had been at it again. His was usually the one I had to fix.

"He sure is determined to be free, isn't he?" Jessica

shook her head and petted the critter as she removed him from the play area to put him in the indoor rabbit run.

"Willy is always up to mischief. It's a wonder we haven't lost him to a wild animal. He wanders away as often as he can." I rubbed his fur, then stepped back as Jess let him take off through the run and then come back. I rushed to open the trapdoor to the outside portion of the run.

Jess watched him go and chuckled. "He certainly is fast."

Bun had joined us and said, *"Huh, he's not as fast as I am."*

I looked at Jess. "Do you think he's as quick as Bun?"

"Mm, I'm not sure. It's been a while since I've seen Bun in action. I'm usually in the clinic when he exercises."

"Well, let's see, shall we?"

I scooped Bun off the floor, then put him into the run.

Bun sniffed. *"I don't feel like running right now."*

"Why isn't he moving? He usually runs through quickly, doesn't he?"

"He'll do the course later, in his own time, I guess. I want to see if Molly left me a note in the shop. She's amazing." I reopened the door of the run and Bun hopped out without a word.

We'd entered the room to find it neat and clean. I walked to the counter and looked for a message, but found none. A car stopped in front of the shop. We greeted Molly as she came in.

In unison, Jess and I said, "Hey, there."

"Great to see you," I remarked. "Unexpected, but still great. What brings you by?"

"I wanted to see if you have any news on Della's death. Is it murder?"

"Nothing new that I know of. When I last saw the sheriff, he was still awaiting the coroner's report. Why do you ask?"

"I heard some gossip at the hop. Two guys from the college were talking about Della. One said she'd been murdered and the other one said he didn't think so. As men do, they went back and forth about who was right, then changed the subject that included some college students who had volunteered."

"Did you hear anything good?" I asked.

"It seems three of the people at your station were doing community service due to misbehaving on campus. They were about to be expelled for their actions when Denton intervened on their behalf. He recommended they work at the hop and help clean up afterward as a community service."

"The dean agreed to that? If their behavior was bad enough for expulsion, why didn't he call the police?"

With a shrug, Molly said, "Dean Jasper considers ugly publicity equal to the plague. He'll do anything to avoid it. He took Denton's recommendation and gave the kids a choice between working at the event or leaving school permanently."

I nodded. "Amazing as that is to me, I understand the dean's reasoning. Do you know who the students were?"

"Out of the three, I know two of them. Frank Poland and Felicia. No one mentioned the third one's name. If you'd like, I can ask around."

Jess and I looked at each other and Jess said, "That might put you in an uncomfortable position. Is there another way to find out?"

Before Molly could answer, I said, "I agree with Jess. Don't take chances, no matter how much you want to help. If anything ever happened to you, we'd never forgive ourselves."

"Wow, you like me that much, huh?"

We both smiled and spoke at the same time, again. I gave Jess a glance and nod to speak first.

"We do; you're an important part of our businesses. We value your friendship. It would never do if you were harmed in any way."

"Before you three become too sappy, why doesn't she just ask this Denton fella?"

"You might ask Denton," I remarked.

"I don't think he'll tell me—privacy concerns and all that—but Dean Jasper's secretary has that information, I'm sure of it. There's nothing she doesn't know about what goes on, good or bad. I often handle her duties while she's on lunch break. Her office is always covered during the day."

"Have I mentioned how bright Molly is? She's one in a million."

I ignored Bun and agreed to Molly covering while the secretary was at lunch. "Be careful."

Her eyes lit up as she nodded vigorously. "I won't act foolishly, I promise."

We talked about her classes until she snapped her fingers and said, "Oh, gosh. I'm supposed to ask if you two would be willing to lecture to Denton's marketing class. The semester is starting to wind down, and he wants the class informed of responsibilities as a business owner and how you two market your businesses. He thinks that could help prepare his peeps for life after graduation."

"Why us?" Jess wanted to know.

"Because you're both successful and well respected in Windermere and beyond. Some students want to be entrepreneurs but aren't quite sure how to deal with the everyday life of operating a business. Come on, say you'll do it. Please?"

I asked, "How long do we have to prepare for this?"

"A couple of weeks, I think. If you agree to speak to the class, Denton will call with the particulars."

Jess said nothing, though I could tell by her expression that she was giving it serious consideration. I figured if I could handle a slew of kids and rabbits at birthday parties, then taking on this onetime opportunity would be easy.

"Okay, have Denton call me," I said. "Jess and I will work out a program to give the wannabe entrepreneurs something to consider. Right, Jess?"

"Absolutely."

"Great. Thanks. I'll let Denton know."

Molly started to leave, then she said, "I'll be in touch as soon as I get the name of that third student. Sheriff Carver might find use for the information. I'm sitting in for Cora Stanley's lunch break tomorrow."

After she'd gone, I turned to Jess and said, "I hope she's careful."

"Me, too. You realize we couldn't have talked Molly out of sneaking through Cora's paperwork, don't you?"

"I do. She's a daring one, for sure."

"Maybe, like you, she needs excitement in her life. Let's face it, Molly goes to college, has to study, and works here. There's not much time left for anything else."

"We have both been down that road, haven't we?"

"Yeah, speaking of roads, I have to be at my mother's

house in fifteen minutes. Gotta go, see you tomorrow," she said as she hightailed it out the door.

Alone with Bun, I busied myself by visiting Petra and her little ones. Adorable as they were, I couldn't spend the rest of the day with them. It was time to deal with Bun's anger over putting him in the run due to his bragging. I opened the run door and picked Willy up, then returned him to his hutch.

In the house, I found Bun sitting on the scatter rug in front of the sink. I stared down at him, but he refused to acknowledge me.

Squatting in front of him, I said, "I know you're upset with me, but you bragged about something that wasn't true. It doesn't matter if you are or aren't faster than Willy. You're special in your own right."

"I might not be faster, but I'm very quick," Bun remarked in a snooty tone.

I smoothed his ears and the top of his head. "Why, yes, you are. And, thank goodness for that."

"You sound impressed by it."

"Of course, I am. Your speed has saved us both time and again."

"I know, and you needn't worry about Molly. She's quite capable of spying for us."

"I hope so."

"Molly is smart. Have a little faith in her."

"She's quite brilliant. I know we need assistance with our investigation. I only want everyone concerned to be safe. Instead of worrying, let's take a walk, shall we?"

"I thought you'd never ask. I'll hop down the driveway with you and then ride in the sling, okay? After so much exercise on Saturday, I found I enjoyed myself."

More like he'd become lazier and I got all the exercise. I didn't mind, but the whole being faster issue just might have caused his change in attitude. I wondered how long it would last and agreed with Bun. "If you insist, then come on."

We strolled the long driveway, taking all the time Bun needed whenever he got sidetracked by something. When we reached the road, he was more than ready to snuggle inside the sling with just his head and ears protruding.

"Who do you think would dislike Della enough to kill her?"

"I'm not sure. We have no solid leads, just idle gossip so far, which makes it hard to point the finger at anyone specific. Jack is trying to keep an open mind over Della's death, but he's certainly acting like it's a murder, isn't he?"

"He is. I was surprised when he let Rob leave the station before answering his questions. I guess that lawyer wasn't about to let Rob say anything. Not that he would; he's got tight lips, that one."

"He acted the same way when we were at the hop. My mother would have said he'd zipped his lips." I chuckled over the memory.

"Your mother is a funny human."

"Sometimes, she is."

Halfway to Lake Plantain, a car drew up next to us. I looked over when the passenger-side window lowered.

"You wouldn't be following us, would you?"

Adam smirked. "Not this time, not yet, anyway. I'm on patrol and thought I'd offer you a ride. You're going to the lake?"

"We are. Thanks for the offer, but I'd rather walk."

"If you say so. It might start to rain before you return home, though, so be ready to sprint."

With a smile, I watched him pull ahead and disappear around the bend. As an officer, Adam was good at his job. As a regular person, I had no idea what he was like, but he had good manners, which said a lot for his upbringing.

"I think Adam is sweet on you. What do you think?"

"Don't be silly. He's being polite. Besides, I'm not in the market for romance. I'm too busy for that. On top of that, you're the only male I have eyes for." I rubbed the top of Bun's noggin and picked up my pace. Adam was right, from the look of the dark clouds moving in, Bun and I could get soaked before too long.

At the lake, the wind picked up speed as it blew in off the water. *"I think Adam was right. Those storm clouds are getting pretty dark and threatening."*

He'd no sooner said it than thunder rolled and lightning pierced the sky. The first few raindrops hit us while I made tracks for the lodge, which wasn't far from us. I broke into a full-on run when rain, mixed with hailstones, pelted us.

Soaked to the skin by the time I reached the wide porch of the huge, empty building, hailstones fell from my hair when I shook it. Some of them were the size of a pencil eraser. I knelt to free Bun from the sling and then sat with my back against the wall of the building to wait out the storm.

It took a half hour before the storm downsized to a drizzle. Bun hopped back and forth along the porch, drawing a little closer to the far end each time. I watched until he stopped at the end of the porch. Still and silent, as though frozen, Bun didn't flick an ear or twitch a whisker. His focus lay beyond the porch.

"Bun . . ."

Suddenly energized, he flipped over backward and raced toward me. *"Th—there's something on the ground,"* he repeated over and over as he flew through the air and finally landed in my outstretched arms.

"What's the matter? You look like you've seen a ghost."

Chapter 10

"**N**—*not a ghost, it's a human in a rabbit costume. Jules, I think he's dead.*" Bun shivered and wiggled closer as if he'd climb inside my body, if he could. Any place to hide was a good place, I guess.

I walked to the end of the porch, peered a short distance beyond the railing, and realized what Bun had seen. Chills crawled up my spine and I began to tremble just like Bun.

My cell phone had become tangled up in the baggie I always carried for cleaning up rabbit turds as I pulled it from my pocket. Bone dry, the phone worked, and I called the police department's nonemergency number.

"I'd like to speak with Sheriff Carver. Tell him Juliette Bridge is on the line."

"Certainly, please hold."

It seemed like forever, but was only a minute or so, before I heard Jack say, "You haven't figured out who our best suspect is, have you? I have the coroner's report. Della was poisoned, and now this is a real murder investigation—"

"Jack, stop talking. I'm at the lodge on Lake Plantain. It appears there's a dead body here. Come as quickly as you can." I ended the call and paced the porch. I wasn't sure if I shook from our find or from the wet clothes that clung to my body. The air had grown cold, as usual in New Hampshire's springtime, especially late in the afternoon.

It wasn't long before sirens sounded in the distance, blaring as they drew closer. I made a mad dash to the body, Bun at my heels, and leaned down to look closely at the crime scene. Blood had soaked the white fur of the rabbit costume head, which was in disarray. The rabbit's head hung at an odd angle as though unattached from the costume. I peered at the skin that showed but didn't touch a thing. I couldn't tell how the body had arrived at this location. With rain-soaked grounds and droplets from the trees, signs weren't visible. I backed up, tripped over Bun, and hit the ground hard.

"You had to take a look, didn't you, Juliette?" Adam remarked.

I turned, jumped off the wet ground, wiped my hands on my soaked, muddy jeans, and plucked Bun up into my arms. "Y—yeah, I—I guess. I wanted to see if maybe I was mistaken and if he was just unconscious."

"And how did that work for you? There's enough blood on that costume head to conclude this person is indeed dead. Now, come away from there and go to the porch. You're interfering with this crime scene and have probably compromised evidence."

Unwilling to admit he was right, my chin lifted in defiance and I said, "I assure you, I didn't touch anything and neither did Bun. We were only looking and didn't trample the scene." With a sniff, I marched past Adam. I climbed the steps and sat on the porch in the same place as before. Only this time, I shivered uncontrollably.

"I guess you aren't taking any guff."

I held him close and watched Adam climb the stairs, a blanket in his hand. "I keep one of these in my cruiser. Wrap up yourself and Bun so you'll be warm."

Thankful for his kindness, I put Bun aside and stood up to wrap the blanket around my body. Before I crushed it to my chest, I sat down and motioned for Bun to climb inside. He was as wet and cold as me.

From our spot, we could watch the comings and goings of the crews that arrived. The sheriff drew to a stop beside Adam's cruiser, and a team of rescue workers parked as close to the scene as they could get. The ambulance, a fair-sized vehicle, took up a lot of space. Two other police cars filled the remaining open area and began to cordon off the grounds with yellow tape.

All too familiar with the routine, my attention turned to Jack Carver, who intently listened to what Adam softly murmured. I couldn't hear what he said, but figured it wasn't good when Jack stared up at me. I pointed to the grounds at the far end of the porch and walked along it, keeping up with Jack until he made his way to the body.

From this height, Bun and I could see all that went on. Jack checked out the rabbit head, then removed it to see who was inside the costume. My breath caught in my throat when Jack stepped aside. I recognized Frank Poland's face. Why on earth was he dead? Why was he dressed in the costume? How did he get here and who had committed this crime?

Stunned by rank death, questions sped through my head like a freight train out of control. Two murders within a few days would add pressure to Jack and his officers. It would complicate my end of things, too. Jack would worry that I'd come to harm if I got close to the killer. He might be right, but it had never stopped Bun and me from doing our best to solve a crime.

I backed up, went to the other end of the porch, and took several deep breaths.

"You okay?"

"Mm, you?"

"He was the last person I would have thought to dress up as a rabbit."

Footsteps sounded on the wooden floorboards of the porch. I glanced over my shoulder at Adam.

"Come with me, Juliette. I'll give you a ride home. The sheriff will stop by to see you after he clears the scene. The coroner is on his way."

When I didn't immediately move, he stepped closer to us and put his hand on my shoulder.

"You need to go home and change out of those wet clothes. Come on," Adam urged gently.

He was right, of course. It seemed he thought I was in shock and not thinking clearly. Instead, I tried to imagine why someone would kill a nice person like Frank.

I settled into the passenger seat of Adam's car and remained silent on our way to the farm. The dashboard clock caught my eye. It was later than I thought and the rabbits needed tending. I must have said so because Adam glanced at me.

"They'll be fine. Don't worry about them."

"I don't like to break their timetable for feeding and such. Rabbits need to be on a regular schedule."

At the farm, Adam escorted us into the house. "You get changed, then tell me how I can help you with your animals." He pointed toward the stairs. "Dry clothes first."

With a nod, I put Bun on the floor and scooted upstairs. It didn't take long before I returned to the kitchen dressed in clean, dry clothes, my hair toweled dry, and a different pair of shoes and socks on my feet. The smell of fresh perked coffee permeated the room.

"I took the liberty of making coffee. I hope you don't mind." He handed me a steaming cup of brew and sipped his own.

After a few sips, I warmed up from the inside out. Saying I was grateful, I beckoned Adam into the barn and pointed to the fridge. "Containers of fruit and veggies are on the shelf.

Take them out and set them on that table, okay?"

He nodded and got busy while I brought over bunches of alfalfa hay. "We need to make some pods of food to leave in the cages. Any empty feeding trays get grain pellets, too. You take a walk around and see how many rabbits need pellets. I'll make the pods."

Within a half hour, we put the last of the pods in place for the bunnies to enjoy. I made certain to refresh feeders and water containers before I called the job done. That was when Sheriff Carver arrived.

"You two done farming?" Jack asked when he entered the barn.

I glanced at him and asked, "How did it go after we left?"

"The coroner took the body. He said I'll have a report

in a day or two, but his preliminary inspection of the man was that he died of a blow to the head."

"What with?"

"He won't know until he does the autopsy. You know the dead man, don't you?"

"Yes. His name is Frank Poland. You questioned him at the hop event."

"I remember. Know Frank well, did you?"

"No, he volunteered like the rest of us. I didn't know any of the students or Denton Clarke until we met that day. Why do you ask?"

Ignoring my question, Jack asked, "What do you think he was doing at the lodge, especially dressed in that costume?"

I leaned against the huge sink and considered my answer. "I think Frank was dumped there."

"Be careful what you say."

I glanced down at Bun and continued. "Furthermore, I saw a costumed rabbit leaving the location where I found Della. At first, I thought I imagined things, then the rabbit looked back, before rushing away. I couldn't believe my eyes."

"You were going to tell me this exactly when?"

"I just did, and don't lecture me. You wouldn't have taken me seriously, Jack. We both know it, so let's move on."

"Perhaps Frank Poland was that same rabbit. But why kill him and leave his body at the lodge?" Sheriff Carver seemed stymied and stood there, shaking his head.

"Were there signs he was dumped there?" I asked.

"The rain washed away any footsteps or drag marks." Jack turned to Adam. "Tomorrow, I want that location combed for any bits and bobs you can find. I don't care how insignificant they may seem. Take a few officers with you."

"Yessir. I'll arrange that now."

Jack nodded as Adam left.

"There's hot coffee in the house if you want a cup," I offered.

"That would be great. I have a long night ahead of me."

In the kitchen, his elbows propped on the tabletop, Jack rubbed his eyes and then drank the coffee I'd set in front of him.

"If you're hungry, I can make a sandwich for you."

"Nah, the coffee is fine. Meredith dropped supper off at the station earlier. Thanks, though."

"I'm confused over why Frank would dress up like that. If he wasn't killed there but dumped instead, maybe the killer thought no one would find him for a while. How long do you think he's been at the lodge?"

"The coroner said it couldn't have been long, but with the rain, he wasn't certain. We'll know more when the postmortem is finished. Why does his being there bother you so much?"

"It's an unusual place to leave a body. People do go there, Jack. The old folks would have been shocked to see that sight. You must have the key to the gate because it was locked when Bun and I were running for cover. I had to climb over. Since the gate was locked, was Frank brought in on somebody's shoulders or by boat?"

"By boat would be the easiest, though not everyone has access to them or is aware of the boat ramp, either. Would you contact Mora Lindsey and fish around for information on who uses the ramp, or even knows it's there? She's more likely to talk freely to you than she would to me."

With a shrug, I said I would. "Mora knows what goes on in town. I think it's due to seeing so many residents' family members. They fill her in on all the gossip."

"That could come in handy for us. Gossip starts with a grain of truth, becomes warped in each telling, but the initial kernel remains. Our job is to sort through it all and dig it out."

Jack swallowed the last of the coffee, pushed his chair back under the table, and left.

I grabbed a notepad and pen from the desk to jot down events of the day and write a list of questions.

At my ankles, Bun asked, *"So, whatcha think of Frank's murder?"*

Flipping the pencil between my fingers, I thought about it for a moment. "I think something's going on at the college. Nobody's talking about it, and the dean needs to realize that when students or staff break the law, it's not okay to hide it from the police. I'm concerned for Molly's safety, now, more than ever. Who would want to kill Frank and why? He seemed like a good person to me. What was your opinion of him?"

"He was sharp as the blade of a knife—not one to miss much. I don't think he and Rob got on very well. I remember when you were waiting for kids to return with their eggs, Frank asked who'd been questioned by the sheriff. Rob didn't say a word until you asked him directly. I saw the look on Frank's face. He seemed pleased that you pressed Rob for an answer."

"We should find out what happened between them that didn't sit well. Rob's a prickly kind of guy, one with layers so you can't get to the real person." I turned to the notes I'd made and added a few questions about Frank and then a few more concerning Rob. I yawned, slapped the pen on the pad, and foraged in the fridge for a snack.

"Do you plan to check the other rabbits again?"

"Yes, why?"

"Just wondering. I want to exercise in the run for a bit."

"Sure, let's go."

While Bun ran the length of the indoor rabbit tunnel, I walked the aisles, spoke to the rabbits, scratched some noses, and stopped in front of Petra's hutch. The kits were moving around a bit to find the right spot to get a drink from Petra. She stood patiently, waiting for them to fill their tummies with her milk. I spoke softly to her and watched her care for the little babes.

Bun suddenly announced, *"I'm ready to get out of here."*

I turned the latch and opened the door for him to gain his freedom. Shortly after, he turned in for the evening. The TV on, I tossed an afghan across my body for warmth. I must have dozed off and suddenly awakened to the sound of the phone ringing. Tangled up in the afghan, I tripped and landed hard when I hit the floor. The phone ceased ringing for a few seconds, then began again. This time, I managed to make my way without a mishap.

"Hello?"

"Jules? Uh, Juliette Bridge?"

I didn't recognize the voice but was curious over who would call this late at night. I glanced at the wall clock as it clicked to one o'clock. "Yes, who's this?"

"Alvin Peterson, from Windermere's events council."

"What can I do for you, Alvin?" Geesh, the guy was old—didn't he sleep at night?

"Something has been bothering me about Della's death. I thought if I told you that you could let Sheriff Carver know without mentioning my name. It seems a killer is targeting people associated with our function, and while I'm no spring chicken, I'd like to live longer if I can. You understand, don't you?"

I rolled my eyes, wondered why I got all the weirdos, and said, "I certainly do, but if you have information that's important to the sheriff's investigation, you should tell him."

"It worries me that what I know could reflect poorly on the council, since our efforts to involve Windermere's residents in our functions is at stake. Bad publicity over what happened before and during the egg hunt might deter people from participation in future programs."

"It could do that, but look at it this way, if you don't let Sheriff Carver in on what you know, then those responsible for their dreadful actions won't be brought to justice."

"I—I can't tell him. Please, Juliette, please pass on the information for me?"

I held back a sigh, ruffled my hair with one hand, and finally said, "I won't promise not to tell Jack where I got the information, but I will try to keep you and the council out of it. That's the best I can offer."

"Uh, okay. I think Frank Poland killed Della."

"You think, or you know he did?" Thinking and knowing are two different things.

"I'm sure. Otherwise, why would Frank have been killed?"

"Maybe for a reason that had nothing to do with your event? Was he dressed as a rabbit before it ever took place? Like on the day Della was killed? I ask because he worked at our station during the event."

"All day?"

"Well, I didn't keep watch over him, if that's what you're asking. I just saw him at various times, is all."

"Oh, then he could have been the one. He came around the day Della died to try on the rabbit costume. He insisted it might not fit because he was so tall. I didn't think much of it, but gave him a costume that might be his size and sent him on his way. An hour or two later, he returned it to me. When I asked what had taken so long, he shrugged and said he took a walk to see how hot it would be when dressed in it. It wasn't long after that when the police arrived to report Della's death."

"I see. What else do you have to tell me?"

"Um . . . uh, that the costume is missing."

I plunked down in a chair, rubbed my eyes and face with one hand, and gripped the phone with the other. "Okay, I'll let the sheriff know. As I said, I can't promise to keep you out of it."

"I know you'll do your best." The line went dead.

I set the phone in the charger and mumbled, "Yeah, right."

With the hope of no further calls, I stumbled upstairs, flopped onto the bed, and fell asleep in my clothes. I didn't awaken until I heard Bun say, *"You'd better get up. Sheriff Carver and Adam are at the door."*

Good grief.

Chapter 11

I scooted down the stairs, unlocked the door, and left the two men to enter while I made coffee. Jessica came rushing in, a look of worry in her eyes. From the grim expressions on the men's faces, I could only guess this was a bearer of bad news mission.

Jessica motioned to the table, then took coffee mugs from the cupboard and put one at each setting, and added the sugar bowl to the center of the table. I brought the coffeepot and milk.

Once Jess and I were seated, we waited for Jack to begin. Instead of getting to his reason for the early-morning visit, he poured coffee for himself and Adam, then handed the pot to me.

Annoyed by the way my night had ended and how my new day started, I gave each man a straight look and asked, "Okay, what's this about?"

Jack gave Adam a slight nod.

"There has been a development in the investigation."

"Oh?" I remarked.

"It has come to light that Rob Brayton is a confidant of Alvin Peterson's."

Surprised by the revelation and that Alvin had omitted it when he called, I took a swig of coffee to let the importance of their relationship sink in. "And?"

"We think Rob and Alvin planned Della's murder. It seems Della tried to get rid of Alvin so she could take over his council position. In the meantime, Alvin found out what she was about to do, and he made plans to get rid of her instead. Rob was Alvin's backup in the whole thing."

I opened my mouth, but Adam raised his hand to stop me from interrupting.

"Wait, I haven't finished yet."

I gave him a nod.

"Before hauling both of them in for questioning, we wanted your opinion."

"Funny you should ask for that. I have information, too, and I would like your opinion, especially now that Alvin's involved."

With a keen look, Jack asked, "What have you got and where did you get it?"

I poured a second cup of coffee for me and refilled Jessica's.

"I had a call from Alvin last night. He asked me to tell you something without mentioning his name due to the possibility of bad publicity for the council. He said he thought Frank Poland had killed Della." I went on to repeat all he'd said, then sat back and waited.

Neither man spoke right away. They digested what I'd told them, instead.

"Gracious, you'd think we were the cops and they were common, untrained sleuths."

While I agreed and wanted to laugh, I couldn't. I leaned down sideways, scratched Bun's ears, and gave him a wink.

With a look of bewilderment on his face, Jack asked, "You mean to tell me Alvin called to implicate Frank in Della's murder?"

I nodded. "Quite a coincidence, wouldn't you say? Frank's dead and can't defend himself. Convenient, huh? The old guy is up to something. What that is, remains a mystery. How did you come by your information?"

"You know I can't divulge that, Juliette."

That's when Jessica entered the conversation. "Oh, but Jules must tell all, though. I hardly think that's fair."

"Be that as it may, I still can't say. Police business and all that."

"Don't forget for one second, Jack, that you asked me to help out. If you don't share all, then count me out of this, as of right now." I pushed back my chair and looked at Jess. "It's time to get to work. My rabbits are waiting for breakfast."

Jack blustered, Adam hid a smirk, and Bun hopped toward the breezeway, waiting for me and Jess to catch up. The three of us left the men behind. I wasn't as irked by Jack's behavior as Jessica was, mainly because I knew he wouldn't have told me anyway. I only asked in case he might.

Jess was on a roll. "He didn't hesitate to put you in danger, though, did he? He won't tell you where he got his info. You know, you might even walk into a bad situation without realizing it."

She was right, of course, but I knew Jack would reach the same conclusion. That possibility would cause him to tell me. I murmured as much to Jess and watched her start to grin. "You knew he'd hold back. It's a game he plays, isn't it?"

"Yes, sometimes it's a dangerous one."

"You're certainly right about that."

We went through the usual morning routine of caring for the rabbits, when Jess asked, "Are you concerned for Molly's safety?"

"More so than ever. I'll have a word with her when she comes in today. Never let it be said I was the cause of harm, should that ever happen."

"Uh-huh. I wasn't thrilled by the offer to use her campus friends and associates for information."

"Me either, but she's got a good head on her shoulders. We need to have confidence in her abilities, to not overstep and cause suspicion. Especially since we know the sheriff is in his dog-with-a-bone mode. He's certain that Alvin, Rob, and Frank were involved in some way with Della's death. Who killed Frank, and why, is another mystery."

We finished up, scrubbed our hands, and I opened the barn doors to receive a delivery. Jess had work to do and left me and the deliveryman to haul the goods inside. I signed the paperwork and noticed the sheriff and Adam had left. Contemplating what the two had said, I put the order away.

Several rabbits played in the exercise pen while a few others were outside in the fenced area. Walkabout Willy remained indoors. He ran back and forth through the clear Plexiglas tunnel, seeming to enjoy himself. Bun waited for his turn and finally insisted Willy should take a break. I complied with his request, knowing full well that he wouldn't stop yammering if I didn't. I guess animals do train us. We don't necessarily train them.

Allowing the rabbits more playtime, I wandered through the gift shop and checked for an inventory list. I found it written in Molly's neat cursive. I tucked it in my back pocket and continued into the clinic.

Two dogs and a cat waited with their owners. The dogs found the cat interesting, though the cat showed disdain for them, as only cats can. I greeted everyone, petted the animals, and waited for Jess to appear. Her mother stood behind the counter, going over appointments and such. She looked up at me and said, "It's quite a busy morning."

"That's terrific."

She smiled and continued working. I wondered if her words were a subtle hint for me to leave, but disregarded the thought. When she glanced up as Jessica walked toward the desk, I stepped back and waved before I left. What I had on my mind could wait.

A second or two later, I heard Jess murmur my name as she scooted into the shop. "You wanted something?"

"I'll make lunch if you have time to eat, and show you what I've come up with for our lecture. I'll give Denton a call, too."

"Okay, great. See you later."

Not only had I not heard from Denton, I wondered if he'd changed his mind. The opportunity to speak to the students was too good to pass up. We'd be on campus, which offered a chance to ask questions of those familiar with Frank and Rob.

Denton's business card held two numbers. One was the college number, the other his cell phone. I dialed his cell. He answered on the first ring.

"How are you, Juliette? You were on my list of calls to make today."

"I'm fine. I hope I haven't interrupted you?"

"Not at all. You must be looking for the particulars of the class, am I right?"

"You are. When would you like Jess and me to speak to your students? I also need the time that the class will start. Oh, and an estimate of how many people to expect."

"I've outlined the information for you and gave it to Molly. She dropped by earlier and mentioned she'd see you this afternoon. Nice young woman, very bright. You're most fortunate to have her work for you."

"We are thrilled. Molly's very smart and fun to be around. The students at my shop adore her."

"I heard you found Frank Poland. That must have been a shock for you. I'm sorry you had that experience."

"It was. Frank's death is mind-boggling. Did you know him well?"

"He was one of my best students—a sharp mind and terrific personality that would have taken him far. His death was not only surprising, but a real shame. His parents fly in tomorrow. The dean will handle that. I'm glad I don't have to."

"Frank seemed well-liked when he worked at the event. I can't imagine why anyone would kill him. He was dressed in a rabbit costume, you know."

Other than Denton's breathing, the line was silent.

"Are you still there?"

"Yes . . . uh, sorry. I have to get going, I look forward to you and Jessica being here."

The call ended before I could utter a sound. I quickly rang Molly. Her voice mail picked up, so I left a message for her to return my call.

"How did Denton take the costume news? It's possible he was aware of Frank's attire and didn't want to let on."

"It had occurred to me. Are you all set for a while? I have to get lunch ready. I think Jessica's mother will be joining us."

"I'm going into the barn and I promise not to get into trouble."

"I'll hold you to that promise. No surprises, okay? Don't instigate Willy to act out, either." Usually, I trusted Bun on his own, though when something mischievous that he shouldn't do occurred to him, Bun acted on it without consideration of the consequences.

His whisker jittered and one side of his lip drew back. I'd never seen other rabbits do this, so I always took it to mean he found it funny. *"I won't. You have my word on that."*

Lunch consisted of soup, salad, and sandwiches. I pulled out two cans of Progresso minestrone from the cupboard, emptied them into a bowl and set it in the microwave. The salad quickly took shape. I set the table for three and got to work on sandwich fixings. Before long, lunch was ready. I heard the two women coming through the breeze-way. They entered as I took glasses from the cupboard.

"There's iced tea or hot coffee, your choice. Help yourselves to lunch." I brought the heated soup to the table and added a ladle to the bowl. We ate, talked, and laughed.

Mrs. Plain enjoyed herself, which was good to see. She'd been a bit short with me in the clinic, leaving me to wonder if all was well.

"You know, dear, Jessica brags about your food all the time. It's very good of you to keep her well-fed."

"We developed the habit of eating together when we first started working together. Jess didn't always have time to run home for a meal before her classes began, and frankly, I find it boring to eat alone."

"I could see where that might happen. Do you have a beau?"

Slightly surprised by the term *beau* and by the question, I shook my head. "Not for me, I'm afraid. The farm is all-consuming."

Jessica nodded. "Same here. The clinic takes most of my time. By the end of the day, I'm too tired or busy to date."

"In my mother's day, it was expected of women to marry and have children. Things sure have changed since then. I didn't marry until I graduated secretarial school and found employment." Mrs. Plain shook her head. "I would like to have had the same freedoms you girls have."

"You don't regret getting married, do you, Mom?"

"Not a bit. I just would have liked to live a little before settling down."

My cell phone rang and Molly was on the line. I took the call on the porch.

Her voice excited, Molly said, "I've got what we discussed, I'll see you later. Oh—and Denton left some papers for you. I'll bring those by, too."

"Great, what time will you arrive?"

"My last class for the day is at one, so I'll come to the farm right afterward."

"Okay." I tucked the phone in my pocket and returned to the kitchen. Jessica and her mother looked up at the same time. "Everything okay?" Jess asked.

"Uh-huh. Now, who would like dessert?"

"What's on the menu?" Mrs. Plain asked.

Bun had just come in from the barn and paused to listen to our exchange.

"Chocolate ice cream and brownies. I bought the brownies at the market bakery," I admitted with a grin.

Jessica remarked, "I wondered when you had time to bake; you've been so busy lately. I'll have a brownie. Mom, what would you like?"

"Both."

I asked Jess to give Bun a snack while I served dessert. She went into the fridge, plucked a Bun snack off the shelf, and herded him into his room.

"That must be your housemate Jessica tells me about. She says you talk to him. Does he answer?" Her words and smile held no sign of sarcasm, just curiosity.

"When I first decided to be a rabbit farmer, I did a lot of research and found these animals are social. While they can't talk, they enjoy being spoken to." I leaned forward when passing her the plate and whispered, "Jessica gets a kick out of it, but I catch her doing it, too."

After lunch, Jess and her mom went back to work, as did I. There hadn't been a chance to discuss our speaking plans, so I got started on my outline.

An hour or more went by before I realized it. Molly walked into the house and took a seat opposite me. First, she handed me the papers from Denton. While I looked them over, she helped herself to a cup of tea. I scanned the basics of the information, then set them aside and looked up.

Her features were animated and her eyes sparkled. It was a wonder she didn't burst before giving me the name and whatever else she'd come across.

"Well, what are you waiting for? Spit it out. Come on."

"There were more than three. Frank Poland, Rob Brayton, Felicia Brandt, and Erin Britman. Does Erin seem like a rule breaker?"

I shook my head. "What was the charge?"

"They were caught partying."

"So?"

"With drugs. Not serious drugs, though."

"Get out—no way."

"Cross my heart," Molly remarked as she did so.

"Who was in charge? Somebody brought the drugs, right?"

"You're never going to guess."

"Then tell me."

"Frank was held accountable for being the druggist."

"Huh." I stared at the sweet girl in front of me and said, "I'd never have taken him for a drug dealer."

"Oh, I don't think he was a dealer, he was a buyer. You see, according to Cora's report, the students admitted pooling their money to buy the drugs. It was marijuana and some other stuff, not cocaine or fentanyl. At least those weren't listed." Molly shuddered. "I can't imagine ruining my life with drugs."

"Glad to hear it. No wonder Dean Jasper had a fit. Did the report say who Frank's dealer was?"

"No, I guess that's when the dean became angry and threatened to expel them all. They still wouldn't give the dealer up. Word got around campus that these students were in trouble and Denton visited the dean. He must have made a heartfelt plea on their behalf because they didn't even have to explain their actions to their parents. Imagine that?"

"Like you said before, the dean would go to great lengths to avoid bad publicity. No college wants that. You were careful?"

"I was. The office wasn't busy, and I had the place to myself for the most part. Don't worry, nobody will be the wiser. I think you like this sleuthing business because of the rush you get. I know I did." Her chuckle was wasted on Bun.

"Oh, yeah, it's all fun and games until you walk into danger."

I repeated what he'd said and watched Molly's reaction.

"I did well, though, didn't I?"

"You sure did. Thanks for this. I'll let the sheriff in on it, but will refuse to share my source."

"Okay, great. I don't want him to nag me or tell my parents. He and my father are Freemasons."

"Really? I didn't know that. Huh, curious."

"Why do you say that?"

"My father is, too. Dad attended the Masonic Hall on Jersey Street when he and my mother lived in Windermere. Maybe he and the sheriff met each other there."

"Could be. I'll be in the shop to prepare for class tonight. Meredith Carver has real talent for spinning. She'll use her spun yarn to make animal beanies and coats. Don't be surprised if you receive one for Bun." With that, she rushed off into the breezeway.

"I refuse to wear a beanie, but a hat would be nice. It gets fairly cold when we go out in the winter, especially at the lake."

I stared at Bun and said, "You should have mentioned that before. I'd have made you one."

"You don't knit."

"I can knit. I simply don't have much leisure time, is all." Self-righteous in my excuse, I added, "But, if you'd rather have Meredith or someone else make you one, then fine." Childish, I know, but there you have it. If I didn't spend hours poking my nose in other people's business to hunt down killers, I might find time to knit. I thought about it for a second and then shook my head.

"I didn't mean to insult you. It's just that we spend our days sleuthing and bringing justice to those who deserve it."

"No worries, Bun, no offense taken."

Chapter 12

During Molly's early spinning class, I noticed a car drive in and stared out the kitchen window. Sheriff Carver stopped and went into the studio, came back out and left. I'd called him in between late afternoon chores and said I had some information he should hear. He'd said he couldn't drop by until tonight, that he'd become inundated with work. I wondered why he went into the shop and didn't stop to see me.

With time on my hands, Bun and I headed for the lake. The air was warm, though the wind had a chill to it. I made sure we sat on the sunny part of the beach.

"I heard you speaking with the sheriff earlier. Will he grace us with his presence later?"

There was no love lost between Bun and Jack. Bun had no patience for anyone who didn't listen to our findings, let alone one who wouldn't take them seriously. Jack, on the other hand, believed that Bun shouldn't roam freely nor accompany me in my sleuthing. Little did Jack know that Bun had saved my skin more than once. I ignored him when he started to get crabby about my rabbit and me.

"He's getting better about respecting our tenacity and realizes we're apt to take chances, even if he doesn't like it. Now that I'm aware Jack's a Freemason and that he surely knows my father, he'll want to make certain that he won't have to explain to my dad if I get killed or seriously injured."

"I wouldn't want to be the bearer of that news either. I'll cut Jack some slack, but if I hear one more insult, he'll be persona non grata in my book."

Bun was probably hoping Jack would step out of line just so he could continue to dislike the man. I smoothed Bun's fur, checked my watch, and said we should go home. Bun didn't hesitate to snuggle into the sling. He wasn't fond of the cold or being out for long periods in a chilly wind. It made me wonder if he was kept in the cold by his former keeper. I had mentioned it once, but Bun refused to discuss the matter. I didn't press him on the subject, but respected his privacy. Why make him live through unpleasantness when it wasn't necessary? I didn't like to discuss my own concerning the car accident that had nearly killed me a couple years back.

We arrived in time for dinner. Once I'd fed the rabbits and given Bun his meal, I made a carafe of coffee, wolfed down a sandwich, and slurped the small bowl of leftover soup from lunch. Jessica had met us in the driveway when we'd arrived from our walk to say she'd been called out to Mr. Bentley's ranch to check on his horse.

Jack showed up as I loaded the dishes into the dishwasher. I set out coffee cups, then asked him if he wanted a snack before I poured steaming coffee into his cup.

"What do you have for a snack?"

"Brownies and ice cream."

"I'll take a brownie. Don't tell Meredith, she thinks I shouldn't have sweets or bread. She goes on about cholesterol and all that crap." He shook his head, nibbled the brownie, and added more coffee to his already half-empty cup. "So, what do you know that I should?"

Giving him the information I'd gotten from Molly, without mentioning her name, I waited while he thought it over.

"Dean Jasper never filed a report? Why is that, I wonder? Would you happen to know?"

"Like all schools and businesses, bad publicity is detrimental. Remember when, it was a year or so ago, I was unfortunate enough to find a dead body. I worried about the effect it would have on the farm. That might be why he took Denton's advice."

"Why would Denton get involved? He had nothing to gain by interfering on those kids' behalf. It does explain why Rob Brayton is so sure of himself, though. After all, he's some kind of associate of Alvin Peterson's, which is nothing short of being favored by the governor. Alvin wields a lot of power, though not many people know that."

I leaned back and fiddled with my napkin. "Really?"

From the rug in front of the sink, I heard Bun's response. *"Well, well, well. That sheds a different light on Rob and Alvin, don't you think?"*

Pensive, I asked, "How many people do know it?"

"A handful at most. Alvin doesn't like the limelight. He's a very private person, yet powerful. That's why it confuses me that Della thought she could oust him from his council seat. I've decided to treat that information as a possible red herring somebody would like us to follow."

"You're likely right. As a member of the committee, Della would surely be aware of Alvin's position." I leaned forward, cupped my chin in my hand, and let my mind run out of control. Sometimes, it was useful. This wasn't one of those times.

"I guess I'll have a chat with Dean Jasper tomorrow morning. Then I might ask Denton Clarke a few questions. You keep digging. The autopsy report showed blunt-force trauma to Frank's skull. He didn't die instantly, but not long after he was struck. Della was slowly poisoned, instead. Whoever did it must have added it to her beverage. Her stomach contents showed nothing."

My stomach rolled at the results of her autopsy. It was just a tad more than I wanted to know. To say she had died from poison was enough. "Any idea what type of poison it was?"

"The coroner isn't sure. More testing is in progress, but it's slow going. I guess his lab is fairly busy and like me, he has a man out sick and one on vacation. Who knows when I'll get that report."

I realized Molly's class had ended. I quickly removed Jack's plate and put it into the dishwasher in case Meredith stopped in. Watching cars leave the property, I breathed easy when hers was one of them.

"Where did you get all this information?"

"Oh, Jack, you know I can't tell you that." I heard Bun thump his foot and knew he was tickled to think I used Jack's own words on him.

"Don't be funny."

"I'm not, but if you can't share with me, then turn-about is fair play. Take it or leave it." I folded my arms across my chest and smiled.

"Fine, but if you get in over your head and your source can't help you, then don't look to me for assistance."

"Ditto. Goodnight, Jack."

He was the last to leave. Even Molly was gone. I went into the shop with Bun hot on my heels and found a note from her. She'd made a list of goods to order and I noted there was no deposit waiting to be made.

Grateful for her business acumen, I shut off the shop lights, looked in on the rabbits, and went back to the house with Bun. He sat on the floor at my feet as I opened the laptop and placed the order Molly had requested.

"Where shall we look for our killer? I have no clue as to who might have killed Frank, but Della certainly had enough people that disliked her for us to choose from. It might take us forever to sift through them all before coming up with a viable suspect."

"Indeed, she was unpopular with many. Maybe we should look into Alvin and Rob to get a better picture of them. Since they are associated, whatever that means, Alvin might feel that he should protect Rob at all costs."

"He can't possibly think Rob is above the law. Right?"

"I can't shake the feeling there's more to Rob than meets the eye. He's hiding something. You must have noticed that."

"Why don't you look him up on your computer? You might be lucky enough to get a peek into his background."

I Googled Rob's name. Several names popped up, so I dug a little deeper by adding his address. This time, the Rob Brayton we were in search of showed up on the screen. When I exclaimed I'd found it, I started to read about the history of the Brayton family. "Oh, wow!"

"Read it aloud so I'll know what you find so fascinating."

"It says the Braytons were industry pioneers and made their fortune in New Hampshire and the Midwest as shoemakers. They closed their businesses in the US and took their manufacturing overseas in order to stay competitive."

"So they died wealthy and Rob inherited, is that what you're saying?"

As I scanned the remainder of the article, I found a link to the family tree and clicked on it.

"Well?"

"Wait a minute. I found the family tree. The way it's set out might tell us the connection between Alvin and Rob." I followed the map and realized Alvin had no relation to the family. Then what was the connection?

I made it clear to Bun that I'd found no mention of Alvin. I watched him sit back on his haunches and wiggle his whiskers.

"Look up Alvin's family."

"Good idea. His parents earned their money in the paper mill industry as owners of three companies. They invested well and Alvin is wealthy because of it. His parents moved to Windermere and retired from the business when he was a boy. Alvin holds a master's degree in business and there's a link to another article. Shall I take a look?"

"Sure, why not?"

"You sound as though you've lost interest."

"There doesn't seem to be much in the way of info on him and Rob, is all."

"Okay." I clicked back to Rob's page and read aloud his sports accomplishments and then mentioned his family problems. His parents had died while on vacation in the Alps. They'd left him well off, but had tied the money up in a trust fund. I wondered aloud if it existed and was administered by someone. It would make sense.

"So his hands are tied when it comes to money. Isn't there a coming-of-age thing where humans reach a certain age and the money is theirs to do with as they please?"

"It doesn't say." I closed the computer down and flopped back against the sofa. "Maybe Jack knows. I'll ask him tomorrow; it's too late to call now."

"I think I've had enough for one day. I'm going to bed."

"The sheriff has had his officers search the crime scene at the lodge. Would you be interested in taking a second look tomorrow after chores?"

"Sounds like a good idea to me. The cops might have

missed a smidgen of evidence that only my nose could find. While we're at it, we should inspect the dock, ramp, and the inlet, too."

"We will. Goodnight, Bun."

My cellphone jingled its merry tune. The screen read Jessica's name and number.

"You're up late."

She chuckled. "I could say the same about you. I didn't have a chance to discuss our presentation with you. If you can, could you email the basics of Denton's outline to me?"

"Sure. I'll forward it to you as soon as we get off the phone. I have a question, though. How well do you know Rob Brayton and Alvin Peterson?"

"They're some sort of friends. Alvin never said how that came about, but he and Rob have done a few good deeds together, like the hop. Why?"

"Wow, I should have asked you first before digging through their backgrounds. How do you know all this?"

Her laughter brought a smile to my face. "It's like this: Just as hairdressers and barbers know more about their customers than anyone else does, I get as much gossip in the examining room. Pet owners always talk about the most unusual things while I am dealing with their pets. Anytime you have a question about somebody, check with me. I may have gossip that always holds a nugget of truth, okay?"

"Okay, I'll keep that in mind. Who told you about their friendship?"

"Judge Moore's secretary. She's on the council with Alvin. Send me that information so I can look it over. I'm nervous about standing in front of a group of students who have more business knowledge than I do. How about you?"

"I agree, but on the upside, it's great publicity for our businesses. I think we can get through an hour or so. We need to make the talk interactive with our audience and make them laugh, too."

"So, that's how you handle the kids at birthday parties and school events."

"I wouldn't have it any other way. Goodnight, Jess." I hung up.

On the laptop, I pulled up my outline and added the basics of what Denton wanted. I sent the entire thing to Jess by email with a two-line explanation of what I'd done.

Chapter 13

The day began on a good note. Bun was in a great mood, he made a few jokes as usual. I didn't get the point of them since I figured they were geared to a rabbit audience, not a human one. I snickered anyway and remarked on his terrific sense of humor.

Pleased that I appreciated his jokes, Bun ate his breakfast and accompanied me into the barn. I did the daily chores while he watched, sometimes prompting me on what came next, as if I didn't know. I'd been a rabbit farmer for some years now with the same routine every day. Ignoring his instructions, I suggested he see if Jessica had arrived.

He took off and raced into the shop and back. *"The clinic door is closed and I can't smell Jessica's scent. She'll probably be here any minute."*

I glanced at the clock, kept moving the cart loaded

with rabbit food, and began to worry. It wasn't like Jess to be this late. She never arrived after six in the morning. My curiosity grew until I couldn't stand it for another minute.

Finished doling out meals, I picked up the phone and dialed Jessica's cell phone number. Breathless, she answered on the third ring.

"Is everything all right?" I asked.

"I'm fine, just going to be a little late. I'm at McPherson's, trying to get his goat to comply with my checkup. So far, it isn't working very well. Talk to you later."

The line went dead. I grinned at what I knew would be a real wrestling match. The McPherson goat was a handful at the best of times. Once I'd asked Sean why he kept such a stubborn goat. He'd grinned and said the goat was the best lawnmower a man could have. Each to his own, I guess.

Knowing Jess would be fine and could handle Charlie, I finished my workload, then took a shower and donned fresh clothes. My hair still damp, I toweled it again and then tried to get it under control. It was a waste of my time, but the snarls came out as the mop of hair sprung into its normal disorder. Dressed in a warm jersey and corduroy pants, I added socks and ankle boots to my attire.

I turned to find Bun at the edge of my bedroom door. "What is it?"

"You'd better come downstairs. Sheriff Carver is here. I heard his car."

"How do you know that?"

"If I say I know the sound of his car, would you believe me?"

"Not for a second. Were you on the buffet looking out the window?"

"Kinda."

"I'll be right down."

"Are you angry?"

"Would it change the fact that you were where you're not supposed to be?"

"Well, no."

"Okay, then I'll see you downstairs. Don't get on the buffet again." I'd said it softly, but Bun got the message.

He was crouched on the kitchen rug when I reached the bottom stair and beckoned Jack in. His hat in hand when he entered the room, he tossed it on a coatrack hook and took a seat at the table. I made toast and poured two cups of coffee for us while gauging his mood, which wasn't easy to do on a good day. Today he seemed in decent spirits.

"What can I do for you, Jack?"

"Why do you ask? He's never got anything worthwhile for us to do."

I gave him a swift glance that said he shouldn't push his luck today. Bun pointedly ignored me as he looked everywhere but at me. Ignoring him, I took a piece of toast to munch while Jack stared at me, an odd look on his face.

"Well, what's up?" I insisted. After all, I didn't have all day.

"I wondered if you had come across any information on the students who worked at your station during the weekend."

"I researched Alvin and Rob, did you?"

"One of my deputies has that job. She'll give me a full

report on what she finds before her shift ends. Tell me what you found."

I gave him a quick rundown and then asked, "Are you meeting with Dean Jasper today?"

"He's on my list. I'll get to his office before the college gets too busy."

"What sort of questions do you plan to ask? Because if you're going to poke into private stuff, you'll be wasting your time. We're both aware of the way schools of any kind protect personal information on their staff and students."

"It's important the dean is made aware that breaking the law is frowned upon, and that just because he has a security staff, wannabes that they are, it doesn't mean he's scot-free to allow underage partying or that he can mete out punishment for drug use that's against the law. I won't stand for it. I'll arrest Dean Jasper right along with the people he's protecting."

"Uh-huh . . . well, I wish you luck with that endeavor. I also wondered if your officers found evidence at Frank's crime scene."

"Nothing. The weather was against us this time. The downpour erased any possible footprints and to top that off, it washed the beach clean as well."

"Another dead end, then?"

"It was. I did learn the reason Alvin is associated with Rob. Alvin was in a situation that I can't talk about, but Rob came to his rescue."

"After witnessing his attitude, I'm surprised to think he'd help anyone. Though, he did step up and help us look for Gerald Coldren."

He smirked. "People can surprise you." He glanced at

the wall clock and said it was time to head for Dean Jasper's office.

"I'll see you around, Jack."

Without a word, he left.

"Okay, Bun, we'll wait until his car is out of sight and then make tracks for the lodge. Let's hope there are no dead bodies this time."

"I'm ready when you are."

I took the bicycle my mother had left behind from the storage shed out back and set Bun in the basket on the front, rimmed with faded artificial flowers. I'd tucked a soft towel in the bottom for Bun's comfort. He hadn't said a word when I loaded him into it. I couldn't tell if he liked the idea or not.

We'd ridden a half-mile when he looked at me and remarked, *"Why haven't we made use of this before? It's great exercise for you. Besides, I'm very comfortable here. The flowers can go into the trash and you can buy new ones to put on. They break the chilly wind. What do you say? It won't be a major investment."*

"I intended to do just that. I hadn't realized Mom left it behind when she and Dad moved. When I opened the shed door, there it was, tucked into a corner behind some bins. I'm glad you like it. This way, you aren't as jostled around when I run with you in the sling."

We left the bicycle at the locked gate. I added a bike lock and put Bun in the sling I'd worn beneath my windbreaker. Once he'd made himself comfortable and was able to poke his head out of the sling to view our trek to the lodge, I started to walk at a quick pace in case we were interrupted by someone, anyone, especially those in law enforcement.

At the scene of the crime, I didn't bother with the porch, but set Bun free and told him to forage for what might be useful to us. I took the opposite direction and let him get to work. His nose and whiskers worked overtime while I dug through long, dead stems of tall grass left from the winter.

About to end that search and begin another, I touched a piece of metal and peered at it. A single silver button lay wedged inside a thick cluster of dead grass. It wasn't tarnished, but seemed fresh and new. I plucked the metal button from its hiding place and held it up to the light, turning it for a closer look. I tucked the button into the inside pocket of the windbreaker and zipped it closed. Somehow the button was familiar to me. I didn't want to lose this tiny gift from the grass gods.

"Hey, Jules, over here." Bun jumped back and forth on the incline, not far from where we'd found Frank. I hurried to see what had him excited.

"What did you find?"

Bun's superior expression meant he'd found something of value to our investigation. *"This."* He stuck his nose into the weeds and lifted his head high enough for me to see a chain with a medallion hanging from his mouth. He dropped it in the palm of my outstretched hand and said, *"Pretty cool, huh?"*

"Yes, indeed. Pretty darned cool, Bun. Anything else up there?"

"Not that I could find. How about you? I noticed you dug through the tall grass."

"I found a silver button that looks new. I'll add this necklace to my stash."

He bounded from the incline and landed at my feet.

When people refer to fleet-footed animals, Bun fits that bill. I tucked the piece of jewelry in with the button.

"Let's check the boat dock next. Imagine that, the cops overlooked this stuff? Maybe they overlooked evidence at the landing, too."

"We are super-sleuths, Jules. There's no doubt in my mind."

Thrilled by what we'd found, we went to the dock and scoured every inch of it, then we searched under it and studied the ground before shifting grains of sand for more evidence. The landing showed nothing, either. Deflated by this lack of success, we started our jaunt back to Mom's bicycle and began our trip to the farm.

A police car pulled up next to us as I pedaled home. Adam slowed to my speed and put the window down. "Out for your daily exercise? Where did you get the bike? It looks like it's from the sixties."

I grinned, as did Adam. "My father gave it to my mother for her birthday in 1966. She told me it was the perfect bicycle she'd been looking for. I found it in my shed behind the house. I never go in there but decided to take a look to see if it could be used for storage. Imagine my surprise when I found it."

"I can tell you're excited about it. What were you doing at the lake?"

"Our usual—just hanging out by the water and walking the beach. It's nice there, don't you think?"

He inclined his head in agreement. "You're right." As his radio went off, he waved and sped off.

I breathed a sigh of relief that we hadn't been questioned longer. Adam could often tell when I lied or sidestepped, and I tried not to push my luck with him.

I emptied my pocket of our finds when we reached the house. The button was dry, but crusted with dirt. I soaked it with dish detergent and warm water while Bun inspected the medallion suspended from the chain. I looked it over and while there was a bit of dirt on the front, it didn't matter. The back of the medallion was engraved, and needed cleaning.

I turned it over again to study the design on the front. An intricate braid pattern wound through itself. I used the laptop to go online in search of Irish and Scottish weaving. Scrolling through picture after picture, I realized the hunt could take much longer than I'd imagined. I put the necklace aside and rinsed the button. Running the medallion under hot water, I gently rubbed it clean and laid it on a towel to dry.

When Jessica came into the kitchen, I almost jumped out of my skin. Intent on the evidence, I hadn't heard a sound, nor had Bun.

"What's wrong?"

"I didn't hear you coming. Bun and I went to the lake and did a search of the crime scene. The sheriff's crew found nothing—at least that's what he said. In my opinion, they didn't look very hard, because we found two items."

"We?"

"Well, me, but I always include Bun."

"Oh. Can I see them?"

I pointed to the kitchen counter, where the two pieces lay on the towel. Jess picked up the medallion and peered at the design. "Have you any idea of this pattern's origin?"

"I did a Google search for British Isle designs. After scrolling through several pages of them, I quit."

"Molly might know. She's got lots of patterns she offers to weavers. Eve McPherson is also a person you might ask if Molly can't identify it. Eve has some beautiful woven rugs and chair throws similar to this." She handed the medallion to me.

"Thanks, I also considered asking at the library."

"Good idea, but try Molly and Eve first. They could point you in the right direction. Let's face it, the fewer people who know you have this necklace, the better. Did you find the pieces close to where Frank's body was?"

"Yeah, not too far away. I figure the button might have been loose and fallen off during the struggle of hauling his body to that spot. The medallion . . . well, I have no idea where it came from but was probably around someone's neck when the clasp broke." I held it up for her to see.

"Hmm, it might have been on Frank's neck. I don't know his nationality, but most of us Americans have diluted backgrounds anyway. It could have been a family heirloom, or could be a good many other things, like something someone had bought at a yard sale."

"Let's not get carried away before you have a chance to look at what's written on the back of it." I flipped it over to show her the inscription.

"It's in a foreign language, like the road signs you see in Scotland that are in English and Gaelic."

It made sense, the design and the language fit together like pieces of a puzzle. With a *yippee*, I hugged Jess. "Of course."

Neart Agus Urram Clan was engraved on the medallion and had only one word I understood. The word was *clan*, which meant closely-knit and interrelated families, such as those in Scotland. What the rest meant was anyone's guess. Another part of the puzzle worth looking into. Even if it didn't pertain to the students themselves, it could reveal who the person was that dragged Frank to the lodge grounds and left him there.

We inspected the button again. Similar to the medallion, it held a tiny woven design on the surface. "I'll ask Molly as soon as she arrives. She has college classes until noon today. Jack was here early this morning. Luckily, I'd finished the chores and showered before he arrived. We talked about the investigation. Like us, he has more on his hands than he can deal with. Leads are nice, but it takes time to follow them up. How heavy is your workload today?"

"Not too bad. Why?"

"I'll put a chicken in the Crock-Pot, and we can eat dinner while discussing the program for the marketing class. I want us ready to engage these students."

Jess nodded. "Me, too. I went over what you emailed me last night and then took an hour or so to write out my thoughts. I followed your presentation. I hope you don't mind. You kept it so positive and fun, I couldn't resist."

"I'm glad we're doing this lecture. I'm sure we'll have lots of questions directed toward the issues of being a business owner—you know, the ones that aren't fun to deal with."

"You must mean cleaning the rabbit poop."

We both laughed as Jessica went to greet her patient and his owner.

With Molly in class, I handled the order that arrived. Surprised it was here so fast, I mentioned it to the delivery driver.

"We're a twenty-four business now. The boss wants to make sure you're happy with us since you order so much.

She got out of bed early to pack this and put it on the truck."

"Tell her that I appreciate it." I studied the man for a moment. He seemed young, but not too young. I took a chance and asked him a question.

"Do you work full-time for the company?"

"Only a few hours a day. I attend college and try to get as many hours in as I can, but it doesn't always happen. I study a lot and work in the warehouse mostly. Why?"

"I hadn't seen you before today, but then, Molly usually handles stock that arrives."

He looked as if he wanted to say more, but hesitated.

"Is there anything else?" I asked.

"Uh, you found Frank Poland, right? And Ms. Meeny, too, huh?"

I nodded.

"You must have the worst luck ever."

"Sometimes, it seems so. Why do you ask?"

"Frank and I were good friends. It's too bad what happened. He was a decent kind of guy, unlike others in his group of friends."

"If you don't mind my asking, who exactly are you talking about?"

He stared at the floor and then said, "I really shouldn't say."

"It will be between us, and I'm simply curious. I had the chance to meet some of his fellow students at the egg hunt event."

"Rob Brayton isn't a bad sort, he's honest, too. Brandt, on the other hand, seems like a real nasty person who thinks she's better than most. Maggie is nice and so is Erin. I don't know why they hang out with Felicia."

"How did you meet Frank? He was genuinely nice when we worked the egg hunt together."

"He and I shared a room at the beginning of the first semester, then we changed rooms and split up. We remained friends even though I'm not rich like the others are." He checked the time and left in a hurry.

"That turned out to be productive. Good work, Jules."

I glanced around and whispered, "It adds to the perspective I had on Frank. He was genuine and a decent man. Where have you been?"

"Making the rounds and talking with my friends. Willy wants to go outside, as do some of the others."

I walked alongside him into the barn.

Chapter 14

Sorting through the shop order, I inventoried it. Some of the hanks of wool roving were larger than others. A few colors were drab, unlike those we usually ordered. I assumed one of the students had requested them for a special project. Meredith came to mind.

Molly and Jason came through the door at the same time. I left them to their respective jobs and went into the kitchen to start the Crock-Pot meal for supper.

Carrots, chicken, potatoes, onions, and spices went into the pot. I added a bit of water and turned the temperature to high. While dinner cooked, Bun and I took a ride to Walmart in the next town over.

"Am I allowed in the store?"

"I don't see why not. If anyone asks, I'll say you're my comfort animal."

"Do people get away with that?"

"Uh-huh, they do. Once a woman took her pig onto a plane and insisted it was her comfort animal. She got away with it, too. Besides, I've seen people with all types of pets in stores around town. The most popular ones, though, are dogs."

"There are those specially trained ones for needy people."

"Those particular dogs have to wear a jacket that designates them."

We left the car in the enormous parking lot in front of the store. With Bun in the sling, we went inside like nobody's business. All went well until we reached the register to pay for the artificial flowers we'd chosen for the bicycle. I put the goods on the conveyor and adjusted the sling. Bun huddled inside after he'd gotten a glimpse of his former owner, Margery Shaw, and was scared witless, though I assured him not to let fear control him.

The man behind the register gave me a rotten look and asked, "Madam, what's inside your sling?"

"Nothing that belongs to you," I said. Okay, so I should have admitted my comfort animal was in the sling, but after the look I'd gotten, I refused to say.

A buzzer went off somewhere. An older man rushed at me. "Hang on, Bun," I murmured.

"Okay."

"What do you have in that contraption you're wearing?"

Unfazed by his manner, I asked, "And you would be?"

He puffed out his chest and hooked his thumb into his security belt. The badge on his uniform shirt listed his name as Homer Ruffian. Why I found it humorous, I couldn't say, but all of a sudden I found myself giggling.

The security guard stared in surprise and then rolled his eyes at the cashier.

Holding back my mirth, I said, "My name is Juliette Bridge. I live at Fur Bridge Farm in Windermere. I haven't stolen anything from your store."

The line behind me had grown and the guard motioned me forward. I paid for what was in the bags. I walked a few steps behind Homer toward what I assumed was his office. When he opened the door, it appeared to be a broom closet. That's when I heard the cashier mumble about shoplifters.

I stopped dead in my tracks.

"Jules, don't respond . . ."

"Excuse me? What did you say?"

"I said that you're a shoplifter. Furthermore, if you are who you say and live on that farm, you should have enough money to pay for all your goods."

I reached inside the sling, hauled Bun halfway out, and said, "This is my comfort animal. Now apologize for slandering me."

"I most certainly will not. You should have identified your pet when I asked."

I stepped close to the register. "You aren't a security guard, nor are you much of a cashier. I don't have to identify anything for you. I know the law." I tucked Bun back into the sling. He poked his head out and watched everyone.

The guard, who'd thought I was right on his heels, returned in a hurry, but not fast enough. The store manager arrived and greeted me like an old friend, as he should have. I had done birthday parties for three of his kids. Edward Wickersham was six-foot-six with skin as dark as mahogany and a laugh that rumbled from deep within his body. A nicer man I couldn't imagine.

"Mr. Wickersham, it's so nice to see you."

Wickersham raised an eyebrow at the cashier and asked, "What's going on?"

"She refused to tell me what was in her sling. I automatically assumed she had pilfered from the store."

"Why not notify me and security instead of making a scene? Miss Bridge wouldn't steal anything. I've known her for some time and she's a friend of my family, too."

Without waiting for the clerk to answer, Wickersham looked at me. "Come with me, Juliette. I'll handle this." As we walked away, I thumbed my nose at the cashier. Childish, I know, but better than punching him in the nose, though less satisfying.

He summoned the guard and entered the manager's office, which wasn't large either. Geesh, the store was enormous, you'd think the manager would have a decent sized office.

"I suppose that is Bun in your sling. I know he goes everywhere with you. My kids adore him."

"He does travel with me and I enjoy having him along. I know how much your kids love my rabbits, especially Bun. How are they doing? Your kids, I mean."

His rich, deep laughter eased my tension.

"They're growing like weeds. They were at that egg hunt thing in Windermere. Were you there? My sister took them."

"We worked there for the day. It was an awesome event."

"Great. Now, give me those bags so I can have your money refunded. Then you can take the purchase home with you."

"Oh, no, don't go to that trouble, please don't. I bought these to decorate an old bicycle that Bun and I ride. I do all the pedaling and he does all the riding."

A smile spread across his face as he brushed my plea aside. He handed Homer the bag with instructions to make the refund and return with the flowers and money.

While awaiting Homer's return from the service desk, I engaged Edward in conversation. It wasn't long before Homer returned and Bun and I left, never to be seen at that store again.

"That was quite a hullabaloo if you don't mind my saying so. We could have been arrested, you know. I don't think I'd look particularly good in striped garments."

"We won't ever be returning there again. It was just closer to the farm than the one in Windermere."

I let Bun loose in the car, removed the sling, and drove out of the parking lot.

"The cashier was rude to accuse you of theft. I wonder if he'll be fired or will get a good talking to by Mr. Wickersham. He is such a nice fellow and large, too."

"Edward is a kindhearted person. All that cashier had to do was apologize. I didn't ask for a miracle, although, maybe it would have been one." I started to giggle and turned into the driveway.

When we walked through the barn, I realized Jason had done his assigned chores and was gone. In the shop, we stopped to help prepare for the students, who, according to Molly's schedule, would show up in about fifteen minutes—leaving enough time to show her what Bun and I found. We rushed through the remaining preparations, and I beckoned her into the house.

Explaining what we found near the lodge, I admitted I had no idea what the engraved words meant, and then I produced the necklace. "Do you know about the origins of these intricate designs?" I asked.

She lifted the medallion into the sunlight. "It appears Scottish. The weave is similar to ones from a book I have in the shop. Amy Briner wove a table runner using a similar design. It's quite lovely."

"Do you know what the words mean?"

"Not a clue, I'm afraid. There's a professor at the college who might be able to help. His hobby is antiquities and stuff like this. I could show him these before class tomorrow."

"I'd rather not let the pieces out of my sight. They were near Frank Poland's body and I think they're connected to the crime."

As if it scorched her skin, Molly dropped the necklace and rubbed her hand on her slacks.

"It won't hurt you. I don't believe it has Druid connotations. It would be nice to know if the person who dropped Frank at the lodge was wearing it, or if Frank was. I'm sorry, I should have mentioned where I got it."

A tad uncomfortable, Molly waved my apology away. "No worries, I overreacted. I'll look it up in my book and mark the page for you to see."

Using her smartphone, Molly snapped photos of the front and back of the medallion and the button's surface. "I'll show them to the professor without explaining where they came from. Let's hope he doesn't ask."

Worried that I would put her in a tight spot, I reluctantly agreed. I don't think I could have stopped her, even if I'd insisted. As if she knew what I was thinking, Molly said, "Don't worry, I can handle this."

I nodded and heard cars arrive. "It seems your students are here. Get going, I'll check in later. Oh, uh, I'd like to see Amy's table runner if she doesn't mind. The students appear to be working hard, and we could display their work at an open-studio kind of thing. You and I did discuss that some time ago, but things got crazy and we never followed through. Would they be open to that? They could even sell or take orders if they chose to. I know they pay a good sum for classes, and nothing is more satisfying than having somebody interested enough in your work to pay the asking price."

"Great idea. Time got away from us after we had initially talked about it. I'll ask if they're interested in an event like that. I believe they'll be quite thrilled."

"Okay, let's plan to give it a try. We had such luck with our open house in the past. I don't see why we wouldn't be able to pull off a show and sell that sort of thing."

"I'll keep you posted on this."

Alone with Bun after Molly left to greet her students, Bun said, *"Do you think they'll do it?"*

"I think so. It's a confidence builder, that's for sure."

"This professor guy, he might give us enough information on the medallion that we can pass on to Carver. We can use it in furthering our investigations. Maybe you shouldn't play cat and mouse with him over your sources."

I slanted a look in his direction. "Really? You're serious about that?"

"He does have responsibilities, Jules. Just sayin'."

"I'll give it some thought." Not.

Jessica poked her head around the edge of the breezeway door and said, "I have to run out to Sean McPherson's. Want to bring your evidence and show it to Eve?"

Willing to make the trip, I grabbed the two articles and tucked them into the soft little bag before tucking it into my jeans pocket. With Bun in tow, I met Jess at her car.

"Charlie is having problems again. He gets sick because he eats anything and everything. I warned Sean about that and recommended he clean up the land where Charlie eats the grass. I think the soil should be tested, too. Maybe it's polluted."

"Are you going to suggest that?"

"I will because Charlie might have eaten poisoned grasses. Goats aren't fussy, that's for sure. Unlike rabbits and other animals that know when something isn't good for them, goats don't."

"Yeah, like lily of the valley."

I glanced down at Bun. It took some doing not to ask why rabbits wouldn't eat them. I mentally filed my question for later.

While Jess inspected Charlie, I knocked on the front door and was invited in by Eve.

"What brings you by, Juliette?"

"I found a couple of oddments. Jessica thought you might be able to identify the artwork. I'm interested in the origins of the saying and design."

Her face lit up and she said, "Let me see them, then." Having come to America from Scotland, her brogue was beautiful, though somewhat difficult to understand at times.

I laid the two items on the table. Eve peered at them for a while before laying a hand on either one. Her concentration intense, I waited for her to speak first.

Eventually, she picked up the medallion by its edges and spun it with one finger without touching the front or back of it. "The engraving says *strength and honor clan* and it's a clan from a century in old Scotland, when warriors defended their clan with much honor. They weren't warring clans who killed other families, like the McDonalds and such. The weave is theirs, as well. Where did you find this?"

Certain she knew more than she was willing to say, I said, "Bun and I were at the beach digging around. I came upon it merely by accident."

"I'm familiar with someone who's a descendant of that clan. I can't remember their name at the moment, but when I do, I'll give you a call, okay?"

"That would be great. Thanks. Any ideas on the button?"

She gently placed the medallion on the table as though it was sacred. Picking up the button, she seemed to weigh it in the palm of her hand. "This is a button that factories use when making suits for those who can afford the marvelous fabric that goes into the making of them. The weight of the button is the tell. Other manufacturers use cheaper fabric and a lesser weight of this button with a similar design. Most people are fooled by it unless, of course, you happen to be from Scotland and are wealthy," she said with an honest chuckle.

I thanked her for taking the time to help me out. She then asked if I'd like to see her family crest and other Scottish wares she'd brought to America. I found my interest piqued when she showed the impressive items from her homeland.

"You're very proud of these wonderful things, and you should be."

"Yes, many came down through generations from long-lost ancestors. You should come to the Highland games the next time we have them. I think you'd enjoy the bagpipes and their soulful, yet joyful sound, as well as the talent it takes to compete in the Highland games. I'll keep you posted on the date."

Jessica appeared and asked if I was ready to leave. I nodded and thanked Eve once again.

During the ride home, Jess quizzed me about Eve's information. "She's not always easy to deal with. At times she broods, and Sean knows that's when she misses Scotland the most."

I ran through what she'd shared and said, "She knows more than she would say, but I didn't want to push."

If you had taken me in with you, I would have found a way to get her to tell everything, but no, you left me in the car. I guess you'll never learn.

I let the comment pass, aware this wouldn't be the end of things. Instead, I said, "Eve is familiar with a descendant of the clan, but she couldn't remember their name. She didn't say if it was a man or a woman."

"That's great, you'll probably get a call from her when she remembers."

"She did mention that, but I'm not so certain. It's just a feeling I got from the way Eve handled the medallion. Molly took pictures of the pieces and plans to ask a professor at the college about them. His hobby is all things ancient and Scottish."

"I wonder how important it is to your investigation."

"It could offer a lead to the killer, or the people involved in one or both deaths. I can't imagine how much strength it took to get Frank out of a boat, up an embankment, and then leave him near the lodge where he'd be found. Frank was a good-sized guy. Deadweight is more cumbersome than lifting a live person, too."

"How do you know?"

"Jack told me when I first started sleuthing."

With a light chuckle, Jess said, "To be specific, Jack

refers to your escapades as sticking your nose where it doesn't belong."

Yup, he'd called my poking around a good many things, some quite descriptive, but in the end, Bun and I helped him solve the crimes. We could get people to talk when police officers couldn't. We also broke into places where cops had to have a warrant to search the premises.

Chapter 15

After dinner, Bun and I redecorated the bicycle basket. Instructed by Bun, once I had stripped off the dilapidated flowers, I got into the job. He wanted the flora to look a certain way, and while it wasn't easy to weave the stems into the basket, eventually it all came together. I picked up Bun and stepped back to survey the job.

"What a splendid basket. I'm going to enjoy riding in style."

"You're a great decorator, Bun."

He leaped from my arms and scooted up the steps of the porch. He sat on the top step and gazed at the bike. *"Can we take a ride, at least to the end of the driveway?"*

"We can. I'll get a small pillow to make you more comfortable." A few moments later, I returned with a sweet pillow I'd had as a kid. My mother had bought it for my dolls, and I'd saved it. The dolls . . . well, they were given away to someone less fortunate than me. I didn't mind. I wasn't a doll kind of kid. Instead, I liked wildlife and would walk through the woods in search of foxes, birds, rabbits, and whatever else I might find.

"That's a wonderfully soft pillow, Jules. Have you been saving it for me?"

He sounded excited and I didn't want to disappoint him, so I said, "I've had it for a long time and can't think of a better use than to make your ride comfy."

With Bun nestled into the basket, I climbed onto the bicycle and pedaled to the end of the road and back a few times, as he went on and on about the new look and feel of his brand new ride.

Twilight had set in, along with dark gray clouds that threatened rain. I said as much to Bun and wheeled the bike into the barn. Bun jumped from the basket, ran up and down the aisles, and then asked, *"Can we go out again tomorrow? I like being able to sit in that classy basket much more than the sling."*

"I guess so. It depends on the weather. Although, I have to make time to speak with Jack."

"About what? You aren't telling him that we found some evidence, are you?"

"I hadn't planned on it. I want to see what he's found out. After his last visit, he had lots to do and interviews to hold. I'm interested in how that worked out for him. I'll keep the medallion and button until I think he needs to know. They might not be worth much in the way of clues, and I won't do a thing until I hear from Molly."

"Smart, very smart."

I gave the rabbits a last round of food and water, then checked on Petra and the babies. They were fluffy and sweet and she let me touch them. Their fur was exquisite, beautiful like Petra's, except for one kit whose short coat and looks resembled its father. Pleased by Petra's care of the little critters, I gazed at them a bit longer before locking up for the night.

I'd had an informative, yet busy day. I flopped on the sofa, reread my marketing business speech for the college kids, and then set about straightening up the house. I'd been lax in cleaning the messes I'd ignored, which was evident by the looks of the dust bunnies that lingered in corners or tumbled across the floor.

An hour later, the dust bunnies were gone. I'd washed the kitchen floor and scouted out what needed to be cleaned next. The breezeway had dirty footprints where we regularly tromped in and out. I refilled the floor steam cleaner and set that job to rights. The entire time I worked, the murders and happenings since then, ran through my mind. Bits and pieces had come together, but not enough to amount to much. After rinsing the steam pads, I put them in the washer, tossed in a few more items, and started the wash.

Thunder rolled, torrential rains came, but no lightning accompanied it. Like a rain cloud, Jack arrived, parked as close as he could, and hurried up the porch steps. I let him in and stared at his stormy face. Uh-oh, now what?

He hung his hat on a hook, draped his jacket over the back of a kitchen chair, then sat down without uttering a word. I made a half of a pot of coffee and served it without speaking. Our waiting game ended after Jack took a few slurps of brew.

"I can't believe Dean Jasper could be so stupid and hold such a responsible position. His predecessor had more going for him than Jasper ever will. When I asked why he didn't report the crime to our office, he had the nerve to say it was college business, and none of mine. Who the heck does he think he is? Because he wasn't smart enough to obey the law, there have been two murders."

Okay, Jack was on a rant. I said nothing, just listened as he went on. Why he did so must have been due to his inability to tell Meredith. Jack tried to keep his wife out of police business. I, on the other hand, always nosed into police affairs, and thought he was probably comfortable using me as a sounding board.

I refilled his cup and set a plate of oatmeal cookies in front of him. He glommed two right away, sucked them down, and slurped the fresh coffee before he started in again.

"I demanded he tell me . . . uh, certain things, and he refused. He used student privacy for an excuse. I'm telling you, if he so much as held back one tiny thing that could lead to an arrest, I'll arrest him for obstruction. My job is hard enough without dealing with his sort." He chewed another cookie, leaned back in the chair, and heaved a sigh.

I guessed the rant was over. It was annoying to be wrong so often.

From Bun's doorway, I heard, *"He's not done yet. If he's not careful, he might have a stroke or something. Get him under control, Jules, for his own sake."*

Certain Bun knew something I didn't, I allowed Jack to keep going for a bit. You never know what valuable crumbs of information might fall from his mouth. Right about now, I could use all the clues I could get.

"Have you found out anything?" Jack asked.

I shook my head and sipped my coffee.

"I spoke to Professor Clarke. He, too, was less than

forthcoming. It seems they've circled the wagons. I won't get a word out of them, which brings me to the reason for my visit."

"Okay, go on, but no more raving, Jack. It's bad for you, me, and especially Bun. He becomes upset when people show aggression."

Jack peered across the room to where Bun squatted in his doorway. He'd flipped his long ears downward as a sign of fear. "I guess I have scared him. Sorry, Juliette. I had to get that off my chest and I can't talk to Meredith about it."

"No harm done. Tell me what I can do."

"I've said this before, but people like you. They open up to you and offer things we would never get out of them. While it annoys the daylights out of me to ask, I want you to get closer to the students and dig deep. You know how to do that, I've seen you in action."

"As a matter of fact, Jessica and I have been invited to lecture at the college. We're giving a special presentation on how we have become successful, and what it takes to do so, to Professor Clarke's marketing students."

"When?"

I checked the calendar and realized the date was coming up quickly. "In about a week. Can you wait until then? If not, I could meet with Denton and use the lecture material as a segue, then turn the conversation toward whatever you want to know."

He smiled. I'd won the day, I knew, and so did Bun.

"Plain to see that idea is appealing."

"I knew you'd be able to come up with a reason to poke around. Will Jessica go with you?"

"Only to lecture. She's far too busy with the clinic to become involved with my efforts to assist you. Besides, if anything happened to us, who would care for the rabbits?"

"Molly. She can handle anything. Never does she seem frazzled—at least that's what Meredith tells me. That young lady has a real fan in my wife. I'm sure the other students feel the same way."

"She is precious. There's no doubt in my mind."

"Meredith mentioned a possible display and sale of work done by the students. She's ecstatic. I hope this isn't going to cost me more money, Jules."

"Don't worry. It's to benefit the students only."

"When will you meet with Clarke?"

After a mental schedule check, I said, "I'll give him a call in the morning and will let you know how it goes, okay?"

"Very well, I'll hear from you sometime tomorrow morning, then?"

"Uh-huh."

"That was easier than you thought it would be, huh?"

"What else, if anything, did you get from others at the college?"

"After being snubbed by the dean and Clarke, I went to the security office and had a cup of coffee with my old pal, Will Johnstone. He's a former police officer, who was injured on the job. He's retired from the department now. A good man. His hands are often tied when it comes to the discipline of students for wrongdoing. Jasper refuses to allow Will to call us in, no matter the crime. Dean Jasper thinks he's the judge and jury. If I can, I'll oust him from that office. He isn't doing those kids, or their families, any favors by ignoring laws that apply to all, not just a few."

"What else did Will have to say?"

"There's a drug problem on campus. Will can't figure out who's at the bottom of it, either. He's frustrated by the way things are handled."

"I can check with Molly to see what she's heard about the drug situation. Do you think it pertains to your investigation or is another avenue entirely that's caught your interest?"

"Once these two murder investigations come to an end, or close to it, I'll turn what I know over to the narcotics department."

"I wasn't aware there was one."

He smirked. "Other than the captain of that squad, there are only three officers. Windermere isn't that big of a city to demand more, not right now."

"I never considered drugs a problem. I guess I'm too busy with the farm to have heard about it. Little kiddies aren't likely to be buying and selling drugs at birthday parties."

"That is a good reason for not knowing." Jack donned his hat and jacket and then left.

"Wow. He was certainly put out by those two men who refused to answer his questions and then showed how unwilling they were to help on any level. Doesn't that beat all?"

"For a moment, I thought he'd have a meltdown. Glad it didn't happen. Jack's a good cop and a good man. He takes his job seriously and lets us get away with a lot. The fact that we are helpful has something to do with his decision to allow us to dig around where we have no right to."

"You say that, but we'd do it anyway, whether he approved or not. We both know it. How do you plan to bring up the subject of the two murders?"

"I have no idea. I'll fly by the seat of my pants, just like always."

"Tread carefully. Drug dealers aren't nice people. Margery . . . uh, well, never mind. I don't want to talk about that."

"As you wish. I do have one question for you, though. When we were with Jess earlier, you mentioned something about lily of the valley flowers. What was that about?"

"Why, I'm surprised you don't know. The plant is poisonous, even though the flowers smell wonderful. People have them growing in their yards, their kids pick them, and they could become very sick. When put in water, the poison from the stems seeps out. If you drink enough of that tainted water, you can die."

Bun began to jump around and yammer wildly; so wildly, I couldn't understand a thing he said. "Stop, just stop and tell me what's got you in a frazzle."

"Remember when we were in that small valley where I found Della's body?"

I said, "Yeah."

"Della had a lily of the valley bouquet on her chest. Her body, surrounded by those awful eggs, caught our attention, and we ignored the flowers. I think they were a taunt from the killer that we didn't realize was one."

I picked up my laptop and Googled poisonous wildflowers and plants. Sure enough, Bun was correct. Stunned, I dialed Jack's cell number. He mumbled hello and I interrupted with, "lilies of the valley poisoned Della."

"How do you know?"

"I was doing a Google search on plants I want to add

to the farm when I read how poisonous those are." I went on to explain how they leech their poison into a container of water and what happens when someone drinks it.

"I'll call the coroner. He's been looking for barbiturates rather than plant poison. Thanks, Juliette."

I hung up and nearly Snoopy-danced. Bun sat at my feet and asked, *"It's a clue, right?"*

"It sure is. In the morning, we're going to visit Della's house. It isn't far from here and shouldn't take us long to see how she lived and whatnot."

"I hope she doesn't live in an enormous house like the one in our last murder case. That was terrifying for me."

"It was an overwhelming place. I don't think Della had that kind of income. She seemed to live like an average person. But then, you never know. I wouldn't have thought Alvin was filthy wealthy, but he is, and it's old family money, too."

"I'm so excited. I don't know if I can sleep tonight. Just thinking we're going to make headway in Della's death thrills me."

That said, Bun rubbed his head against my ankle and wandered off to his room murmuring a soft goodnight. I said the same and called Jessica.

Her voice groggy, I realized it was later than I'd thought. "Sorry to call so late, but I have a question. Was Della living on Mulberry Lane?"

"Yeah, she had a sweet cottage there. I want a home like that. I was never inside it, but the outside was adorable, kind of like those in kids' storybooks. Maybe it's for sale. Can you look into it for me?"

Jess had gone from groggy to wide awake in a New York heartbeat. I said I would, but wanted the house number if she could remember it. She gave it and said good-bye before I could utter my thanks.

I jotted down the house number and Googled driving directions. Mulberry Lane wasn't too far from the farm, which was a relief. Jason would be here after school, as would Molly. Since Jessica was interested in the house, she probably wouldn't mind checking on the rabbits between pet appointments.

What would I find at Della's home? Unsure, since I didn't know what to look for, I figured I might come across an important clue or two. At least her home was a humble cottage instead of a gargantuan house that had caused me no end of trouble in my last investigation. Anxious to see what the house looked like, I searched in the Windermere Real Estate category.

A slew of listings popped up on the screen. I entered Mulberry Lane in the search box and was surprised to find three homes for sale. Only one was a cottage and the house number matched Della's. I'd hoped for a virtual tour, where the Realtor would record the inside and outside of the home, but there were only a few photos of the exterior of the place, front and back yards, and a photo of the one-car garage. A white picket fence surrounded the property, which I found whimsical. Della hadn't struck me as whimsical or flighty, but hard-nosed, bossy, and a bully. I guess you never know about folks.

Chapter 16

Rain, blown by the wind, pelted the bedroom windows and awakened me. I opened my eyes, glanced out the nearest window, and then noticed Bun had entered the room.

"What are you doing up here? Is everything all right?"

"Of course. I was just wondering if you were awake yet." He bounded across the room onto a chair near the window. With his paws on the windowsill, he peered out and then flip-flopped his ears.

"Crummy day, Jules. I wonder if it will clear up enough for us to go to Della's. I'm not interested in getting soaked to the skin or freezing my bones. It looks pretty chilly and blustery out there."

"I'll check the weather station once I'm organized. Has Jess arrived yet?" I glanced at the clock on my bedside table. It was six in the morning, late enough to put me behind on chores—good thing I didn't have as many rabbits as in the past. I tossed the covers aside, got out of bed, and told Bun that I'd be downstairs shortly.

He hopped away and I prepared for another busy day.

I'd made coffee and put sliced bread in the toaster when Jessica walked in. Without even a hello, she said, "Della's house is for sale. I looked it up on the internet this morning, that's why I'm late. Not too pricey, either. Will you scout around there today?"

"Good morning to you, too," I said with a wry grin. "I had thought Bun and I would do some sleuthing there after I finished the chores. I don't look forward to doing that in this rain, though. Why do you ask?"

"It's going to clear up this afternoon. At least that's what the weatherman predicts. My mom will call the Realtor who has listed the house to see if I can look at it. It has one of those combination lockbox things on the door, so I'll need the code for it. My mom knows the man and said she'd ask for me. Interested in snooping legally, yet?"

"Well, heck, yeah. It's much easier than picking a lock or to search for a key in daylight. From the looks of Mulberry Lane, the homes aren't very far apart, so there's a good chance of being seen."

"My last appointment of the day is at one this afternoon. It would have been later, but Fred Allen had to change the one he'd set up for Jackson. Fred and his wife have a funeral to attend. You'll never guess whose it is."

"I haven't seen a newspaper in ages and you're teasing me, so it must be Della. Frank's parents have made arrangements to bring his body to their hometown for burial."

"It's Della's funeral. Fred said he and his wife heard

about it from the council secretary. I can ask questions about their friendship when he brings Jackson in tomorrow if you'd like."

"That would be super. I'd never considered the scope of people you and Molly deal with before now. It's great to be able to tap into those acquaintances, don't you think?"

With a nod, Jessica gulped a mouthful of coffee, snatched the last slice of toast, and made for the door. She glanced back and said, "I'll let you know what my mother says."

"Okay. See you later."

After Bun was fed, I started the barn chores. Hungry, the rabbits greedily accepted their breakfast. Even Petra and the kits perked up when I reached their cage to tuck a food bundle inside.

Halfway through the daily work, Jessica popped into the barn. "We're all set for one-thirty this afternoon. My mother gave me the combination to the lock. The Realtor said I could call him with questions I might have."

"Okay. Jason will be here by one o'clock. Are you eating lunch with me?"

"Sure. Oh, my mother isn't at work today. I hope she didn't make you nervous at lunch the other day."

"She seemed uncomfortable at first. I have no idea why. Did she mention it to you afterward?"

"Mom was just surprised that you asked her to lunch. She'd never been treated like that in her old job."

"Oh, that's too bad. I'll finish up here and we'll eat before we head out."

Her next appointment on their way into the clinic, Jess hurried off.

A half-hour later, I'd finished up the chores. Some of

the rabbits were in the barn playpen, the others in the inside run. I scrubbed my hands and followed Bun into the house to prepare lunch.

"Will you take me along this afternoon?"

"I planned on it, but if you'd rather stay here with your friends, it's okay."

"I wouldn't miss this in a million lifetimes. You won't be able to chat with me, but if I see anything you should check out, I'll let you know."

"That works for me. You often notice more than I do." I pulled a couple of cans of tomato soup from the cupboard, peeled the tab-top lids back and dumped the contents into a casserole bowl. I didn't have cold cuts on hand, just sliced cheese. Grilled cheese sandwiches always went well with a bowl of tomato soup. The sandwiches were ready to grill, and I set them aside until Jess came in.

"Have you heard whether Molly got any information from that antique collector she knows from school?"

"Not yet. I'm sure she'll have news for us soon. Professors don't always teach every day. Molly might not have been able to meet with him."

"Maybe today, then."

"Keen to learn what he has to say, aren't you?"

"If it matches what Eve told you or is more than she said, then yeah, I'm interested. Aren't you?"

I heard Jess's footsteps in the breezeway and whispered, "I am."

Bun silently huddled on the rug at the front door while I microwaved the soup and grilled the sandwiches. Jessica came in and set the table.

She sniffed the air and said, "I do enjoy a hot meal on a day like this. It looks like the rain is lighter than before.

The clouds aren't quite as dark, either. Tomato soup and grilled cheese, huh?"

"Is there anything that goes better with either one of those things?" I grinned, set the plate of sandwiches on the table, checked the time, and dug in.

"I'm glad we're going to see the cottage today. I showed the pictures to my parents. I'll need their help if I decide it's a perfect place for me. Small, but not too much so, and sweet from what I read online."

"I see you've already made up your mind."

She began to deny it, then shrugged and said, "I hope I'm not disappointed. The pictures didn't show as much as I'd hoped, and the neighborhood looks decent. You know, no junk cars lined up in yards or on the street, along with discarded furniture and such."

"Indeed, I thought much the same. Windermere stays on top of that, so it doesn't become an issue."

We finished lunch, cleaned up, and were about to leave when Molly and Jason arrived. "I thought Molly wouldn't be here until later," I said and watched them run through the raindrops onto the front porch.

Bun leaped away from the door as Molly opened it.

"Are we interrupting you?" Molly asked.

"We were getting ready to leave. Is something wrong?"

"No. I spoke with the professor this morning."

She went on to tell me almost the same as I'd learned from Eve. When she drew a breath, I asked, "Is there more? By the look of you, I'd say you've saved the best for last."

Her eyes wide, Molly said, "The medallion came down through the centuries and was only awarded to women, not to men. It was a symbol of favor to the man who received it from a woman."

"And?"

"The name of the clan was McDonough. The professor said the clan was redheaded and extremely fair, like the Irish. Does that bring anyone particular to mind?"

I gasped, my brain running at top speed. "But her name is Brandt, not McDonough."

"I know, but it could have been her grandmother's or mother's maiden name. The necklace would only have been passed down from one female to the next. Only firstborn girls received it."

"You've done well. Thank you for taking the time to dig up this information."

"I have to get going. I wanted to tell you what I found out and give Jason a ride. No need to get soaked by the rain."

Jason nodded and left for the barn. Molly went out the front door, followed by Jessica, Bun, and me.

In the car, Jess said, "I wonder what Eve's maiden name is."

"It isn't McDonough. She knows Felicia, though. Eve didn't want to tell me that tidbit, and I didn't insist. She became vague and said she'd call me if she remembered. I doubt that will ever happen."

We rode through town as the sun peeked through the clouds. We took a left onto Mulberry Lane.

"This is an omen. I can feel it in my lucky foot," Bun remarked.

I opened my mouth to repeat that to Jess, when she took a sharp turn into a driveway and said, "It's as if I'm supposed to have this place. The sun is out, the day is going to be marvelous, and we'll find evidence to give the sheriff."

I left the car with Bun in the sling that hung off my shoulder.

"You could be right." I watched Jess finagle with the lockbox, then retrieve Della's house key to open the door.

Inside, we stopped dead, looked around, and both said in unison, "This is adorable."

I said, "I'd never have thought Della would live in such a darling place. She was such a negative and rude person. I would have thought a cave might suit her better."

"Wow, that was mean."

"Very much like her, though. She had a mean streak and had no consideration for the feelings of those she insulted. This home is her saving grace as far as I'm concerned. Let's check it out."

Jess went in one direction, Bun and I took another. The house had five rooms, two of which were open to each other with a set of sliding doors that could separate them should there be a need. An oak desk, with a comfy-looking chair, faced windows that overlooked the tiny yard. The house and garage seemed set on a postage-stamp-sized piece of property, compared to the farm, but had a homey atmosphere.

A large area rug covered hardwood floors that gleamed in the sunlight. Pictures filled the painted walls. Nothing fancy about the place, simple and clean, with a sense of grace about it all. The rest of the rooms had the same feel to them. The house itself gave me pause to re-think my opinion of Della. There was more to her than what she projected to others. Maybe she'd used that attitude as a protection device. Hmm. Food for thought.

"It's a terrific house, just what I hoped to find. I'll be

out in the backyard." She peered through the window and said, "Perfect little yard, sweet like the house."

I watched her saunter out back to inspect the yard. About to turn away, I noticed a young girl in the yard next door. She watched Jessica from beyond the picket fence, until she called to Jess. The two of them talked as Bun asked, *"Would you like to rifle the drawers and file cabinet while I check under the beds and in any nooks and crannies that I might find?"*

I agreed and got started as Bun did his thing. In the past, when Bun searched under beds, he'd found evidence that proved useful to us and the sheriff. I walked the room, stared at a snapshot of Della and the girl next door. There was one picture of them with a few other people I didn't recognize, propped on a shelf with odd bits of memorabilia. I removed that picture from the frame and tucked it into my jeans pocket.

All but one of the desk drawers were empty. The last drawer I opened caught halfway, as if it was somehow stuck. I gave it a good tug, but the drawer didn't budge. I knelt on the floor to look underneath for the reason I couldn't get it open. Nothing blocked it from beneath. I stuck my arm inside the drawer as far as I could and touched what felt like a large binder. I peered in at a huge, black, hardcovered notebook wedged in place.

I leaned back on my legs, wiggled closer to the desk, and ran my fingers over the interior walls of the drawer. Impatient, I almost gave up. Being a tenacious sort, I ran my fingertips over the entire inside again and felt a small indentation that I had initially taken as a flaw in the wood. I pushed my fingertip into the dent and heard a faint *click* before the notebook sprung free.

Bun came in as I tossed the notebook onto the desktop.

"I found nothing, not even a dust bunny. Why are dust balls called dust bunnies? They don't look like bunnies, but like tumbleweeds. It's rather insulting to bunnies, you know."

Okay, Bun was rambling. Why? He was undoubtedly disappointed, since he found nothing, not even a dust bunny. I pointed to my find. "This notebook was secured into the bottom drawer. It took some doing to get it out, and it might be of importance."

"Well, let's have a look, then."

I heard voices as the kitchen door opened. Jessica and another person had entered the house. I slid the notebook onto the desk chair.

"How does the yard look? Any flower gardens or rows of blooms? Did you check out the garage?"

Jessica nodded and said, "I peeked in the windows and saw a Volkswagen Beetle. It doesn't look new, but it's clean, just like this house is."

The teenage girl nodded and added her two cents' worth. "Della was a fanatic about this place and her belongings. She told me once that it was all she had and kept it in perfect condition." She reached out her hand and shook mine. "I'm Valerie, by the way. I live over there." She thumbed to the house next door.

I introduced myself and Bun. She leaned over and stroked his ears, which won her a spot of favor at the top of his likeable-people list.

"I was sad to hear Della died. She was a nice person."

I didn't disagree out loud. "Did you have many dealings with her?"

"Oh, yeah. Della used to watch me when I was younger, so my mom could go to work. My dad died when I was little, so it's just Mom and me. Della was really nice to us. She even spent Christmas Day at our house."

An eye-opener, for sure. I mentioned how wonderful that was for her and her mother, and also good for Della, since she was alone.

"Oh, she wasn't alone; she liked to spend the day with us. Della had friends at the local college. I'm surprised she didn't tell you."

"The subject never came up. Ours was more of a business association. You were quite lucky to have a neighbor like that. Did she ever mention who she was friends with at the college? Jess and I might know some of the same folks."

Valerie's eyebrows drew together as she thought hard. "I can't remember exactly, but one day when I was mowing the lawn, a tall woman with a huge amount of auburn hair came to visit."

Ah, Felicia Brandt. The woman got around. What exactly was her connection to Della? Interested enough to find out, I would dig deeper into Della's life as I'd done on other suspects. The internet had turned into a place where one could find out just about anything they wanted to know. I said goodbye as Valerie turned to leave.

She stopped and stared at Jess. "Will you buy this cottage? I hope so, 'cause I like you." With that said, she zoomed out the door before Jess could answer.

"I take it your answer is a resounding *yes*?"

Her head bobbed up and down as her grin widened. "I'll bring my mother by later. She'll fall in love with it, too."

"Okay, let's get a move on. I found a notebook to look at before I offer it to Sheriff Carver."

We left the house, the notebook tucked inside the sling

with Bun, so no one, including Valerie, would see what I had pilfered.

"This book is crowding me."

In the car, I removed the sling, let the notebook slide onto the floor at my feet, and let Bun snuggle in my lap for the ride home.

Chapter 17

Later in the afternoon, Molly stopped by to pick Jason up. While he collected his belongings, she walked around the shop with me at her side.

"There are two girls from the hop that have shown interest in our classes. One of them is an awesome knitter, too. She wants to discuss the possibility of teaching students to knit here in the shop. What do you think?"

"Gosh, I'm not sure. Does she plan to attend Denton's lecture that Jess and I are giving?"

"Yes, she's quite excited, too. She won't graduate for another year, but she'd like to start a knitting business that she'll eventually offer as an online course. Cool, huh?"

"I'll say. You know, I had thought of doing something similar, but the course would be about raising rabbits.

The problem is, I have no idea how or where to get started with what it would take to do that. Besides, I have enough to keep up with. Can I bring these women in to meet you? They were rabbit portrayers at the hop event."

"Ah, I knew there was another reason why you brought it up. Bring them in. The sooner, the better. I've got more leads than I know what to do with at the moment and hope to hand them over to Jack, so he can handle them.

"Is he aware that you and Jess went to Della's cottage?" Molly continued.

"Not to my knowledge. Have you spoken to Jessica about the house yet? She's fairly bursting with excitement and will take her mom to take a look. If Jessica can swing it, she'll buy the house with the help of her parents. It is adorable and a perfect place for her to live."

Gleeful, Molly squealed. "Oh, how wonderful. Not long ago, Jessica complained that her landlord had raised her rent twice in the past year or so. I think he wants to get rid of her and charge a higher amount of rent to some unsuspecting fool. She's never late in paying her rent, either, and is a good tenant. Some people are just plain greedy, I guess."

"She never mentioned it to me. This house might be the answer to her dilemma."

Jason walked into the shop and said he'd see me the next day. He and Molly set off, but not before Molly promised to bring the women by. I waved and took the notebook into the house with Bun at my heels.

"Can we go for a bike ride? It's still warm out and I think a trip to the lake is in order."

"Oh? Well, since the rabbits are all taken care of for now, I guess we can cycle on over there. You like that basket, don't you?"

"Sure do."

The phone rang as I put the notebook on the table.

I didn't recognize the number but answered the call.

"Hi, Juliette Bridge speaking."

"This is Eve McPherson. I wondered if we could meet somewhere private? I want to talk about the things you found."

"Sure, I'm going to Lake Plantain. We could meet there if you want."

"I'll see you in a little while, then." While her Scottish burr wasn't as evident as usual, I thought nothing of it and readied to leave.

In a lightweight windbreaker, I added a pair of thin fabric gloves to the zipper pocket in case it grew chilly. Bun settled in the freshly decorated bicycle basket. Unnecessary to secure him, Bun enjoyed the ride and wouldn't jump out to go off on his own. I pedaled fast to gain momentum and chuckled when Bun lifted his face to the wind as his ears flew back. His joy made me happy.

I encouraged Bun to jump onto the sand when we slowed to a stop at the lake. I pushed the kickstand down and lodged the tires against a log so the bicycle wouldn't topple over. The sun, bright and delightful on my face, left the sand dry enough to sit on. I relaxed on the beach while Bun investigated anything and everything nearby.

It wasn't necessary to be vigilant where Bun was concerned. Rarely did he take off for parts unknown and he had a tendency to stay close. Occasionally, his curiosity took over and he would leave me, especially when he was on the hunt for clues.

Leaves crunched as he bounded into the brush. I peered in the direction he'd gone, but couldn't see him. I rose to take a look and turned away from the water's edge as I caught a glimpse of a length of wood that swung in my direction. I raised my arm to ward off the attack, but I wasn't fast enough. The force of the wood hit me hard. My vision blurred, I lost my balance and landed in the lake. While I floated, Bun splashed about in the water yelling, *"Get up, wake up. You'll drown in this water."*

He stopped short when I opened my eyes, peered into my face, and sank his teeth into my windbreaker. He backed up, tugged furiously at my collar, to no end. I was too heavy for him to haul ashore.

"Let go, Bun. I think I'm okay, just give me a minute." That said, I closed my eyes and drew a deep breath. I lay there, on my back, in the frigid water, trying to remember what had happened. My mind fuzzy, the incident began to return.

I rolled over and dragged my drenched self to dry land on my hands and knees. The water wasn't deep, but enough to drown in. Thankfully, I'd fallen back and not face-first. I reached the beach, shivered like mad, and pushed bedraggled clumps of hair back from my face that I'm sure left traces of sand from my hands in the sodden locks.

"I only left you for a few minutes—what happened? I heard a splash and came running. When I saw you were

out cold, and in the water, I panicked. I thought I was going to hop 'til I dropped. Whew, I'm tired."

"Did you see who did this to me?" I touched my head, looked at my fingers, and found them bloody. I knew I'd been close to being pulverized. Why had someone left before finishing the job? Had they thought I was dead? Could they have hoped I'd eventually drown? Had Bun scared them off when he thrashed through the undergrowth just a few yards from them? In rapid-fire, the questions added to my headache of enormous proportions.

"My focus was on you, sorry. You scared the rabbit fur right off my head. See?" He tipped his head down so I could take a look. His fur was fine, but rather than disagree, I nodded to placate him.

"Let's go home."

"Wait, is that blood on your jacket?" Bun's voice sounded horrified and fearful. At least it seemed like horror. I'd never seen Bun shocked like this.

"Looks that way. I should get home and see how bad the damage is. Don't panic, Bun. Head wounds always bleed a lot. It's nothing to worry about, honest." I left out the headache and dizziness part.

"Come on then, let's go." He must have been concerned. He looked back at me when I slowly moved toward the bicycle.

"Better yet, why not call the sheriff and let him rescue us? I think that's a better idea, don't you?"

I felt my pockets, but my cell phone was no longer there. I waded into the water, peering into the crystal-clear depths. The phone lay at the sandy bottom and was no use to me now. I plucked it out of the water. I tried to make a call, but nothing happened.

"I'm afraid the sheriff isn't an option, Bun. My phone won't work."

He hopped onto the log near the bicycle to wait for me to catch up. When I reached him, he said, *"I can't look at you, the blood is upsetting my tummy. Can you help me into the basket?"*

I did as he asked, realizing Bun was as traumatized as I was. I tried to pedal the bike, but the effort was too great. We wobbled erratically along the road until I heard him say, *"Why don't you walk the bike rather than try to pedal it. You're unsteady. I'm worried we might crash, then where will we be?"*

His advice was sound. The bike wobbled once more, and I knew we wouldn't get home without a mishap. I got off and pushed Bun and the bike toward home. It was tough going. I'd become more unsteady, just like the bicycle when I'd pedaled it.

The upper right side of my windbreaker soaked with blood, Bun sat with his back to me. All I wanted to do was get back to the farm.

A car slowed next to us when we'd reached the main road. I glanced sideways and tried to smile. That's when things went dark. My grip on the handlebars went limp, my sight blurred, and I went down with a thud.

I came to and found myself on a gurney headed through a corridor.

Dr. Sommers nodded at me when I looked up. He said, "Nice to see you again, Juliette."

"What happened?"

"You lost consciousness. A police officer brought you to the hospital. How did you get that laceration to your head, can you remember?"

We'd entered the X-ray department while I considered his question. Dr. Sommers stood aside until I was transferred to a table for X-rays. He didn't move, but waited for me to answer him. Technicians stood nearby, without a sound. Nobody dared question the doctor or ask him to leave.

"I was at the lake when someone struck me from behind. I fell in the water, came to, and found my rabbit splashing about in a panic."

His look, long and thoughtful, he didn't question my explanation. Instead, he nodded to the technicians and said we'd talk more after he'd viewed the X-ray results. I lay still, then turned my head as best I could when told to do so, and held my breath while my injury was captured on film.

With the photoshoot finished, I was taken to a curtained area and left to await Dr. Sommers. The curtain opened a crack, and Adam peeked in.

Glancing over his shoulder, he stepped to the bottom of the gurney, and murmured, "How are you doing? You gave me quite a scare."

"I'll be fine, I've been through much worse. You should go to Lake Plantain and search the beach for what my attacker used as a weapon. It might have traces of blood on it."

"Jules, don't worry about that now, just relax."

The curtain parted slightly again, and Sheriff Carver sneaked in.

Good grief, was this a convention, or what? I opened my mouth, but Jack told me to be quiet. That's when Dr. Sommers made his entrance and ordered both officers out.

His glare and annoyance were evident. "You can't question my patient right now. I'll see you in the waiting room."

Jack nodded at me. Adam dipped his head in acceptance and smiled before he left.

At my bedside, Dr. Sommers said, "Lucky for you there's no cranium damage, just a laceration that I'll suture."

"Do you have to? Just put a Band-Aid on it, it's probably fine by now."

"Yes, I have to. Don't give me a hard time over this." He prepared the suture kit and got started after the area was numb.

A short time later, he said, "There, twelve sutures, and you're all set. You'll have a serious headache for the next few days, so take it easy and you should be fine. If you have vision problems, or that sort of thing, come in right away."

"I will." Not if I could help it. Hospitals gave me the heebie-jeebies.

Much aggrieved, I was forced to ride in a wheelchair while taken to the waiting area where Jack and Adam sat and drank coffee.

"Where's Bun?"

"I took him to the farm after I brought you here. Bun's fine. Molly is taking care of him. Your bicycle is also there."

"Thanks, I don't know what happened. You stopped on the road right next to us and then I woke up on a gurney."

Adam glanced at Jack and kept his mouth shut while he stared at the bandage covering my sutures.

"You were a mess when you arrived," Jack uttered softly. "What happened? Do you think you can remember?"

Okay, these two tough guys were shaken right down to their toes. I could say, ask, or do anything at this juncture and not get lectured for it. Pleased to no end, I knew it would be bad form to take advantage of their worry.

I shared what I could remember of the incident and then fell silent. More due to my growing headache than any other reason.

"I'll take you back to the farm. Molly must be anxious." Jack took over from the orderly and pushed me outside after a brief stop at the front desk.

Adam followed and held the wheelchair steady while I got up and into Jack's car. Jack looked at Adam. "Follow us to the farm."

No time wasted, Adam handed the wheelchair over to the orderly and drove behind us toward the farm.

"You scared the daylights out of us, Juliette. Don't ever do that again, you hear me?"

"Listen up, Jack, I've got a headache the size of Montana and can't handle a lecture from you or anyone right now. If you can't be civil, I'll ride with Adam."

"I'm sorry. It's just that you do things that normal people don't. Like, take chances when you shouldn't."

"Jack, there were no chances taken this time. Bun and I went to the lake to enjoy some downtime. I got a call from Eve McPherson saying she wanted to meet and talk somewhere private. I didn't think I'd be assaulted. I told her to meet me at the lake."

"Did you see Eve?"

"No. I didn't get a look at who swung the wood in my direction. I only caught sight of the wood."

"Uh-huh, well . . . we'll investigate this, starting with the McPherson woman. Why would she attack you?"

"I don't know. Jess and I were at their farm a week or so ago, and I showed her a necklace I had found. Eve, quite taken with it, said she knew someone who owned one, but couldn't recall their name at that moment. It was obvious she lied, but I couldn't accuse her of it. There was no proof, other than her reaction to the piece."

"What does the necklace have to do with anything?"

"That's what I tried to find out. I found it not far from the spot Frank Poland's body was found. The necklace is an old relic passed down through the centuries from first-born Scottish women to their firstborn daughter. There's an engraving on the back of it written in Gaelic, which says it's from the strength and honor clan."

Jack parked the car. The shop door flew open with Bun and Molly in a race to reach me first. Bun won, of course, considering four legs are better than two.

It was clear by their shocked expressions that I still looked pretty awful. I opened the car door and said I could use some clean clothes before I shared my experience. Molly offered help, but I waved it away and asked her to make coffee, instead.

In my bedroom, I peeled off the disgusting clothes, left them in a heap on the floor, and went into the bathroom. The image of me in the mirror darned near caused me to faint. I gripped the sink as I swayed, until my vision cleared once again. The swollen bruise on one side of my face appeared to spread along my cheekbone and up into my hairline. I looked pretty bad, but mostly due to crusted blood that matted my hair.

I cleaned the blood out of my hair with a moist wash-cloth after I removed the bandage that interfered with the process. Dressed in clean clothes, I felt human again. I flipped a few locks of hair over the sutures so it wouldn't be apparent and bring about any possible vomiting by those who saw it.

Chapter 18

In slow motion, I entered the kitchen where the guys and Molly were deep in discussion. All went quiet when I sat at the table. Molly poured a hot cup of brew for me and Bun sprawled across both feet.

"I thought you were a goner, like in those cowboy movies. One and done, you know?"

I reached down and ruffled his fur, then stroked his ears in answer. A tiny puff of air crossed my hand as he sighed.

"Bun was terribly upset when I was struck and landed in the water. When I came to, he splashed me with water as he hopped around. I'm glad you took care of him, Molly."

"He's okay now that you're here. I didn't mind staying with him at all."

Sheriff Carver grunted and sipped his coffee. "I suppose you think the rabbit saved your life, don't you?"

"If he hadn't splashed about as he did, I might have drowned, Jack."

He dipped his head and said, "True. It was a good thing he was with you, then."

For Jack to give in so easily put me on guard.

"Do you have that necklace?"

Molly gasped when I admitted that I had it. I took it from the drawer and laid the bag in front of Jack. He wasn't going to take it because I didn't want him to have it.

He slid the medallion onto the table, ran a finger over the surface, then picked it up and flipped it over. He squinted at the engraving before he set it down. I snatched the necklace, slipped it into the velvet bag, then tucked it in the drawer.

"It's quite nice. You found it near Frank's location?"

I nodded.

"I'll look into this, but will put the piece into our evidence locker for safekeeping."

"I don't think so."

His narrow-eyed stare said more than words ever could. It seemed to say it wasn't a request, but instead, he wanted me to know he could keep it safer than it was in my desk drawer.

Standing my ground, I said softly, "I would rather it didn't leave the premises, Jack. I think Frank had it around his neck."

Surprised, Jack asked, "How did you reach that conclusion?"

"I remember that before you arrived, I noticed a red line on his neck. I thought it was a scratch from the brush when Frank was hauled to the spot where he was left. The medallion belongs to a woman, and that woman chose him to wear it. You see, when passed down from mother to daughter, the daughter gets to choose the person she wants to marry. If he agrees to wear it, then a bond forms. I know it sounds far-fetched, but that's how the story goes."

I was about to go on when Molly interrupted me. "Sheriff, from what my professor said, the medallion is old, very old, and is part of a custom that has pretty much fallen by the wayside."

His look centered on me, Jack barked, "You let her take this to show a professor, but you don't want me to keep it at the police station?"

In a soft voice, the kind of softness that can defuse a volatile situation, Molly said, "I never took it anywhere. I have photographs of it. Jules was worried the person searching for it would see it, and that might put me in danger."

He sighed, leaned back in his chair, and glanced at Adam. Why? I wasn't sure, but knew Adam would try reasoning with me. Not.

"Juliette, the medallion would be safer at the station than it is here. If the owner knows you have possession of it, then that could be more dangerous for you."

My head pounded. He was right, but some unknown reason held me back from agreeing to let the medallion go. "I can't let you take it."

"Why?" Adam asked gently.

"I don't know. I have to keep it here for now. I'm not trying to be difficult. The medallion might have more meaning than we're aware of." I raised my hands, palms up, and said, "You have every right to take it from me, and I understand if you do."

Jack nodded at Adam, who slid his chair back and retrieved the medallion from the desk. That Jack refused to understand my reasoning pushed my patience to the limit. The headache might have had something to do with it, as well.

I pointed to the sack and remarked, "If anything happens to that, I'll hold both of you responsible. It's an ancient relic with major history behind it. If the person who owns the medallion killed Frank, then she shouldn't have it, but if she didn't, I must return it to her."

"And who would *she* be?" Jack waited for my answer, an answer I didn't want to give him.

I fiddled with my coffee mug handle and said, "Felicia Brandt."

"How do you know?"

"I do my homework, Jack. Now, you do yours." I left the table, marched upstairs, gripping the handrail for all I was worth, and slammed the door to my bedroom behind me. I took a couple over-the-counter pain relievers and settled into the softness of my bed. A light scratch sounded at the door, then I heard, *"Are you okay? I want to come in and see for myself."*

I let Bun in, rubbed my cheek against the top of his head, and began to cry. Between tears and sniffles, I whispered, "I know you were frightened. I'm sorry, Bun."

"It's okay. I knew you'd be fine. Get some rest. I won't leave you, all right? I had to be certain you were okay. The sheriff and his sidekick have left. I think Molly is making you a cup of tea."

Footsteps on the stairs and the rattle of a teacup in its saucer meant Molly was on her way. Bun backed out of my hold and eyed Molly from the doorway.

I rose and thanked her for the tea.

"I've called Jessica. She's on her way over to help finish up with the rabbits and settle them for the night. I'll give her a hand with that while you rest. Jessica will make your supper, so don't worry about anything."

"Thanks again, Molly. You're the best."

"I don't say this to be mean, but you need to resist the temptation to investigate this sort of thing. It's too dangerous, Jules."

"I know." Teacup and saucer in hand, I turned toward the bed.

She waited until I'd settled in, and then said, "Your hero is right here. I don't think he'll leave you for a minute."

Her footsteps receded as she returned to the kitchen.

Bun huddled in the hallway across from my door. I set the teacup on my nightstand, smiled, and closed my eyes, sinking into the mattress and huddling under an afghan. Huddling felt rather good right about now.

At seven o'clock in the evening, I awoke with a start. Deep shades of twilight filtered through the windows. What had awakened me? It wasn't apparent. Yet.

Footsteps sounded on the stairs and in the hallway. Bun sat next to my bed, his ears straight up in anticipation. *"Jess is bringing you food."*

His senses on high alert, he could smell her essence and identify her footsteps much better than I ever would.

Jess entered the room, a bright smile on her face that failed to reach her eyes. "How are you?"

"Hungry, less of a headache, and happy to be home."
And alive, but I didn't say it.

"Good, then you'll enjoy supper. Mashed potatoes, steamed carrots, and pork chops with bread and butter on the side. Would you like coffee or tea?"

"Ice water would be fine. I'm parched." I sat in the chair near the window and set up the small folding table beside it. I'd spent many a day in this room, eating meals and practically living in here while I recuperated from the car accident I'd had some time ago.

Jess perched on the bed while I ate. Bun never left my side and Jess noticed.

"Bun's been up here the entire time you were asleep. He hasn't even taken a snack break." She reached for my tray and lifted a food bundle from it, then placed it on the floor for Bun.

He jumped at the meal and ate to his heart's content until not a morsel remained.

"I'll be downstairs for a few minutes, and then I'll come back."

I watched him hop away and looked at Jess. "He's such a cutie."

"He certainly is, and from his actions, I think he was concerned for you. Molly filled me in on what took place. You're lucky to be alive."

"I know. I think Bun saved the day."

"How's that?"

"He was in the underbrush and probably heard the person coming at me. The leaves and debris crackled and crunched when stepped on. Maybe my attacker heard the noise and thought somebody was nearby. It's the only logical explanation I can come up with."

"Sound thinking. What did the doctor say?"

"I'll be fine, a headache from the assault, and he said to take it easy for a few days. He has no idea what it's like to run a rabbit farm. Enough about me. Did your mother like the cottage?"

Jessica nodded. "She loved it on sight. She and my father agreed to cosign a loan for me if my offer is accepted."

"Does the Realtor know who will end up with the money from the sale?"

"Are you digging for information again?"

"Not at all. I wondered if Della had any family to speak of."

"Sorry, I jumped to conclusions. I'm not aware of Della's private affairs, or her last wishes. She may have made a trust or some such thing."

"That's a possibility. I hope this works out for you. You work hard and deserve to have a home of your own. How soon will you know if the offer is accepted?"

"I'm not sure." She stared out the window as the sky darkened. "I'm not nagging you or anything, but you could have been killed today."

"I realize that. I can't believe Eve struck me. Jack is going to speak with her and also with Felicia Brandt."

"What do they have to do with each other? I don't understand."

"I believe Felicia owns the medallion and gave it to Frank. Eve knows her somehow and put me off the day we were at her farm. She had called to ask me to meet her somewhere private to talk."

"Are you sure it was Eve?"

"She said she was Eve, and it sounded like her voice." Silent for second, I said, "But now that I think about it, her brogue wasn't as strong as usual. Someone could have impersonated her. I didn't see my attacker."

"All I can say is that you were darned lucky. Bun protected you once again." She stared at Bun, who had returned to his position in the hallway, to guard me from anyone he thought shouldn't enter. Jess said, "You're my hero, Bun."

Bun crouched as bunnies do, and relaxed.

I watched Jess leave, finished my meal, then set the tray and table aside. I motioned for Bun to join me and closed the door behind him when he came in.

"Are you certain you didn't glimpse the person who attacked me?"

He remained silent for so long. I realized he didn't want to admit what he'd seen.

"Well?"

"A human dressed like a rabbit."

Flabbergasted, I sank into the chair and studied him.

"You're sure that's what you saw?"

"I didn't want to tell you since the rabbit costume was the same one I had seen before, but somehow different. A tad dirty and ill-fitting. Maybe that's what threw me off."

"Ill-fitting in what way?"

"The costume was sort of big, not like the rabbit impersonator at Della's crime scene. That outfit was the right size and it fit perfectly."

"So what you're saying is today's rabbit wasn't the same as the one we saw before?"

"Exactly. Who do we know that's shorter?"

"Let me think about it. I thought that Della's rabbit was about as tall as Adam. How much shorter was this person?"

"How would I even begin to know the answer to that? I only got a glimpse as I was trying to save you."

"Okay, don't get upset, we'll figure it out. It doesn't need to be right this minute." I left the chair and took the tray downstairs. Food and medicine had made a difference in how I felt, as well as Bun's information.

At the bedroom door, I looked down at Bun and asked, "Why didn't you want to tell me? You know you can share anything with me."

"I didn't want to get you all riled up so you'd run off and start hunting for him or her. You weren't feeling all that great, and I was worried."

"Thanks for being so thoughtful."

We walked along the hallway. At the top of the stairs, Bun said, *"I figured tomorrow would be a great time to start."*

So much for a couple of days of rest. I rolled my eyes and whispered, "Right, I thought that was your angle. Jessica and I give our lecture at the college this week, and I'll need all the rest I can get before that takes place. No investigating until that's over if we can help it."

"Sure thing, you betcha."

Chapter 19

Two days later, Jessica wandered into the house as I practiced my part of the lecture. She stood just inside the breezeway door, her arms folded, and watched me walk back and forth talking about my business. When I stopped, she applauded.

"Great work. Maybe we should get together and practice. That way, we can be more relaxed and possibly urge each other on or even play off each other. What do you think?"

"Perfect, when?"

"After work tonight? My last appointment is at four this afternoon. I should be ready by dinnertime."

"Okay, I'll cook and we can practice after we've eaten."

"Sounds good to me. I'll see you later. Oh, how are you doing today?"

"Well enough to feed the rabbits and get some of the chores tended to. Jason came in early and handled the rest. All said, I'm better. The stitches will come out on their own, so I won't have to see Dr. Sommers."

"That must be a relief. I know you aren't a fan of hospitals."

"No, I'm not."

"Have you heard from Sheriff Carver?"

"Not a peep. Have you?"

She shook her head.

"He's got plenty of work to keep him busy. Did Molly mention if Meredith came to class?"

"She hasn't said. Maybe Meredith will stop in to see you if she comes to the spinning class tonight. Molly did say the plans for the student open house are progressing nicely, though. The students are excited about it."

"I'll have a word with Molly about advertising. The ads must be placed in advance of the event if we want a good turnout. It's nice to offer a giveback. The students and Molly work so hard and their talent shows."

"My mother is looking forward to it. She's good at organizing and has assisted with details."

"That's nice of her. Molly has a lot to handle these days, and I wouldn't want her to become overwhelmed."

Jess headed for the door as a car arrived. "That's Mrs. Chandler, she's ahead of schedule, so I'd better go. Her cat is old and nearing the end of its life. I hope she doesn't want me to euthanize it."

"See you later." I couldn't think of a thing to say about the subject. I know I would be hard-pressed even to consider it.

"I can tell by the look on your face that you think you couldn't do that, but sometimes, it's the right thing to do.

Animals shouldn't have to suffer because their partner, in this case, Mrs. Chandler, can't bring herself to help her cat move on. She's not doing that animal any good by dragging out the cat's agony. It isn't fair."

"I suppose so, but humans are emotional, and feelings of guilt increase our loss of perspective over what's right. We love our furry friends so much we can't imagine living without them."

"Hmm." Bun went to his room to snack on fresh veggies and fruit I had left for him.

At his doorway, I asked, "Want to take a ride? We can take a spin down the road and back. I could use some fresh air."

"We aren't going to the lake, right?"

"We are not. We'll ride in the opposite direction, instead. How's that?"

"Okay, I'm ready."

Pedaling along the driveway, I stopped midway as Molly drove in. The passenger-side window went down, and she greeted us with a smile.

"Glad to see you're out and about. You're not going far, are you?"

"No, why?"

"I wanted to speak with you concerning our event."

"Sure, we won't be gone long; our ride will be a short one. I'll see you when I get back unless you want to discuss it now."

"There are a few odds and ends in the shop that need attention. I'll be there when you get back. Don't rush."

I pedaled off as Molly drove to the shop.

"I hope this event will be spectacular. Molly has worked endlessly to keep everyone on board. I heard her talking to Mrs. Plain about postcard advertisements."

"We did that for our last open house and attendance was fantastic. I'll see what she has to say and get more involved. I seem to have put everything aside for this investigation, and ignoring the farm isn't smart. It's my livelihood, and we know how important that is to all of us."

Bun wiggled around in the basket and faced me. *"Are you saying we should let the police do their job?"*

"Not exactly, but I can't keep getting attacked by somebody who wants me out of the way. Where would you and the other rabbits be if I ended up dead?"

"True, you frightened all of us, that's for sure. This last attack was the worst yet. I think the rabbit impersonator would have finished you off if I hadn't made so much noise in the brush."

"I suppose we could always help the sheriff without physical involvement. Possibly in an advisory capacity. That way, danger wouldn't be such a problem. It does seem to find us, doesn't it?"

"Yes, and when we least expect it."

A police cruiser slowed to a stop when I did. Adam put his window down and said, "You must feel better."

"I thought fresh air and exercise would be good for us. What's Jack up to? I haven't heard a word from him."

"We're following up leads and questioning people. Why do you ask? Have you remembered anything that might be helpful?"

"Kind of."

His brows arched, Adam waited in silence.

"I think my attacker dressed in a rabbit costume. I saw what looked like bits of fake fur on the beach when I came ashore." I lied, but couldn't very well tell him what Bun had seen. "Did you guys check the scene for evidence?"

"Yeah, but if there was fake fur lying around, the wind must have taken it, because we didn't find any. I'll look again."

"Okay. This person might have been short, too."

"How's that?"

"The wood he swung didn't come from above, but from the side like a bat. If he was tall, then it would have been swung from a higher position, don't you think?" From the look on his face, I got the impression he didn't think my information viable. I didn't press the issue. Again, I couldn't very well say that Bun told me the outfit was ill-fitting because the person in it wasn't tall enough for it to fit correctly.

Adam gave me a nod, said he'd tell the sheriff what I'd said, and then drove off. Bun and I cycled for another half mile before we turned toward home.

Silent on the trip home, Bun snuggled in the basket. His fur ruffled gently in the breeze created by the bike's motion. Refreshing as it was to be outside, my thoughts were on the upcoming lecture and the shop's event.

"He didn't believe you."

"I know. But, that's not my problem, it's his and Jack Carver's. We have to focus on Molly's open house and ask what we can do to assist her and the students."

"I'll get focused, then. You know how brilliant I am at coming up with ideas."

I let the comment pass, not because I questioned Bun's brilliance, but mostly because he could get underfoot while he tried to be helpful. I pedaled up the driveway, set the bicycle in its usual spot, and then went into the shop with Bun at my side.

Molly looked up from behind a pile of yarn jumbled across the counter. "You seem refreshed."

"We are. At least I am. What can I do to help you?"

"These skeins of yarn were stored under the counter. If you'd sort out the colors, I'll add them to the display."

"Sure thing. What did you want to talk about?"

"The event plans. They're coming along nicely, but I wondered if we could afford to have postcards printed like the last time there was an open house. It made such a difference in attendance, don't you think?"

"It did. I dropped them off everywhere I could think of and even got calls for more. I'll place an order if, or when, you have sample artwork ready. I'll also need a mock-up ad for our website and to put in the newspaper. Can you handle that, or would Mrs. Plain be able to do it for us?"

"Funny that you ask. Mrs. Plain and I have discussed those things." Molly hesitated a second and then said, "You don't mind, do you?"

"Not at all. I've been lax about business lately, and that's got to change. I'll help you any way I can. Mrs. Plain is a valuable asset and can help as much as she wants to. It's necessary to have input for this sort of thing. I'm not creative when it comes to ads. If you two can put your heads together for an advertisement, I'll do my part by putting it in place and delivering postcards."

"That's wonderful. I'll let Mrs. Plain know."

The yarn sorted, I carried arms full over to the diamond-shaped display attached to the wall, and handed skeins to Molly, who tucked them into their respective spots. We both stopped when the door to the clinic burst open and Jessica flew in.

"My offer for the house was accepted. Isn't that great?" She Snoopy-danced in place as we watched and chuckled over her excitement.

When she came to a halt, I said, "Congratulations. What comes next?"

"My parents and I have the financing in place. We'll have a home inspection and then hopefully close on the deal. I'm so thrilled, I can hardly stand still."

Molly chuckled. "Apparently. Anything we can do?"

"Not yet. You two can give me a hand packing and moving in, though."

I agreed. "Whatever and whenever, it'll be fun."

"Okay, back to work." Jess rushed from the shop and greeted the next patient.

Mrs. Plain sidled in as Jessica closed an examination room door.

"She couldn't be happier. Keep your fingers crossed that the inspection goes without a hitch. Jessica will enjoy living there. She does like that little cottage." She looked at me and asked, "Weren't you familiar with the former owner?"

"Only through the Hop 'Til You Drop event at Perkins Park. We hadn't met prior to that."

"Oh, I thought you were well acquainted with her."

"Why would you think that?"

"I wondered that, too."

"Why, Mr. Clarke thought so—at least that's what he said."

"Denton Clarke?"

She nodded and glanced back at the clinic. "I must get back to the clinic. We'll talk again later. I know you probably have more questions."

"I do."

She scooted through the doorway, closing the door behind her.

"That was odd," Molly murmured. "I wonder why she'd think you knew Della well?"

"Yes, it is very strange. Mrs. Plain doesn't come right out and say why she wants to know something. Instead, she leaves you wondering what's really on her mind. Anyway, if you two can get that advertising information together for me, I'll order the postcards and place the ad. I don't want to leave it until the last minute. Have you considered refreshments?"

"Not really. When there are demonstrations using yarns or fiber supplies, the last thing I would want is to have someone spill their beverage on the work. If you think we should have snacks, then go ahead and make arrangements."

"I hadn't considered that aspect. We won't have food or drinks in here, then. Will there be some small freebie given away, you know, like favors or discounted tickets for a class?"

"The students mentioned making small items to hand out when people leave. It's good business to promote the shop with business cards attached to the front of them."

At the counter, Molly took a notepad and pencil from a drawer, then sketched out how the gifts would look.

"Attaching Fur Bridge Farm cards to them would be perfect, don't you think?"

"I'll look in my stash for business cards and small notepads advertising the farm. Maybe the printer will be able to print labels, too. Might as well support local businesses, right?"

"I like that idea, and it's wise to use businesses in town instead of ordering from companies across the country, when we don't have to. I'll get this completed right away."

I left her to it. Bun and I walked into the barn to visit the rabbits. All was quiet and the barn was clean and in good shape, as were the rabbits. Jason was worth his weight in gold as far as I was concerned, just like Molly was.

"I've been thinking about Alvin Peterson. He could tell you more about Della and her life. She'd been on the council for quite some time."

"I'll tell you what: When we order stuff for the open house, we'll stop by to see what Alvin has to say. He and Della weren't best friends, but you don't work closely with your fellow council members without knowing what makes them tick. At least, it would make sense, right?"

"Absolutely."

Supper was over. Our rehearsal session ended in fits of laughter. Jess sobered and asked, "What would make someone like Della so miserable?"

I shrugged. "There could be any number of reasons. Maybe Della's childhood was terrible; she could have had a relationship gone bad, or maybe she just became cold and vicious when life didn't go her way. She probably felt she deserved more than she got. It's hard to say. I didn't know her that well. Why do you ask?"

"Today, my mother mentioned Della. It seems she— Della, I mean—had met my mother once and was extremely rude. Mom didn't get into what exactly took place, but she did say Della was forthright and nasty. She also asked if you knew Della very well."

Before she could utter another word, I remarked, "Your mother asked me that very question just this afternoon."

"Did she, now. That's curious, isn't it?"

"Molly and I thought so. Your mother came in while we sorted yarn and asked how well I knew Della. I said I only knew her from the egg hunt. Why would she ask that? Do you think she knows something about Della that she should tell Sheriff Carver?"

"I have no idea. My mother can be an oddball at times. My father and I are always taken by surprise at the things that pop out of her mouth." Jess grinned and said she'd see me in the morning.

She left me with no idea of what went through Mrs. Plain's mind. I shook my head and went into the shop, where students spun yarn, knitted, or crocheted, and some spent time at the swift and ball winder.

Fascinated by their proficiency with the swift and winder, I watched in silence until one woman glanced up at me and asked quietly, "Would you like to try your hand at this?"

I whispered, "No, thank you. I find it interesting to see how it all works together, though."

"There is a knack to getting the yarn to wind smoothly. The hank of yarn must be in order. It can't get tangled, or it won't work. My first time doing this was a nightmare." She grinned at the thought of it.

The class took a break, a kind of recess if you will, to stand and stretch, to walk around and see what went on at other stations in the shop.

I noticed her name badge and asked, "Will you participate in the open house, Maggie?"

With a nod, she said, "I'm looking forward to it. It's good of you to offer this to us. We'll have a chance to connect with the public and show our work, and it's also good for your farm. A win-win, for sure." Maggie glanced around before she sidled closer to me. She said in just above a whisper, "Has the sheriff made any progress in his investigation of Frank Poland's death?"

"I'm not sure. Jack hasn't said a word to me."

"Oh, I've heard you and the Carvers are quite close, and thought he might have taken you into his confidence. You did find Frank, didn't you?"

I nodded. "It was awful. Frank was a nice person."

"He was, uh—until, uh—"

My Spidey senses perked up and I whispered, "Until what?"

"Never mind, I shouldn't talk about the dead."

"There's nothing wrong with talking about the dead. People do it all the time when sharing memories and anecdotes. There's no harm in telling me."

"If you insist. I didn't want to speak out of turn, that's all."

"No worries, you're not."

"Until he got tangled up with Felicia Brandt. Then his life took a completely different direction."

"In what way?"

"He went from a fun and cheerful guy to someone secretive and pensive. Several of us noticed it."

"Secretive in what way?"

"Frank often disappeared for hours on end, missed classes, and he seemed besotted with Felicia. I didn't understand his actions then and I still don't."

Molly called time's up, recess was over. The students had another hour to go and I didn't want to interfere with their progress. I joined Molly as she turned to a basket of hanks.

She handed me the ad mock-up along with the postcard sample, saying Mrs. Plain had done them on Jessica's computer when business in the clinic was slow. I studied the artwork, pleased by the look of it. With all the necessary information addressed, the setup worked beautifully. "Nice work. She's talented, isn't she?"

"I think so. I don't have time to fool with the computer. Mrs. Plain has the know-how, and that's good enough for me. When she brought these in, I was thrilled. I'm glad you like the way they look."

"They're perfect for what we need. Great job done. Do you have time for me before you leave for the night?"

"Of course. I'll be done in an hour."

I waved to Meredith before leaving the shop and took the mock-ups into the house, all the while chewing over the revelation of how Frank had changed after his involvement with Felicia. The woman was a challenge. I'd check with Jack on my way to the printshop to see if he'd spoken to her yet.

After the students left class, Molly walked into the kitchen and flopped in a chair.

"This has been a long day."

"Is something wrong?"

"Not really. I just need to reorganize my schedule and learn to say no at the college when I'm asked to take on one more job."

"Oh?"

Using her fingertips to massage her temples, Molly said, "Denton asked me to handle refreshments the evening you and Jessica are speaking. He has an assistant, so I said I couldn't help him out. He had a few questions about you, too. I think he'd like to ask you for a date."

"I got that feeling, but I'm not interested. My schedule here is enough to keep me busy."

"What did you want to discuss?"

Concerned that Molly had taken on too much, I said, "The supplies you need to increase the shop classes are on hold. The distributor can't ship what you need right away. There's some sort of strike, I guess. I'm sure the wait won't be too long. Will it make a difference in your expansion plans, or should I find another distributor?"

"The wait is fine. I had hoped to get the plans in place by the end of May, which isn't that far off. Give the Franklin sales rep a call tomorrow and ask if there's any way he can expedite the order." Molly hesitated and then asked, "Has he mentioned what the strike is about?"

"The shipper they use has union problems; the shippers won't sign the new contract. All the spinning wheels are handmade, and the delivery of the raw-materials delay is due to that. The company is seeking another shipping company, but it's not easy when there's a strike."

Shaking her head, Molly said, "Union people tend to support one another, and while I think it's feasible, it slows everything down." Molly yawned and then said goodnight.

Chapter 20

Chores over with, I showered and changed into clean jeans, a multicolored cotton sweater, and a pair of snazzy gold-edged loafers. I didn't wear the loafers often but wanted to break them in because they were part of the outfit I planned to wear for the college lecture.

My first stop was the printshop. Gary and Edna Erikson had owned and operated their business since I'd attended elementary school. The new look of the shop surprised me when I walked in. Streamlined with computerized machines, along with immense layout and packing tables, I gazed at the changes before greeting the most unlikely matched couple I'd ever met.

"Good morning," I said, noticing how Edna's attire and hairstyle had gone from frumpy to sweet and smart. It was as though she'd had a makeover that looked great

on her. I turned to Gary and saw that he, too, had under-
gone a major change. The couple had finally stepped into
the here and now, leaving their old selves behind.

"This place and you two look wonderful. How's business?"

Gary answered before Edna said a word. "Great.
We've changed our lives and stepped into the future of
printing. What can we do for you today, Juliette?"

I handed him the file folder. "We've planned an open
house for the shop. I wanted to know how soon you could
have these postcards ready? Uh, I'll also need a price."

"Certainly, Edna can handle the pricing, can't you,
honey?" He gave her a wink.

Her blue eyes sparkled as she said, "Of course, sweet-
heart."

I stifled a grin. The couple may have changed their
look and that of their business, but the two of them still
used honeyed words for each other. They'd been married
for years and were friends with my parents.

"I see you've got Bun with you. Is the farm doing
well? How are your parents?" Edna asked as she tapped
computer keys.

"Very well, to both of those questions. My parents
love their new home and have become involved with
folks their age. With trips to the casino, riverboat cruises
and such, they're having the time of their lives. I'll let
them know you asked after them the next time we speak.
We have a new bunch of baby bunnies at the farm. It's
been pretty hectic these last couple of weeks."

"Wonderful to hear your parents have settled in and
that the farm is doing so well. We hear great things about
you, Juliette." Edna handed me an invoice. The cost wasn't

high for the number of cards I wanted. I nodded and gave the go-ahead.

"We'll have them ready for you, no problem. Stop back at the end of the week, okay?"

I handed Edna a company check and promised to come in Friday. On my way to the door, Denton Clarke entered carrying a bulging satchel. He sidestepped me with a warm smile.

"It's good to see you, Juliette. Are you and Jessica ready for your evening with my students?"

"We sure are and we're hoping for a great turnout."

"There are a lot of students registered due to yours and Jessica's business reputations." He hefted the satchel onto the counter and stared at Bun, who stared back.

"There's something special in the satchel that Denton doesn't want us to know about. I can feel it in my bones."

I couldn't remark on his views and nodded in response to both Bun's and Denton's remarks. The couple and Denton smiled and wished me well as I went out the door. None of the three had made a move toward the satchel.

At the edge of the storefront, I sidled up to the window and peeked in. Denton had opened the leather bag. Edna stared inside. Gary appeared gleeful. For the life of me, I couldn't imagine why, until Gary reached in and withdrew stacks of banded cash. I jumped away from the window and took off for the police station. The *Windermere Gazette* stop would have to wait.

At the front desk, I asked to see Sheriff Carver. Told to take a seat, I walked toward a bench when Jack called my name and beckoned me to join him.

I set Bun on the floor and walked into Jack's office.

With Bun at my feet, I relaxed and waited until Jack sat down. His elbows propped on the desk, he asked, "What brings you by? I hope you've got news for me."

"I do." I launched into the conversation I'd had the night before with Maggie Charles, a student attending the college, and mentioned she was a student in my shop. He listened without interruption, for which I was most grateful. My mind kept jumping back to Edna and Gary, their newfound update, and their possibly illegal money.

"What else? I know there's more. I can tell by the expression on your face."

"How astute of him."

"Very astute of you, Jack. I just left Erikson's Print Shop." I went on to explain what I had seen and then clamped my mouth shut to wait until the sheriff sifted through what I'd just suggested without saying it outright.

"In essence, you think Edna and Gary are laundering money? And that money is being brought to them by none other than Professor Denton Clarke?" He tipped back in his chair and shook his head with a smirk on his face.

"Uh, did I hear a tone of disbelief?"

"Don't tell me I've wasted my time bringing this information to you. I know what I saw. Why would anyone bring that couple huge bundles of banded cash in a satchel, a heavy satchel, which means it held lots of money."

"Good point, but there's no proof that the money is being laundered through their business. It is odd that Edna and Gary have stepped into the present instead of looking like people who lived in the fifties. I always wondered why they dressed that way and why they never updated their business, or how they kept it going. You might be right, or Denton is loaning them money."

"Which begs the question of where Denton would get that kind of cash, Jack. Professors his age who work at small colleges don't make satchels of money."

"Uh-huh. We'll look into the Eriksons' and Clarke's accounts to see what's what. I'm not sure there's enough information to get a warrant, but I can try. Judge Moore is rather good about issuing them to me without dotted i's and t's crossed."

"I'll pick up my order on Friday. Maybe I can learn more about Denton's actions then. I think he's sweet on me, at least he's flirtatious every time we meet. I can play that angle. What do you think?"

"That you'd better be careful. You've had one attack on your life, you don't need another."

"Mmm. True. I wouldn't want that. Maybe I'll just let you do your job, then." Not.

"Don't do a thing until I get a warrant. My tech guys can then look into their banking, which will give me cause to go further. I won't accuse any of those people of a crime until I have enough proof to take to court."

"Right, got it. I'd better be going, I have other errands to run."

"How are you feeling since your attack?"

"I'm well, thanks for asking. I saw Meredith in class last night but didn't have a chance to speak with her. Her work is beautiful."

He harrumphed and said, "It should be. Those classes cost me a small fortune."

I snorted. "You know you don't care. You complain,

but there's no chance that you would refuse Meredith anything her heart desires."

His face turned a light shade of pink, and he agreed in good humor as he brushed me away. "Get out of my office, I have to call Judge Moore."

Bun and I made our exit with Bun talking nonstop while we walked through the police station. Outside, I scooped him off the step and tucked him into the sling that hung off my shoulder.

"I guess you convinced Carver there's something worth looking into, huh?"

"Surprisingly enough."

"Are we going to the Gazette now?"

"We are, and then I want to see if Mr. Peterson's in his office before going to the market for a few items. You'll have to stay in the car at the market, okay?"

"Sure, I have a lot to think about anyway."

"Like what?" I drove into the Mayfair Center complex and parked in the visitors' section.

"I'm trying to make a connection between Frank, Felicia, the Eriksons, Clarke, and the drug trade."

"It might take you a while to connect those dots. I'll be right back, okay?"

"Can't I go in with you? I could pick up something that you might miss when you and Alvin get to talking."

"Okay, come on." I held the sling open for him to climb in. We set off for the city council's office in the humongous building that housed so many other city-related offices.

Directed to Alvin's suite, Bun and I rode the elevator to the third floor. The door opened and we stepped into the corridor. I turned left, walked past a few official-looking businesses, and ended up in front of glass doors with the Windermere city council's logo on them.

Alvin entered the foyer, where a smartly dressed secretary sat behind a semicircle-shaped counter. He handed the woman a sheaf of papers and then turned to me.

"Good morning, Juliette." His greeting warm, I matched mine to it and proceeded to follow him into his office.

"I see you have your pal with you." He reached out to scratch Bun's head, but Bun ducked back into the sling.

"Something's off with this guy. Take care, Jules, he's dangerous."

"I guess he isn't very sociable today. Sorry about that, Alvin."

I took the seat Alvin motioned to as he walked behind his desk and sat down facing me.

"To what do I owe the pleasure of your company?"

I smiled and said, "I have a question for you. My friend, Jessica Plain, is in the process of purchasing Della Meeny's cottage. Would you happen to know if Della had any relatives? Jess would like to meet them."

He leaned forward, his hands lightly folded, and said, "She had no children that I know of. No husband, either. I think she was single all her life. If she had a family, they didn't live in Windermere." He paused a moment, then said, "Frankly, I have no idea about her background. She worked here for quite some time. As you know, Della wasn't an easy person to work with, and I believe she was about to lose her job."

"What, specifically, was her job, if you don't mind my asking."

"As weird as it sounds, Della was in charge of community relations. She was good at the paperwork end of it, but didn't have the personality for it. Della had an assistant, a college student interning at our offices. That young woman did the footwork and attended meetings Della disliked so much."

"I see. What's her name?"

"Felicia Brandt. She's an asset when dealing with our community projects. She and Della weren't related that I know of if that's what you were thinking."

"Not at all. I was merely asking about Della on behalf of Jessica. I can't imagine who would be capable of dealing with a person as strong-willed and cranky as Della was." I readied to leave.

Alvin walked me to the door. "I hope you'll consider helping us out in future programs, Juliette. You are one in a million, and we need more community-minded people like you to help us out."

"Thank you, and thanks for your time. It was good of you to see me on such short notice."

Bun and I went on our way without looking back. I could feel the bad case of jitters Bun was in the midst of. The vibration of his body filtered through the leather sling.

In the elevator, I murmured, "Are you all right?"

"Don't be fooled by his charm and false pleasure at seeing you. He's a bad, bad man."

"Okay. I'll take your advice. Alvin does seem too good to be true. Our next stop is the *Windermere Gazette*."

We placed the ad, set the date, and went to the market. Bun was quite happy to remain in the car while I shopped. Unwilling to leave him alone for long, I raced through the market as if the devil rode my heels.

Back in the car, Bun glanced up and then snuggled

back down into the leather sling and closed his eyes. I'd tuckered him out.

Our trip back to the farm uneventful, I parked in my usual spot, and let Bun run free before taking the groceries into the house.

The door opened as I reached the top step. Jess took a couple of the bags from me and Bun raced inside.

"I'll give him a snack," she said.

"What's going on? Were you looking for me?"

"The sheriff called, he wants to speak with you. He said it's important."

"All right, I'll call him while you take care of Bun."

She nodded and assembled a meal for Bun while I dialed Jack's number.

"Where are you?" Jack asked.

"Home, why?"

"I just spoke to Jessica. She said she didn't know where you were."

"I said I had errands to run, Jack. Geesh. What's so important that you had to talk to me right away?"

"The information you passed on proved fruitful. Good job in coming to me with it, rather than acting on your own. It seems the Eriksons have come into large sums of money that quickly disappear from their accounts."

"Well, well. I guess I learned that purely by accident. What else did you find out?"

"Not at liberty to say."

"What?"

"Hold on a minute." The sound of his voice became muffled as though he'd put his hand over the speaker. Suddenly, he was back on the line. "I was interrupted. Sorry."

"You have my undivided attention."

"I'm in the process of a warrant approval from the judge to look into Denton Clarke's accounts, and whatever else I can find out about him. Thanks, Juliette, great job. I have to go, the other line is ringing."

The phone went dead. I hung up and found Jessica staring at me.

"What's happened?"

"Let's have a bite to eat and I'll fill you in."

She made a couple of sandwiches while I looked in on the rabbits. By the time I entered the house again, the food was on the table.

We sat down, munched away, and in between eating and drinking, I explained the morning's happenings.

"There's never a dull moment in your life. Smart of you to take the information you gleaned to Sheriff Carver."

"That's what he said. He's also looking into the Eriksons and Denton Clarke."

"Gosh, my hopes for a relationship between you and Denton are dashed. He's quite sweet on you, Jules."

"Don't be fooled by him. People who launder money aren't dumb enough to become involved with someone like me, who can't refrain from poking into things I shouldn't. The last thing Denton needs in his life is a snoop."

"Is he looking forward to our lecture?"

"He said we'll have a full house. However many that is."

"I'll bet it's a roomful. Denton didn't mention using the auditorium, did he?"

"Good lord, no. If that happens, I think a case of stage fright will be the outcome for me. I've never been a public speaker, have you?"

"Once or twice in college, but not to a huge audience, only to my classmates. Let's not get jumpy about this, or we'll both be wound up tight before we even get there. By the way, what did Alvin say about Della?"

I gave Jessica an overview of the conversation between Alvin and me, then dropped the subject. I left out the part about Felicia Brandt. No sense in bringing that up. Jess would only think I had returned to sleuthing and I didn't need a lecture about it.

"Smart of you to keep Felicia out of the conversation. We'll look into things on our own, being careful not to find ourselves in another situation like the one at the lake. The next time somebody wants to see you for a private conversation, invite them here, and call Carver or Adam for our safety."

Jess and I went back to work while Bun took a turn in the exercise run. Once he was situated, I brought Petra from of her cage and took the kits to join her in the playpen. They were the only rabbits there. It was time Petra exercised and introduced the little ones to more than their hutch. Petra kept them in sight the entire time they moved about the pen. I took the opportunity to give her hutch and cage a thorough cleaning.

With gloves that reached past my elbows and donning a heavy rubber apron, I emptied the hutch and cleaned the inside. I washed down the cage, emptied the fecal tray, and then put all of it back together again. I gazed at Petra, as she herded the kits into a group and then stood guard over them. I took it as a sign to return them to their home.

I spoke to Petra in a soft tone of voice, smoothed her lovely coat, and picked up the kits as I opened the pen door for Petra to accompany me back to her hutch. Surprised when she did, it dawned on me she wouldn't let them get away from her. We reached the hutch, I tucked the kits inside, and then put Petra in with them. She settled down without a backward glance.

A few minutes later, Bun said, *"I'm ready to leave this run. I'm exhausted."*

"You've had a busy day, that's for sure. I'll finish feeding the other rabbits. After that we'll take a bicycle ride if you want."

Chapter 21

Our ride was refreshing. When we reached the lake, I turned the bicycle toward home just as it started to sprinkle. Damp from the raindrops, I rolled the bike into the barn, then entered the house with Bun hopping beside me. The house phone began to ring.

I didn't recognize the phone number but answered the call. "Hello, Jules speaking."

"This is Eve McPherson."

"Hi, Eve, what can I do for you?"

"You can tell the sheriff to back off, that's what you can do. He's been here asking questions about your medallion and the person to whom it belongs. Felicia Brandt is the owner, I told him that, and now I'm telling you."

"Did you attack me at Lake Plantain a few days ago?"

There was a long pause before she asked, "Why would I do that?"

"I have no idea, but somebody called claiming they were you. The person asked if we could meet for a private conversation. Was it you, or someone pretending to be you?"

"It wasn't me," Eve insisted. "Were you injured?"

"I was. I'm all right now, but I could have been seriously harmed."

She'd instantly calmed down and sounded pensive when she said, "I'm sorry you were hurt."

"I wouldn't have told the sheriff you wanted to meet me in private if the caller hadn't sounded like you. Their accent wasn't as noticeable as yours is, though."

"Juliette, I'm so sorry. I didn't do it and I don't know of anyone who would. If I can be of any further help with the medallion, please let me know."

Eve's change of heart and attitude was evident in the tone of her voice. I thanked her and rang off, knowing for certain Eve wasn't the culprit. If I was in danger, she might be, too. I wanted no responsibility for bringing harm to anyone else and reported the call to Sheriff Carver.

As the day sailed toward twilight, I made supper for myself and fed the animals their dinner. Jessica had evening appointments where she visited housebound owners' homes instead of seeing their pets at the clinic. After a solitary meal, I returned to the barn and tended to a few leftover chores, then looked the rabbits over before I called it a night. I locked the barn and shop doors on my way out.

No classes were scheduled for the evening, which left

the farm quiet. Bun and I hung out in front of the TV for a while before Bun said, *"I've been thinking about connecting the dots. The main dot is Felicia. The rest of the lines seem to emanate outward from her. Frank was involved with her and went from being Mr. Nice Guy to a secretive man who often took off and never mentioned where he went. Maybe he told Felicia but didn't tell the rest of their friends. We also have Denton Clarke. We know he's involved in illegal activities of sorts. I'm not quite sure how that came about, but Carver will get to the bottom of it for us."*

"Where else do the rest of the lines intersect? I can visualize a pattern of dots, but I can't connect them all. I do believe it all starts with Felicia."

"Felicia's a forceful woman; I realized that at the egg hunt. The others don't seem to care for her much, but they tend to listen to what she says. The one person who shows disdain for her is Rob Brayton, and that's evident when they're in the same group. If either one is at your lecture, it would be worthwhile to keep an eye out to see how they act toward each other. It might show us whether Rob truly dislikes the woman or not. After all, we only saw them at the egg hunt."

"Good idea. A different setting could tell us more than what we have previously witnessed. If both Rob and Felicia are present, I'll try to do that. It will be a hectic evening if all the students that registered are there. Thank goodness I'm not handling this on my own, and Jessica will field some of the questions asked."

"Too bad I can't be there."

He sounded so wistful, I said, "While you'd be my extra set of eyes and ears, I don't think it would be wise for you to go." I'd be giving my half of the program and

Jessica would give the other, then together, we would hold a Q and A session. Even if Bun remained with Jess during my half, he was a distraction for me.

Disappointed, Bun went off to bed. I made a cup of tea and sat at the table to drink it while reviewing my lecture again. Headlights flashed as a car approached and parked at the walkway. I peered out the door window and saw Sheriff Carver coming my way. The automatic lights came on and I opened the door to greet him.

"Come in, Jack." I stepped back as he walked by and hung his hat on a coat hook before he sat at the table.

"Would you like a cup of coffee?"

"No thanks, I stopped by to discuss what we found out about Denton Clarke and his association with the Eriksons."

I took my seat, sipped my cooling tea, and waited.

"The tech guys at the station couldn't find irregularities in Denton's bank accounts. It seems he lives pretty close to the vest financially. You're right about professors not being wealthy. With the education professors are required to have, you'd think they'd make serious money."

"Does he have accounts in just one bank, or did your people search wider than local banks?"

"They searched far and wide and found nothing. Then one of the guys called a friend at the FBI office in Boston and called in a favor. We're still waiting for the results of their search. If Denton has an offshore account, they'll find it."

"I'm certain you'll hear from them soon. The FBI will probably want to take over that end of the investigation if accounts are found. Are you prepared to let them have it?"

"I may not have a choice. Once the FBI gets involved,

they pretty much do whatever is needed, whether local officers like it or not. Agents even step on the toes of the state police, and you know that doesn't go over well."

"I hope they don't get in the way of our finding out who murdered Della and Frank. I think those two killings are connected."

"It would seem so. I spoke with Eve McPherson the other day."

"I know, she called me this afternoon—madder than a wet hen, too, I might add. I've come to the conclusion she didn't strike me at the lake."

"We agree on that. I tend to think it has nothing to do with Eve, but somebody wants us to think so. It's a red herring of sorts. If we centered our attention on Eve, then we would waste precious time. As it stands now, the murders have gone cold and the longer that continues, the less likely it will be to find the killer."

"You think it was one person?"

"Don't you?"

"I'm not sure. The deaths might have something to do with drugs, money laundering, and Felicia Brandt. Frank Poland changed dramatically after becoming involved with Felicia and now he's dead. There didn't seem to be any love lost between the college students and Della Meeny, either. They were forced to put in time at the egg hunt due to misbehavior, and Denton Clarke arranged for them to do community service. Every way you look at this situation, all the same people are involved. The only one I don't consider part of it is Rob Brayton."

"I've reached the same conclusion. After speaking with Alvin Peterson, I realized Rob was assigned to keep an eye on all the students who worked at your station.

Alvin said he felt it was the best way to make certain there weren't any issues throughout the day."

"Rob stayed in the background and didn't get involved with the others much. Now and then, he'd make a remark to Felicia, causing her to become annoyed. It seemed odd, but I didn't think much of it at the time."

"Rob comes from a wealthy background. The others don't. He considers himself above them. I can't figure out what he's doing in our local college instead of a university. He's smart enough and certainly rich enough. It might be worth a look."

"You do that, Jack. Let me know what you come up with."

With a sudden change of subject, Jack remarked, "Meredith has been yammering on and on about this shop open house you and Molly have arranged. Is that a good idea right now? You were attacked, the college kids are taking Molly's classes, and there are two murder cases open."

"It'll be fine. Molly's students have eagerly worked to become great spinners and weavers. I wouldn't dream of cancelling the event. Besides, the murders have nothing to do with the farm. Don't worry, Jack, all will go according to plan."

"If you say so," Jack grudgingly remarked before he left.

As he drove off the property, I thought over the proposed schedule for the open studio. I jotted questions on a tablet from my desk. No doubt Molly had the entire day organized down to the finest detail, but it would do me good to see what activities she'd lined up during the event.

My cell phone beeped. A text from Jessica filled the screen. I clicked the phone open to read the entire message. I glanced at Bun's room and listened for his tiny snore. About to text her, I went into the barn and called her instead.

She answered on the first ring. "I wasn't sure you'd still be awake."

"I had company. Sheriff Carver stopped by for a bit. What's up?"

"I'm at Della's—uh, my house. Can you come over?"

"What's wrong?" I could tell by the sound of her voice something wasn't right.

"Just come over."

"I'll be right there."

I hurried into the house for car keys and a sweater.

I left the house lit and locked the doors as I tiptoed out. I wasn't taking Bun with me. I backed up and drove helter-skelter away from the farm. It wasn't long before I arrived at Jessica's cottage.

Parked in front of the house, I noticed Jessica on the doorstep, standing under the old-fashioned lamp next to the front door. Her arms folded; she shook.

"What happened? Have you called the police? Are you all right?" The questions tumbled from my mouth, one after another, without allowing Jess time to answer any of them. I stopped talking and waited.

Tears rolled from her eyes, down over her cheeks. "Come inside."

Cautiously, she opened the door. When she pointed to the small living room, I moved forward and halted not three feet from the body. I stared at Jessica and asked, "Did you look?"

She sniffled and shook her head.

Careful not to destroy the crime scene, I tiptoed over and gasped when I recognized who lay at my feet.

I took my cell phone from my jeans pocket and dialed Jack's number, anxious for him to answer the call.

"This better be important."

"I'm at a crime scene. You need to see this. We're at Della's house." I disconnected the call and just as quickly, the phone rang.

Chapter 22

"Who is *we*?" Jack barked. I heard the engine of his cruiser rumble and knew he'd arrive shortly. "Me and Jessica."

"What's this about?"

"There's a body in the living room and you'd better call out the troops, Jack. I'm uncertain if the culprit is still in the vicinity."

"For God's sake, don't touch anything. Get out of the house and lock yourselves in your car. I'm almost there." He must have set the phone down because all I could hear was his police radio squawk a few times as Jack gave orders.

Jess and I followed Jack's instructions. Locked in my car, I tried to console Jessica, to no avail, I might add. "You'll be okay. Jack and his people are on their way."

"You don't understand. There's a body in my soon-to-be living room. How can I buy this house now? The neighborhood isn't safe. My parents will have a fit over this and probably refuse to close on the sale."

"Okay, okay. Let's deal with one thing at a time. Try not to get ahead of yourself. Just because there's been an incident doesn't mean the neighborhood isn't a decent place to live. Look at what's taken place at the farm in the past. It's still a great place and a wonderful area."

Saved from arguing by Jack's police car's flashing lights, followed by those of the emergency services truck and crew, and a barrage of other cops in cars, I breathed a slight sigh of relief. Enough police arrived to hopefully scare the rest of the neighborhood into staying indoors. Though, a few brave souls stood on their front lawns and porches. They were immediately ushered back indoors by officers.

We waited until Jack stood next to my car door and then got out to accompany him into the house. He sent officers around the back of the property in search of an intruder and to see if the house was forcibly entered.

Jack focused on Jessica. She explained how she'd found the house turned upside down upon her arrival. That's when she mentioned the body on the living room floor and began to tremble. Jack beckoned to a paramedic. "Take this woman to the ambulance and stay with her."

With a nod, he walked Jess to the vehicle and draped a blanket around her shoulders as she perched on the edge of the truck's step. I accompanied Jack indoors, followed by a rescue team. I recognized it as the same team that had come to my aid a few times. Some of them nodded at me while others walked past without acknowledgment.

The crew chief offered a murmured hello and passed

me as I stood at the corner of the living room entrance. He and Jack spoke in low tones while police officers did a room-to-room search and called them all clear. While I waited, a gurney was brought in without a body bag secured to it, which gave me pause.

I opened my mouth to ask where the bag was when the crew chief stepped forward. "Did you touch her?"

"No, I stayed away. Seeing all that blood, I thought she was dead."

"She isn't, but she's badly injured. What do you know about this?"

"Nothing. Jessica called and asked me to come here. She never said why. I knew something was wrong and drove right over."

The crew tended the victim gently and loaded her onto the gurney. She was rolled from the house and into the ambulance, then driven to the hospital. Still draped in a blanket, Jessica strode into the house and stood beside me.

Her eyes wide, Jess asked, "She isn't dead?"

"No. I didn't want to touch her because I thought she was dead."

Having heard us, Jack left his group of officers and joined us. "You didn't touch her, either?"

Jess shook her head.

"Why not?"

"I thought she was . . . uh . . . you know, dead."

His expression softened as he stared at her. "I'm sorry, I should have realized how difficult this has been for you. What were you doing here?"

"After I finished my home visits tonight, I stopped by to measure the windows for curtains. Nobody was around when I arrived. I entered the house, flipped on the lights, and found this mess." Jess swept her hand out to include the rest of the house and said, "Then I saw the body. I panicked, worried the intruder was still present, so I called Jules. I'm sorry, Sheriff Carver, I should have notified you first."

"The back door was jimmied open. Forensics will dust for prints, along with everything that was overturned or torn apart. You did the right thing by not invading my crime scene, but if there should be a next time, call me first."

With a slight tip of his head, Jack gave me a pointed look. I left Jessica watching officers do their jobs.

In the kitchen, Jack asked, "Who would have attacked Felicia Brandt?"

"It's impossible to say. Some dislike Felicia, those who find her bossy and arrogant, and then there are students who follow her every wish and command. At least that's what I've heard. You know, secondhand information and such."

"Who told you all that?"

"One of Molly's students."

"I see. Did you find it credible?"

"She seemed very honest. I didn't get the impression she held a grudge against Felicia. You know, I'm really curious as to what Felicia was doing here. Was she the one who jimmied the door, or was she with someone?"

"Good questions. I wish I had the answers. Maybe Felicia can tell us when she regains consciousness."

"You might ask the teenager next door. Not much gets past her. She and Della were best buddies. When Jess and I first visited this house, she came over and greeted us like old friends. I'd say she knows more about what goes on around here than a neighborhood watch group would."

"I hope she saw something helpful. I've got to get to

the hospital, I want to be there should Felicia come around."

"I won't be far behind."

"Why?"

"You might need me as a buffer between you and Dr. Sommers." I snickered at the thought of the two of them blustering. It wouldn't be the first time, or the last. Neither man cared much for the other. "I'll send Jessica on her way home after I make sure she's all right."

"Very funny. I'll see you later." He strode off.

I started after Jessica, who had discarded the blanket as she headed out the door behind Jack.

I caught up with her and asked, "Where are you going?"

"There's nothing I can do here tonight. I'm going home."

"Would you feel better if you stayed at my house? You have had quite a shock."

"That isn't necessary. I'll be fine now I know that woman isn't dead."

"I'm going to the hospital. Jack is on his way there now. The woman is Felicia Brandt and Jack isn't sure she was alone. He'll question Valerie later."

As we stood on the walkway in front of the house, I saw Jessica's eyes pop wide and her chin lift a tad as she motioned to something behind me. She murmured, "You and I can ask her right now if she saw anything unusual."

I swung around with a smile on my face and greeted the teenager. "Hi, Valerie."

"Wow, what's going on? I saw the ambulance and all those cops."

"We know you keep an eye on what goes on around

here, and we're so glad you do. Jessica and I have a mystery of sorts to solve. You know Jess is going to be your new neighbor, right?"

Valerie nodded.

"Well, it seems someone wanted to access the house without her knowing, to plan a surprise for her, or something of that sort. Anyway, I wondered if you saw who was here before Jessica arrived."

We stood on the walk, a trio of amateur sleuths, with Valerie's face to the lamplight. Her eyes sparkled as she grinned. "Oh, I love mysteries. My friends always say I'm nosy, but I'm simply curious." Her ponytail bobbed up and down, as did her head, while she spoke.

"Two people came by. They weren't together, though. The woman got here first, then about twenty minutes or so later, a man drove up, parked in front of my house, and then walked down the driveway to the back door. The woman was already inside. I think she had a key because she went in by the front door." Valerie grew silent before continuing. "Anyway, I saw the man struggle with the door, as if it got stuck, you know? Then he went in. After that, I couldn't see anything because the curtains were closed and not all the lights were on. A while later, he drove away. When I looked out the window, the house was completely dark."

"You never saw the woman leave, then?"

"No, but I wasn't watching for her, either. I thought maybe they left at the same time. What happened?"

"The couple had an altercation and the woman was injured."

"She's not dead, right? It would be creepy living next door to a house where a person died in it." She shivered. I couldn't tell if it was from the damp chill in the air, or if she was frightened by the thought that a death took place so close to home.

"Thanks, Valerie, you've been immensely helpful. If Sheriff Carver comes by, make sure you tell him what you saw." About to leave, I stopped and asked, "Did you get a look at the man, by any chance?"

"The lighting wasn't good. His clothes were dark, I think. I didn't see his face, but he was slim and shorter than you. He wore a hat, too."

"Okay, thanks again."

Seeming happy that we took her seriously and listened to what she said, Valerie hurried along the driveway and crossed over to her yard. She waved from the doorway as she went inside.

"That was amazing. Valerie's quite the watchdog." Jessica peered at Valerie's house before walking toward her car. "I don't know if I would want to leave a child alone at night."

"There may be no choice in the matter. That could be why Della took her under her wing, as mystifying as that reason is to me."

"I'll see you tomorrow. My appointments begin early, so have breakfast ready, okay? It is your turn to make breakfast, you know." She smiled a bit, and then got into her car.

I was certain Jess would be okay now that she knew Felicia was alive. Since we had an idea of what had happened, I set off for the hospital.

Jack's car sat near the front entrance. I drove into the visitors' parking area and scurried across the lot. The double doors slid open. Jack paced the hallway of the emergency room. Dr. Sommers was nowhere in sight when I joined Jack.

"Any word on Felicia?"

"No, Dr. Sommers is still with her. They've taken X-rays, but nobody has said a word to me."

"Let's sit in the waiting room. It looks like a slow night, so Dr. Sommers will probably be with us soon."

"He doesn't like me."

"And you feel the same toward him. You and I both know it, as does he, I'm sure."

With a harrumph, Jack stated, "It took you a while to get here."

"Jessica and I were leaving the house when Valerie, the teenager next door, came out to talk to us."

He rolled his eyes and said, "And, you couldn't pass up an opportunity like that."

"She's expecting a visit from you. I said you'd be by to ask questions."

"And? I know there's more, so let's have it."

Within a few minutes, Jack was aware of what Valerie had shared and seemed pleased that she'd been so observant. Unfortunately for me, he didn't feel the same way when I was observant.

"I'm looking for a man just shorter than you, then? She didn't see his face, huh? Did she say if he was fat or thin? Did he limp or anything like that?"

"It wasn't light enough for her to see his features and he wore a hat. He could have had his head turned away, too. She didn't say that, though. Valerie did mention he was slim." Geesh, did I have to ask her everything? Jack always insisted it was his job to make inquiries, not mine.

Dr. Sommers entered the room. He glanced at Jack and

then greeted me. "Hello, Juliette. How are you after that thump on the head?"

We went to meet Dr. Sommers and Jack let me take the lead. "Fine, fine, no after effects. Thanks. How is Felicia?"

"She's unconscious. I've called in a neurologist and a neurosurgeon to have a look at her."

"She's not in a coma, is she?"

"She shows no signs of needing assistance to breathe. I'll have to wait for the Drs. Fielding to arrive and get their opinions." He turned to Jack. "Please notify Ms. Brandt's parents."

"I will. Keep me informed of her condition, won't you?"

"Certainly." He turned away and then back. "It's good to see you are well, Juliette. Stay that way."

"I'll certainly try." I grinned and watched him amble from the room.

In a sly sounding tone, Jack murmured, "It seems to me that Dr. Sommers has a soft spot for you."

"It seems to me that you might pay attention to police work and leave romantic conjecture out of the conversation." I glanced at the wall clock and said, "I'm going home. Five o'clock comes around pretty fast and I need some rest. If you hear anything at all, you'd better call me."

He didn't say a word but gave me a slight nod, instead.

Chapter 23

The alarm clock blared. Seeking the top of it, I reached out and slapped the button to make the noise stop. Awake, I saw Bun sitting just inside the doorway and said, "Good morning. You're up early."

"I'm up and want an explanation of why you were out last night and didn't think to take me with you."

Okay, his nose was out of joint because I didn't take him. I hoped this didn't set the tone for the entire day. Jessica and I would be at the college this evening to lecture, and a calm day would be nice.

"You were fast asleep; snoring, even. I didn't have the heart to wake you. I'm sorry, Bun."

I trotted into the bathroom, did what was necessary, and then went downstairs to make breakfast. Bun accompanied me, asking what was so important that I was out so late in the evening.

"Jess called. She found Felicia Brandt unconscious in the house she is buying. Poor Jess was frantic. I left right away to get to her. We called Jack and his crew did their thing. All I know is that Felicia is in the hospital."

I popped bread in the toaster, made omelets for breakfast, and perked coffee. Bun yammered the entire time.

"I guess her attacker was absent by the time Jessica found Felicia?"

I nodded and buttered the toast.

"I could have been helpful, you know. I can smell better than you, hear better, and tune in better than any human can. I might have been able to identify the attacker by using any one, or all, of those attributes. Just think, an opportunity to solve that little mystery was missed because you didn't want to wake me."

Yup, he was rankled, all right.

"I said I was sorry. Can we move on?"

"Were there any witnesses?"

"Valerie, next door, saw a short, slim man enter the driveway and watched him break in through the rear entrance."

"Jess was lucky he was gone when she arrived. She might have ended up in the bed next to Felicia. Valerie didn't get a look at his face, huh?"

"It was too dark."

The breezeway door opened and Jessica remarked, "Talking to Bun again, huh?"

"It helps to sort out the facts and events of the attack and break-in. Don't you ever talk out loud when you want to figure something out?"

She snickered. "No, but maybe I ought to."

I set the table while Jessica petted Bun. When I turned around, I could see how tired she was. My guess was she hadn't slept well.

"Tired?"

"You can tell?"

"I can. Eat your breakfast. Omelets and coffee, toast, and juice."

"Sounds yummy. Have you heard from Sheriff Carver?"

"Not yet." I went on to share what Dr. Sommers had told Jack and me. That way, Bun would know, too.

"Are you ready for tonight's gig? I can't believe it's time to speak to these students."

"We've had a fairly busy schedule these past few weeks. I'll be glad when the evening is over so we can focus solely on the open house. Jack has his hands full and probably won't bug me to death over the case, especially now that I've backed off somewhat."

"I noticed you have been distancing yourself from the investigation. Did the attack on you at Lake Plantain have anything to do with your decision?"

With a mouthful of food, I nodded.

"Well, I, for one, am glad of that. You belong here at the farm, not out chasing killers."

"Easy for her to say. Sometimes that falls into our lap, and we have to handle it the best way we can."

I gulped a glass of orange juice and then said, "It's a matter of taking care of myself, so I can run the farm and care for the rabbits. They're important to me."

Jess nodded. "I guess it wasn't helpful of me to call and insist you come to the house last night. You and I could have been in trouble if the guy who assaulted Felicia was still about. Did you share what Valerie told us with Jack?"

"He found it most interesting and will speak with her." The phone jingled and I saw Carver's name on the screen.

"Hey, Jack, what's up?"

"Dr. Sommers called to say Felicia had a bleed in her brain, and the neurology brothers—the ones that are doctors and brothers—took her into surgery to fix it. She's still unconscious, but they agree that she will recover. And, before you ask, they don't know how much damage the injury caused. I've contacted her parents. They'll arrive sometime today."

"Thanks for calling, Jack. I appreciate the news."

"I'm off to speak to Valerie before she heads to school. Keep me posted if you find out anything that will help my investigation. You and Jessica are speaking tonight, aren't you?"

"We are."

"Take care, Juliette. There's a killer at large and I think he lives on that campus."

"I'm not so sure, but I'll consider that." I hung up, gave Jess a quick rundown of what Jack said, but left out the part about helping with his investigation. I didn't need or want another lecture from Jessica. She lived her life the way she saw fit while I lived mine—take it or leave it. Did I want to be safe and alive to care for my rabbits? Of course. Did I need to poke my nose where it didn't belong? Sometimes. Could I leave a rock unturned? Not a chance. Bun wouldn't allow it. I heaved a sigh and pushed back from the table.

"Chores await me."

We cleared away breakfast bits and dishes. I set the dishwasher to run when Jess went to the clinic. I prepared a pork roast and tossed some raw veggies into the Crock-Pot to cook for dinner.

The chores went smoothly. Petra's babies could now move about pretty well and were sweet. Bun was in the play yard with his fellow rabbits while I cleaned hutches, sanitized cages, and emptied trays. The rabbits had eaten before I started to clean, which made my job easier.

I'd emptied the last fecal tray into the hopper when the barn door opened, and Jason walked in. "Let me do that for you," Jason said.

"Too late, I'm done. You can handle those hay bales and each hutch needs some of it. What are you doing here so early?"

"It's a teacher-learning day of sorts and there aren't any classes." He grinned and got started.

I left him to his job and went into the house to shower and change my clothes. I struggled with my snarled hair before I dressed, and won the battle. Returning to the barn, I went in search of Jessica. She stepped from the clinic into the shop.

"What's going on?" Jess asked.

"Nothing. I wanted to ask if you planned to eat supper here and then we'd go to the lecture together."

"Sure, what's on the menu?"

I told her what was cooking.

"Consider me included, then."

"I'm going to distribute more of the postcards I picked up the other day. I'll take Bun with me. Jason's here and has taken over what's left for chores."

"Okay, I'll see you later." Jess drew close and glanced over her shoulder toward the clinic. Then she whispered, "There hasn't been anything about the attack on the news, has there?"

I shrugged. "I haven't had the radio or TV on, but I'll listen while I'm driving. I take it you haven't told your parents about last night?"

She shook her head and went to greet her next patient.

I returned to the barn in time to see Bun looking around. When he saw me, he hopped over to the pen wire and said, *"What's going on?"*

I glanced at Jason and said I'd be taking Bun with me while I ran errands. He waved and went back to work.

"For a minute there, I was worried that you'd gone off without me, yet again."

"Come on, we have things to do and places to go." I donned the sling and leaned down so he could climb in.

While I drove into Windermere, my cellphone rang.

"Hello?"

Jack said, "Did you ever go back to the Eriksons for the postcards?"

"I did, why?"

"You were supposed to talk to them about Denton Clarke."

"The store was busy and I couldn't wait for people to leave. There were several customers ahead of me."

"What were they picking up?"

"I don't know. Packages, that's all I saw. Some large, some not." The reason he asked hit me like a brick. I sucked in a breath and said, "You think they're distributing drugs, don't you?"

"I had considered it, didn't you?"

"Not at all."

The line went dead. I continued on to the library, where I left stacks of postcards. The next stops were the supermarket, Carrie's diner, and finally Stacey Farnsworth's corner deli, The Eatery. Inside, I instructed Bun to stay in the sling. The shop was animal-friendly, but I refrained from allowing Bun to roam free.

Stacey greeted us from behind the counter with a wide smile of welcome. She poured a cup of coffee and handed it to me. "Great to see you again. I didn't think you'd remember to stop by after what took place at the hop was over."

I sipped the brew and watched as she read the postcard. When she looked up, her smile widened.

"This is a fantastic idea. I didn't realize you offered classes like this or even taught them."

"I don't teach, one of my employees does. There's also a student waiting list."

"You certainly are fortunate. What can I do for you, other than leave these out for my customers?"

"There won't be refreshments inside our open house, but I will have an outside tent in place for them. I wondered if you'd be able to cater sandwiches and desserts for our guests? I'd like to keep it simple."

"Sure, I'd be happy to bring the food. A cup of soup is always a big hit, too. How many people do you expect?"

"If the crowd is like the last one, food for up to a hundred people should be enough."

Her eyes brightened at the number. I could almost hear a *cha-ching* sound go off in her head. This would be costly, but one month of the student fees Molly charged would more than cover it.

I gave Stacey the date, set up the menu, and what time I wanted her to arrive. On my way out, Stacey remarked, "That was terrible news about Felicia Brandt. You heard about it, didn't you?"

At the door, I glanced over my shoulder and said, "I have. Yes, terrible news." With that, I tried to make my getaway.

"I've always considered her an aggressive woman, but she didn't deserve that."

"You're right. Thanks for being a part of this event, Stacey. I appreciate it."

"You betcha, it's my pleasure. Do you mind if I bring brochures and business cards to give out?"

"Not at all. They're good promotional tools to use during your day there." I left before she could say more.

On our way to the car, Bun remarked, *"Odd that she'd mention Felicia? I wasn't aware that they were acquainted."*

"Me, either. Curious that Stacey brought it up, though, isn't it?"

I called Jessica to say Felicia's attack was now common knowledge. She groaned but said she knew it would come out sooner or later.

Bun's ears flipped forward and he burrowed back inside the sling when Margery Shaw approached.

"I see that despicable animal is with you again. I'd keep an eye on him if I were you. He's worthless, you know."

"You're the despicable one. You should move on."

Margery blocked my path. I started to sidestep but she did the same. I stopped, gave her a look, and loudly insisted, "Out of my way, now."

"Tell me—he talks to you, doesn't he? What does he say? Does he rant and rave?"

"The only one who raves is you. Bun's a rabbit and rabbits can't talk. Now, step aside, or I'll call the police to say you're harassing me."

It took her less than a second to rush off, yelling epithets with each step she took. I shook my head, rolled my eyes while people watched, and then I sauntered off.

A cruiser pulled close to the curb as I reached my car. Adam stared at me from behind the steering wheel, then he got out and stepped onto the sidewalk.

"I received a call that you were having problems. Is that true?"

Bun popped his head out of the sling. *Tell him. Tell him the truth, that the wicked witch taunted us. Maybe he can put an end to it.*

"Margery Shaw was on a rant. She blocked my path and refused to move until I said I'd call the police, which I didn't do, by the way. She's stark raving mad, Adam. She believes Bun can talk. Nuts, I tell you, the woman is nuts." Okay, so my anger was on a roll, even though I hadn't thought I was angry at all.

"I'll have a word with her. Which way did she go?"

I pointed in the direction Margery had taken and then said, "You might be better off to speak with her at her home. I don't know where she was going. But, she was on foot."

He studied the direction she had taken and then nodded before he left. On our own again, we made a few more stops to drop off additional postcards before we returned to the farm.

"It's nice to be back. I don't think I'd enjoy living in the city."

I put the car in park, shut off the motor, and agreed. "Me, either."

Dinner was luscious. The food, cooked to perfection, nearly melted in my mouth. Jess commented on its tastiness as we overindulged. I sat back, replete from the meal, and glanced at the clock.

"It's almost time to go. Are you nervous?"

"Not really. I'm looking forward to it. It's going to be fun and just think, Felicia won't be there to heckle us."

"That was mean, even if you're right. I wondered if she might show up to annoy us. We've got so much to share about being small business owners, that the audience is sure to find interest in what we have to say."

Jess agreed. She began to clear dishes from the table while I stored leftovers in the fridge, and then filled the dishwasher. Earlier, Jason and I had fed the rabbits, then given them extra water and a snack before Jason left for home on his motorized bicycle, which I thought was pretty cool. While I'd looked the bicycle over, he talked of how he'd saved his earnings to buy it.

Pleased to think he was smart with money, I said so and watched him swell with pride as he rode away.

"Jason's motorized bicycle is quite the item. Have you seen it?"

Jess grinned. "He showed it to me when I was between patients. Even my mother thought it was a neat way to get around."

Taking Bun with us, I drove to the college and left the car in the visitor parking area. As I walked toward the entrance of the room assigned for the lecture, Bun said, *"I'll be all-ears tonight. Don't worry about me, okay?"*

"Uh-huh, I can only hope you won't be underfoot," I murmured.

We joined Jessica and headed into a small, eight-row, curved amphitheater.

Chapter 24

Seats filled while Denton consulted with Jessica and me. We were ready, or thought as much, until we saw the number of students. I took a deep breath, let it out slowly, as did Jessica. Bun sat on the top step of the aisle and flipped his ears at me. I smiled and walked over to the microphone.

"Welcome, everyone. I'm happy to be here with you tonight."

Jessica added her welcome and the show began. We shared our backgrounds, explained our businesses, and how we had come to be entrepreneurs. Then we went into the nitty-gritty of what to expect in the real business world. We entertained the audience with our mistakes and shared how we had turned those *oops* moments into opportunities. Our honesty and openness were rewarded with a round of applause.

The time flew and before we knew it, we were at the question-and-answer portion of the program.

Some students were familiar to us, while others were not. Those who had worked the hop event had an advantage over the others due to their familiarity with us and Molly, who sat in the front row. I'd noticed Bun move from step to step and back again. When he heard something of interest, he'd let me know with an ear wag of sorts.

A student with a question would stand and ask away. Jessica or I addressed the question or added to the answer given. This went on until Rob Brayton stood up and asked, "Is it true you were attacked at Lake Plantain, Miss Bridge?"

"I was, but it has nothing to do with tonight's discussion."

"I understand that, but you found Frank Poland's body, too, is that right?"

"It is, but again, it has nothing to do with this evening."

"Are you worried you might be assaulted again at any moment?"

"Not at all. Does anyone else have a question on tonight's topic?"

Rob smirked, resumed his seat, and stared at his fellow students.

Jess fielded the next few questions while I noted the response Rob had gotten from others near him. Some glared, a few wouldn't meet his eyes, and several turned away completely. Remarkably interesting. Rob had given me food for thought. Was it intentional, or had he simply heckled me?

The evening came to an end and not soon enough. Rob

had caused a stir, as he'd intended, by offering me a peek at who might know why Frank was dead. His questions were intentional, but why? Why would this man pull a stunt like that when he knew there would be problems for him from Denton Clarke afterward?

As I contemplated Rob's intentions, Molly stepped forward with Bun in her arms. "That was an awesome presentation." Her eyes sparkled as she placed Bun in the sling that I had donned and held open.

"Thanks. It was delightful to see so much interest in our lecture and be able to respond to the intelligent questions asked."

"All but Rob's questions, of course. He was rude."

"It's okay. I handled it. Now, let's get out of here."

The three of us and Bun went down the hallway with some of the stragglers who'd had extra questions for Jessica. Molly left in her car, while Bun and I stood outside the main entrance. Jessica lagged behind to answer queries.

"We have company."

I heard his murmur before Rob moved into the light from behind the potted tree. "I hope I didn't annoy you with my questions, Juliette."

"Not at all. It was poor manners to bring those questions up, but I didn't mind. I found the responses from other students quite fascinating."

His laughter soft, he said, "I thought you might. The sheriff is running in circles and he's lost valuable time. Instead of dragging me into the station on a whim, he should follow the drug money."

"I'll be sure to tell him that. Thanks."

"I'll see you around. Watch your back, Juliette."

I turned as the double doors opened. When I glanced over my shoulder, Rob was gone.

"That was creepy."

"Yes, it was."

"I hoped you were waiting out here. Glad you didn't leave me behind, Jules." Jessica chuckled as we started down the steps.

"Oh gosh, I forgot my handbag." Jessica abruptly went back inside.

"I'll get the car and wait for you here."

She waved and rushed down the hallway.

Bun settled in the backseat of the car. While we waited for Jessica to join us, Bun filled me in on what he heard the kids talking about.

"All was fairly quiet until good old Rob opened his trap."

"I watched the students around him react to his questions. When Frank's name came up, some students looked anywhere other than at Rob or me. It seems he struck a chord with them."

"He did it on purpose, didn't he? I heard remarks from those around him after the lecture was over. Rob left right away, but a few people lingered, commiserating among themselves. He isn't popular with the drug crowd."

"How do you know they are the drug crowd? Hurry up and answer, Jessica's coming down the steps."

"They talked about making a buy."

Jessica climbed into the front seat, heaved a sigh, and then yawned. "That was a wonderful, but exhausting, evening."

"You had fun and you know it."

She nodded. "We both did, until Rob goaded you with those questions."

"He was just being Mr. Attitude." I didn't relate what Rob said on the front steps. Jess didn't need to know, but Jack Carver did.

"If you say so. I'm surprised Rob didn't get under your skin."

"Early in the investigation I saw him questioned by Jack at the police station. He was calm and unshakable, much to Jack's dismay. Rob refused to answer the questions, did his best to annoy Jack, and then walked out of the building as though he hadn't a care in the world. I wasn't about to let him get to me in front of everyone."

"I thought you handled it well. I don't know if I could have been as coolheaded, Jules."

"Were we successful tonight, or what?"

"We did a great job. Denton said he was pleased by our program and the response of the students to us."

We arrived at the farm and Jess left for home. I opened the car door for Bun to get out and folded the empty sling over my arm as he hopped up the sloped walk beside me. The spotlights were on and now brightened the front yard. We climbed the stairs to the front door.

A breeze brought the sweet smells of spring grass and blossoms with it. I inhaled the scent of new leaves, apple blossoms, and unlocked the door before I looked out over the grounds. Dorothy was right. There's no place like home. If I'd had on her sparkling red shoes, I'd have clicked my heels together. Instead, I just grinned like a silly fool, happy to be alive and living here.

The feeling fled as fast as it had arrived the moment Jack Carver arrived. He entered the house after we did.

"How was your college lecture?"

I measured his mood for a moment, mentioned coffee, and set it to perk when he nodded.

"We had a wonderful time, a full house, and I had an interesting exchange with Rob Brayton."

"Did you now?"

"I did. Is it a coincidence that you happened by right now? Was I being watched by Adam, or one of your other officers?"

He smiled and nodded. "So tell me what Rob said."

I filled him in on the questions Rob asked and how nearby students reacted. I added our brief exchange on the front steps while I waited for Jessica. It was daring of me to repeat Rob's comment about Jack running in circles.

"Rob's a shrewd man and he gives nothing away, either. You saw that when I interviewed him. Why did he bring up your assault, do you know?"

"I think he wanted to show me the way some students would respond. It was a smart move."

"It is curious. I want a list of people who attended. Can you get one from Denton? Give him a story about how you'd like to thank the kids by sending them a note or offering them a mentorship. You know what to do. People open up to you, Juliette."

"A mentorship? Does he have any idea how much of your time that would take? The rabbits and I wouldn't be happy about that."

In a way, Bun was right. Mentoring can become all-consuming if the student is needy. As for the other rabbits not being happy about it, Bun was more than likely the only one to be unhappy. I nudged him with the toe of my shoe as he nestled under the table next to my feet.

"I'll see what I can do, but don't expect miracles. Rules of privacy bind the college."

"I realize that. Just give it a try, then."

We drank coffee in silence for a bit. I mulled over the evening. What Jack mulled over was anyone's guess.

"You're ready for the open house, then?" Jack asked.

"We are. I stopped by Stacey Farnsworth's deli to ask if she'd cater refreshments for the guests. She agreed to set up under a tent outside the entrance to the shop. Having refreshments indoors wasn't a good idea. If spills occurred, it could be disastrous for the garments displayed or the demonstrations scheduled. I've ordered a tent to be erected first thing that morning."

"It's coming up fast. Meredith can hardly contain her excitement."

"She'll demonstrate spinning and several of her finished pieces will be displayed. All the students can sell or take orders for the items they've made. I'm delighted by their response to this. Every place I've left postcards has called to ask for more."

"Good. My people will be here in civilian clothes to keep an eye on you and the others."

"Is that necessary?"

His expression cool, he said, "It is, and I'll not tolerate any argument about it."

"Okay, fine. It'll be good to have them present."

His brows hiked a tad. "My main reason for stopping by was to tell you Felicia has regained consciousness. She will recover, but it's going to take time, from what Dr. Sommers said. Her injury was serious and further tests will be run to see what's what."

"Thanks for the update. I'm glad Felicia is on the mend. No doubt you'll question her."

"When I'm allowed." His sour attitude toward obtaining permission to do his job tickled me to no end. I held back a chuckle, though my expression gave me away.

"It isn't funny. I have a job to do, a killer or two to catch, and I'm blocked at every turn. It's downright aggravating. After all, I am the sheriff."

"I know that. Dr. Sommers also has a job to do that involves those who are alive, not those murdered."

With a grunt and a dip of his hat, Jack left. I set the coffee cups in the sink and filled Bun's water container, then made a light snack for him. While he munched away, I looked in on the rabbits and found all was well.

Sunshine and Bun's chattering woke me. Having fallen asleep on the sofa and still dressed in my clothes from the night before, I sniffed the aroma of fresh coffee that wafted into the living room.

Jess called, "You'd better get up, you're running late."

That was the start of my busy, yet fruitful, day. When you think you have fragments of information that don't make sense, you finally find bits begin to fall in place by the mere act of kindness from the last person you'd ever consider.

Jess and I ate a quick breakfast, fed the rabbits, and then started the remaining chores. I was glad to have her help. Halfway through, Jess said, "I'm finalizing the purchase of Della's house tomorrow morning."

My mouth hung open. I hugged her and asked, "So soon?"

"My mother called me this morning to say it would happen tomorrow. Everything is complete, the bank is ready, and by golly, so am I."

"That's wonderful. Did she ever hear of Felicia's assault?"

"If she did, she kept it to herself."

"How soon will you move in?"

"Not right away, but it won't be too long. Some things need tending and I want them done beforehand."

"If you need help, just let me know. I'd be happy to give you a hand."

She glanced at the wall clock and said, "Thanks. Let's finish up before my first patient arrives."

Chapter 25

A week, then two, passed without incident. Days filled with last-minute preparations for the open studio were the norm for all of us. We squeezed every free minute we could from our schedules to make this a day to remember.

The sheriff was busier than usual, or so Meredith said. I hadn't heard a peep from him or his people, which was a good thing, yet it bothered me somehow. Molly got the list of the students who attended the lecture. When she initially requested the list from Denton Clarke, he insisted it wasn't possible due to privacy concerns. Unwilling to take *no* for an answer, Molly produced the list after covering Cora Stanley's office while Cora and the dean attended a meeting.

Molly left it at the police station for Jack with an explanation of who he should speak to at the school.

The day of our open house, Molly, always cool as a cucumber, inspected the shop and adjusted this or that as she went along. Her students arrived early to make sure all was in order. Molly walked them through what would take place, at what time, and reminded them of who would do what. I listened and realized there was no need to worry about a single thing. Molly had the whole affair in hand.

A clear plastic-sided, white-topped tent squatted outside to the left of the shop's entrance. It wasn't a huge affair, but large enough to seat up to fifteen or twenty people at small folding tables. A counter stood at the rear, with long tables for food and beverages along two sides of it. Sunlight filled the interior and gave the tent a welcoming atmosphere.

At ten o'clock, the first horde of guests arrived. Jason directed drivers where to park along the edge of the fields. It was times like this that the long driveway, bordered by fields, came in handy.

Molly and I welcomed those entering the shop. A student gathered a few people at a time to show them around, stopping at displays and explaining the art of spinning, along with a brief history behind it. Visitors were quite taken with that history and asked questions. Guided through the room, the group was then handed off to another student who left them in the hands of two women behind at a table filled with garments. Most merchandise was either knit or crocheted in delicate designs using hand-spun yarns, while others were colorfully handwoven. A book lay open with a pen next to it for those interested in a class, or who sought a specific item.

Sales went well and splendid pieces of artwork—for each garment was indeed a work of art—left in the hands of many a happy visitor. Women, as well as a few men, readily placed orders with the students while Molly handled the payments.

As the day progressed, the real show began with spinning demonstrations given by Meredith. Weavers offered people the chance to get a feel for weaving by using the shuttle a few times. That's when it dawned on me that the studio should be larger. If only I knew how to make that happen.

Refreshments were served in the tent at a steady pace until the supply was exhausted. By then, the event had nearly drawn to a close. Standing just inside the tent opening, I sipped a hot cup of tea when I heard a voice behind me say, "You've had quite a turnout. Great job, Juliette."

I turned to Rob. "Thank you. Molly has performed the magic here. She's an amazing woman."

He murmured, "That she is. Did you take my advice and remind the sheriff to stop running in circles?"

"I did. I also shared what else you said."

"Good."

"I have a question, if you don't mind."

"Sure."

"Why the sudden change of heart? You couldn't be bothered to answer questions or offer information before. Why now?"

He drew me outside, tucked my free hand into the crook of his elbow, and nonchalantly strolled toward the far end of the shop. We'd reached the corner when he glanced back and drew me away from possible prying eyes, before he said, "You consider me a self-centered and arrogant man without many friends. Well, the ones I do have should be alive and well, and remain that way for a long time."

"So what you're saying is that you are as appalled as I am by Felicia's assault and Frank's death."

"Something like that, yeah."

I stared out over the field while I contemplated his answer. "Is there anything else you want to tell me?"

"Such as?"

"That you're an undercover cop?"

He hesitated for a mere fraction of a second before he shook his head. "Not a chance. Me and the law? Give me a break."

"I'll give you some advice, instead. If all the awful things that have happened could have been avoided because you're an undercover cop, then you should be ashamed of yourself." I walked away without another word.

Indoors, I noticed how much the crowd had thinned and that the event was at an end. Her van packed, Stacey was about to leave. The food was gone, as were the beverages. Amazed at how time had flown, I handed her a check with thanks for a job well done. A few cars remained. A newspaper reporter and a local TV station newsman had arrived while I conversed with Rob.

They were close to finishing an interview with Molly when she motioned to me. I joined her and gave the interviewer my best and most heartfelt comments on our event and said how grateful I was to those who attended and offered their support.

Pleased with my gushing—at least that's what it sounded like to me—the media folks left on the heels of the last visitors.

Dead on my feet, I thanked everyone for their participation and hard work. When I'd finished speaking,

Meredith said, "The day was such a success. We sold almost every garment. I found that people adored our woven items. We took orders for lots more. Thank you, Juliette and Molly, for hosting this wonderful open house."

Other students chimed in and chatted on for another half hour or so until Jessica stepped forward to say our success mainly came from teamwork. When Jess suggested the students were free to leave, they did so, except for Meredith.

The room was quiet once there were just the four of us. I wondered why Meredith hung back when the door opened, and Jack walked in.

He gave us a long look and asked, "Everybody have fun today?"

Molly chuckled and asked in turn, "Do we look that tuckered out?"

He nodded, then turned to his wife. She had her jacket on, slid her handbag on her arm, and said goodbye.

We watched from the window as they walked in silence to their car. Jessica laughed and said Meredith must be exhausted. We all agreed she hardly ever stopped chattering. Molly and I sank onto the nearest bench.

"I'm beat, aren't you?"

Molly and Jess spoke as one. "We are."

I looked around for Bun, who insisted he attend the event, but now was nowhere to be seen.

"Anyone see Bun this afternoon?"

Molly shook her head.

Jessica said, "Bun's in the house. I think the crowd proved too much for him. A couple of times he nearly got crushed."

"Oh, dear. I'd better check on him and feed the rabbits, too."

"Not a problem; we'll get started. I think Jason filled their water containers before he left," Molly announced.

With the rabbits in good hands, I took off for the house.

Bun stood at his bedroom door as I walked into the kitchen. "Was the crowd too much for you?" I asked and leaned down to pet him.

"I was nearly trampled to death. There were too many people for my liking. I decided to take a nap. Jess saw me at the door and opened it for me. Where were you all day?"

He wasn't whining, just curious. I was okay with that. Any whining . . . well, I didn't want to handle that right now.

"In and out of the shop all day, I greeted visitors before they went off with students, who charmed them into making a purchase or convinced them to register for future classes. Then Rob and I talked a bit."

To say he was all-ears was an understatement. They popped up straight and then Bun slightly tipped them forward. I held back a smile and shared my conversation with Rob.

"So, you think he's undercover, huh? What made you jump to that conclusion?"

"His sudden change of heart, his current attitude, and him not looking for information, but giving it instead. I can't offer more of an explanation than that. I just have a feeling."

"Then go with that. It'll never let you down. I don't understand how I didn't figure that out. I do have superpowers, after all."

"I know, Bun."

"We've gotta help the sheriff solve these crimes before there are any others."

"A visit to see Felicia might be in order. I can't take you, sorry."

"I know, do your best to get as much out of her as you can. Then, we'll talk about it."

"I will. You'll be okay here while I'm gone, right?"

"I'm fearless. And demonic if you listen to Margery Shaw."

I slanted a look in his direction. "Right, you are fearless. To heck with Margery Shaw. I've got to help Molly and Jess feed the rabbits before I visit Felicia, okay?"

"Okay, I'll keep watch over the farm."

I entered the barn, finished the chores, and sent Molly and Jessica home. After they'd gone, I stood in the silence and relaxed. It was nice to be alone with the rabbits.

"It's so quiet. I like it this way."

I hunkered down next to Bun, who had sneaked up behind me, and smoothed his soft coat. He crouched on the floor and closed his eyes. Gently, I scratched to top of his head and smoothed his ears before I stood up.

"I won't be gone long. Keep an eye on things." I knew he couldn't contact me by way of telepathy if I were too far away, but watching over his friends and the farm fed his ego.

The doors to the shop and barn locked for the night, I slipped my jacket on and drove to the hospital.

Hospital corridors teemed with staff. Visitors milled about in the foyer as I walked to the information desk. I asked for Felicia's room number and then took the elevator to the fourth floor. When the doors slid open, I stood face-to-face with Dr. Sommers.

"Hello, there," I said.

"Are you here to visit Felicia?"

"I certainly am. The desk clerk said she could have visitors. Is something wrong?"

"No, not at all. Ms. Brandt had several people stop in today. She's probably quite tired, so don't stay long. I'll be in the lunchroom. Stop by to see me before you leave."

"Uh, sure. I just wanted to see how Felicia's doing. I'll be down shortly."

He nodded, entering the elevator as the doors started to close.

The nurses' station was on my way to Felicia's room. I stopped to notify the nurse who I would visit.

"She might be asleep. If so, don't wake her. She's had a busy day," the woman remarked.

I continued down the hall, turned into the room to find Felicia wide awake and engaged in conversation with Rob Brayton, who held her hand. Well, well.

He slipped his hand from hers and rose from the chair. "Sit here, Juliette. I'm about to leave."

"Thank you. I can't stay long, so don't leave on my account." I looked Felicia over. She was pale, her features drawn, but otherwise, she appeared to be doing fine.

"How are you feeling?"

She gave me an odd look and said, "You would have no idea how I'm doing after being left for dead, would you?"

"I've been where you are now, but much worse off, and that's why I came to visit you. I can see it was a mistake." I was ready to leave.

Her expression changed. "Who did that to you?"

"A local guy, who spent years in prison for it." Why I shared this with her was a mystery. The only reason I could think of was that she thought she was the only one to go through something traumatic. Maybe she just struck a nerve. Whatever.

"I didn't know. Sorry. You were left for dead?"

"Yeah, but let's talk about you."

"I'm told that you and Jessica Plain found me."

"We did and just in time, too. You're one lucky woman. Tough, too," I said with a grin.

"Thanks for that. I could have died."

"Did you see who struck you?"

"No, I was hit from behind. I never heard or saw a thing."

"Too bad, I'd like to find who did this. Why were you at Della's house?"

"We are . . . uh—were—related. Didn't you know?"

I shook my head, let the news sink in, and asked, "Related in what way?"

"She was my aunt. We hadn't seen each other in years, but when I was assigned to work for her and at the hop, I gave her a visit. Good thing, too. She was killed not long afterward."

I sat back in the chair and stared at Felicia. I found no likeness when I compared her and Della. This woman was tall, broad-shouldered, and big-boned. She had a shock of rich auburn hair and would have been called a hearty lass in Scotland. Della was short, stumpy like a tree trunk, not ugly, but certainly not pretty, with short arms and legs. Her hair had no richness in color like Felicia's, either.

"I can't see a likeness, but if you say you were related, so be it."

"She was from my mother's side of the family. My father and I look alike."

Somewhere along the line, this woman had decided I wasn't such a bad person after all. I took advantage of the moment and said, "I met Dr. Sommers at the elevator. He said I shouldn't stay long, but I have a few more questions if you're up to it."

"Go ahead."

"Why were you assigned to work at the hop?"

"Some friends and I indulged in a drug buy—simple marijuana, mind you—but we got caught, and the hop was our punishment."

"Why weren't you turned over to the police?" I knew the answer but wanted to hear it from her.

"Professor Clarke felt it would be foolish to notify the police and bad for the school."

"Where did the drugs come from?"

"I can't tell you that."

I stared at her.

She heaved a sigh and said, "Frank Poland bought them. He didn't want to, but I convinced him to. He got them from Denton Clarke."

"Does anyone else know that?"

She shrugged and then winced. "I don't think so. Frank and I kept it between us. Oh, and Della's house was a mess when I arrived the night I was injured."

"I see. Oh, I wanted to tell you something I think you'll be delighted to hear."

"What?"

"I found your medallion. The sheriff has it for safekeeping at the moment."

Tears filled her eyes and rolled down her cheeks. She

sniffled. I handed her the box of tissues from the bedside table.

"I gave it to Frank. He was my choice."

"I know. I'm sorry he's dead. He was a very nice person."

"We planned to marry next year after graduation. We had great jobs lined up, too."

"You will still be able to carry on, Felicia, you're a strong woman. I know you can."

I rose from the chair and said goodbye.

"Come back and visit me again, if you can."

I promised I would and set off to meet Dr. Sommers. I scanned the busy cafeteria and found Dr. Sommers at the far end. I bought a cup of tea and snaked my way to him, weaving in and out of crowded tables. He glanced up and did a double-take before he motioned to a chair.

"I thought you might not show up."

"The visit with Felicia went better than I hoped. She seems to be recovering."

"Indeed, she is. We, the doctors, are surprised by it. She's a tough and determined woman, that's for sure."

"Bossy, too," I added.

"Like someone else I know." He chuckled.

"You're right. I won't deny it. You might want to keep an eye on who goes in and out of her room. She knows things that make her vulnerable. Someone tried to kill her once, and they may have better luck next time."

"Are you sure the perpetrator was out to kill her?" Dr. Sommers murmured.

"After what she told me, yes, I think so. Has Sheriff Carver been by to see Felicia, at all?"

"Not that I'm aware of." He gazed across the noisy

room, his eyes fixed on someone, and I looked up to see Jack Carver walking this way. "Speak of the devil," he said.

Jack stood beside a chair until he was invited to join us. I remained silent as the two men greeted each other. Then, I asked, "What brings you in search of Dr. Sommers?"

"I wasn't looking for him. I was looking for you."

"Oh?"

"We have much to discuss—if you don't mind, that is."

I glanced at Dr. Sommers and said, "If you'd like, I can meet you at your office sometime."

He nodded.

"Right now," Jack insisted with a meaningful glare.

"Sure." I hadn't planned to leave just this minute, but it seemed Jack had to tell me what was on his mind, which left me with no choice but to do as he asked.

We left Dr. Sommers at the table. I followed Jack to the police station. My curiosity ratcheted up with every moment that passed. What was so important that he had to speak to me immediately? It didn't matter. I had much to impart, as well. I rolled to a stop next to his SUV and we entered headquarters together.

When he'd taken a seat behind his desk and I sat in one of the two in front of it, I waited.

"You visited Felicia?"

"I did."

"I wanted to go in to see her, but the nurse gave me a runaround, so I didn't. What did you two talk about?"

"She never saw who struck her, the house was trashed when she got there, and she was supposed to marry Frank Poland next year after they graduated."

"Is that all?"

I mentioned her connection to Della and said Felicia last saw the woman not too long a time before Della was murdered.

"Anything else?"

"Well, it would help if you'd ask outright what you want to know," I snapped and then heaved a sigh.

"Did she say why she worked at the hop?"

I studied Jack for a minute or two and then said, "Why ask me that? It's apparent you already know the answer."

"I want you to confirm what I've heard."

"She and her friends were caught with marijuana. Frank made the buy."

"Okay, who from?"

"Denton Clarke."

"That's what I wanted to hear. Why didn't she speak up, did she say?"

"They kept it between them for fear of retribution from Denton. It didn't matter, though, did it? Frank was killed and she was next on the list."

"Right."

"Are you going to arrest him?"

"I don't have any physical proof. Just hearsay." He pounded his fist on the desk. My bones rattled in the chair at his sudden explosive anger.

"Calm down, Jack. Together we can come up with a plan. We've done it before."

A knock on the door came just before Adam's entrance. I glanced at him, gave him an eye roll, and then settled in my chair again to face Jack.

He beckoned Adam to take the seat next to mine. I listened while they discussed the information I'd shared. Adam slanted a look my way and said, "You've been busy."

I nodded as Jack ordered an officer placed outside Felicia's room. "It's for her safety. If these cases are ever solved, I'll need her testimony. Put Jenkins and Anderson on the job. They're reliable and won't spend their time flirting with the staff."

"Yes, sir. Anything else?"

"Not now."

Adam left to carry out the assignment.

"Have any ideas popped into your overworked brain, yet?" Jack asked.

"Not yet. Give me time to think over the options. You wouldn't consider a drug buy using an undercover officer, would you?"

"Since none of them attend that college, it would be pretty risky to assign anyone at this point in the semester. We'll have to do better than that."

I rose and said I'd be in touch.

Chapter 26

Work at the farm rolled on well-greased wheels, with Jason assuming as much responsibility as he could fit into his school schedule. Molly's college classes were at the final-exam stage of the semester. Studying in between classes at the shop, she began to show the strain of holding onto the crazy schedule she had maintained these last few months.

"Why don't you take the evening off and get some rest? You're worn out."

"I have students coming tonight; they aren't spinning or weaving, or any of that. Instead, we'll discuss where they want to take their skills next. People become complacent as they advance and often take their knowledge for granted. For example, Meredith has thrived in this environment, but I've noticed she's a bit bored at times. She's ready for more challenging projects, though she's hesitant to take that step. By doing so, she tends to create the same thing over and over."

"You'll have your hands full if you try to convince her to do otherwise, you know."

"I'll handle her with kid gloves, and she'll think it's her idea." Molly snickered and then said, "Thanks for your concern. I only have two more exams before the semester ends. I can deal with it, don't you worry. My biggest decision concerns changing from my original study plan to an increased fiber arts program. My parents have agreed to support me in that, especially after they saw how successful the classes are. Now is the time for me to make it happen. I've finished my core classes and dallied with marketing. I don't know why I'm not jumping at the challenge."

"As I said before, you're tired. Make tonight an early one, dismiss the students after an hour or so, and get some rest. You're a straight-A student who shouldn't worry about exams. Now go—catch a nap before it's time for class, you'll feel better."

"You're beginning to sound like my mother. She goes on about burning a candle at both ends, whatever that is supposed to mean. I will take your advice, though. I'll be back in time for the students."

I watched her drive away and then addressed the rabbits' needs.

"How did it go with the sheriff?"

"He's very stressed. His boss must be on his back about the murders and Felicia's near-death experience. Jack lost his temper while we were talking and pounded his desk with his fist. Everything rattled, including my bones."

"Glad I wasn't there. You know how shaky I get

*around violence. Oh, did Felicia ever mention why she
was at Della's house?"*

"They were related, so she probably wanted the family
photographs or some such thing. She didn't say. It's conjecture on my part."

I freshened his water supply and added a lettuce leaf
wrap of raisins, grain pellets, and thin carrot shreds to his
bowl. "I'm going to give the other rabbits their snack. I'll
be in the barn when you're done."

He never said a word but munched his snack. Knowing Bun wouldn't want to miss a thing, I figured he'd
come join me as quickly as he could.

Quick to hand out the portions of goodies, I checked
the water levels of each container inside the cages attached to individual hutches. The job done, I returned to
the front of the barn when Bun raced through the breezeway, went past me, and on into the shop, where he skidded to a halt.

"Where's Molly?"

"I sent her home. She's exhausted and it shows. She'll
return for class tonight, don't worry. Why do you want to
see Molly?"

"Well, she gives me awesome treats."

"Oh, does she now?"

*"Can we take a bike ride? I could use some fresh air
and time with you."*

Bun intended to appease me over his wanting to see
Molly, but it wasn't a big deal to me. He just thought it
was. With a tiny grin, I agreed to the ride, and we set off
to retrieve the bike from the shed.

Comfy in his basket, I pedaled out of the driveway
onto the road and turned toward Lake Plantain. Bun's
nose wiggled as he caught scents while we rode along.

We coasted for a while, slowing when we'd reached the unlocked gate that stood wide open.

"I've noticed you aren't as physically involved in this investigation since you were attacked."

"I've decided to handle my own business instead of handling the sheriff's. Does that bother you?"

"I admit, I enjoy the edginess of sleuthing, but I do fear for your safety. I don't know what would happen to me or the other rabbits if you died. I'd be very sad."

"Let's not think in terms of death and dying. We're more aware than ever before of how we should handle ourselves, right?"

"Right. Let's go see the lodge."

"I'm not sure we should take a chance of being put-upon."

"That was a one-off. You know it's unlikely to happen a second time while we're here. Besides, rather than on the beach, we'll be in a different portion of the property."

I sighed a bit, rolled the bicycle past the gateposts, and slowly pedaled toward the lodge.

Imagine my surprise when I found an empty car in front of the building. The hairs on the back of my neck jittered, and my nerves whined like an off-key violin. Yep, we shouldn't have come.

"Hurry up, let's leave."

Quick to turn the bike toward the gate, I didn't move fast enough to avoid being caught out.

"You needn't leave," he said from the end of the porch.

I glanced over my shoulder at Alvin Peterson. I stopped short and faced him.

"Oh, Alvin, I didn't realize that was your car. How are you?"

"Well, thank you. Join me, won't you? It's such a nice day."

"Don't do it, just don't."

I glanced down at Bun and murmured softly. "Why?"

"I'm not sure, but danger lurks here. He's not a nice man, can't you see that by now?"

I leaned the bicycle against a tree and set Bun on the ground. "Come on, Bun." I urged him to slowly follow me up the front stairs of the lodge. As I drew closer, I noticed the coolness in Alvin's eyes. Why was he here? What was his purpose? Hmm.

His slight smile filled with what appeared to be melancholy, he said, "I've come to this place since I was a kid. It has a calming effect. Not that I need to calm down, but other old folks enjoy the soothing atmosphere that surrounds this lodge. Too bad a dead man was found here."

"You must mean Frank."

"Indeed, I do. He made a mistake."

"What kind of mistake?"

"He told someone a secret he had no right to share. It made him a target, and his girlfriend, too."

My nerves grew tighter and tighter by the second. If I wasn't careful, I might spring like an overwound pocket watch. My heart pounded. I was certain Bun realized it.

"Where did you hear that?"

"Around. People talk."

"What brings you out here if it isn't to unwind?"

"Take it slow, remain calm. We can outrun Alvin, you know. He's dangerous."

Alvin smirked and turned his now-cold gaze on me. "My time has just about run out. You see, you're too nosy for your own good. So is the sheriff, and Rob. Speaking of Rob, I'm thoroughly disappointed in him."

"Why is that?"

"He came to me with a story, but it wasn't true. I recently found out what he's really doing in Windermere, and that he's been talking to you. He has, hasn't he, Juliette?"

I shrugged. "We've spoken a few times, but he hasn't shared anything important with me, if that's what you're asking."

"I don't believe you. But then, you're quite adept at saying what you think people want to hear. Sheriff Carver's one of your biggest fans. He thinks you're amazing. Why, he even suggested you work at the hop. If I'd known that you'd be the one to find Della's body, I'd never have allowed you to participate. You've interfered in things that have nothing to do with you, and now I find I must take measures to correct that."

"You think I know something of value? Like what, Alvin?"

"You figured out the human rabbit you saw was one of my helpers, didn't you?"

I refused to utter a word, hoping he'd keep going.

"Take care, Jules."

I shuffled my feet on the step where Bun and I stood. A few more steps and I'd have reached the porch. I had stopped when Alvin started talking. Flight or fight, I'd have to choose flight. I had the advantage of youth and speed that Alvin didn't.

My plan fell apart when Alvin produced a gun. Oh, my.

"Be calm, we can handle this. Don't let him scare you. I'll jump off the steps and act like I'm running away."

I said nothing and didn't take my eyes off Alvin. The man's face and eyes were now like cold steel. My advantage meant nothing, nada, not a thing. What to do? I had no idea until Bun vaulted from the stairs and raced away.

"You scared my rabbit. Now, I'll never find him."

"You won't need to worry about that, not where you're going."

My hands on my hips, I stated, "I know nothing concerning anything you've said. If I did, by gosh, I'd admit it."

"That's a lie if I ever heard one. Your reputation for interference and figuring out who committed crimes is well known in Windermere. Because of your abilities, people end up in prison. I'll tell you right now, that won't happen to me."

"Why would it?"

"Because I killed Della Meeny, Frank Poland, and nearly finished off Felicia Brandt. They were in my way, you see. They knew too much."

My voice low, I asked, "What did they know?"

"That I'm a killer, and that I have a money-laundering scheme going."

My curiosity hiked to an all-time high level. I snorted and remarked, "In your dreams, maybe. I happen to know that Denton Clarke deals drugs and is in cahoots with the Eriksons, who launder money for him through their business." Fairly good at bluffing, I lifted my chin and glared at Alvin with what I hoped was a look of disbelief. It's tough to be wrong.

"Who do you think is the boss of all that? Not Denton Clarke, that's for sure. He doesn't have the brains for it, just enough greed to do as he's told."

If anyone had sworn on a stack of Bibles that Alvin was all the things he'd have me believe, I'd have called them an outright liar. Unfortunately, the man made sense, and it scared the bejeepers out of me. Gone was the man who played a convincing role as one of the shakers and doers in the community. I wondered how many others were tangled up in this scheme. "Before you kill me, I have to ask: What was the meaning behind the eggs surrounding Della and why leave lilies of the valley on her chest?"

He smirked. "I'm surprised you didn't figure it out. Della was mean and ugly. Those disgusting eggs were befitting. As for the flowers, I had been poisoning her for days when I added water that I soaked the flowers in. The poison leaks from the stems into the water. I mixed it with that stupid energy drink she always carried with her."

"I see."

"Walk down those stairs, and don't think you can run away, Juliette. I promise to shoot you if you make one wrong move."

I turned and slowly took one step at a time until I reached the ground. I'd raised my hands, praying Adam or Jack would come to see what was going on. With a last-ditch ending to the prayer, I begged for somebody, anybody, to rescue me.

I'd reached the path and was shoved toward the dock. Trees and foliage bordered the path as it widened. I continued my journey and dragged my feet in hope of coming up with a plan.

"I'm right behind Alvin. My superpowers are ready when you are. Give me a sign so we can take this guy down."

Bun would do his best, but it might get me killed. I'd gone past a huge, overgrown rhododendron bush and caught sight of movement. Unwilling to turn my head, I stumbled and slid my eyes as far to the side as possible and breathed in relief.

I'd taken a few steps past the bush and then turned to yell, "Now, Bun."

Bun flew from the ground, onto Alvin's back, his teeth snagging Alvin's shirt collar. Alvin's arm flew up in the air and the gun went off. Thankful the bullet didn't hit anyone, the next thing I knew, Alvin was face down in the dirt and was read his Miranda rights.

I gawked at the man who handcuffed my would-be killer. Rob Brayton dragged Alvin upright, shook him once or twice, and asked, "Do you understand your rights?"

Alvin's voice angry, he also seemed disheartened when he said, "I do."

Rob looked at me, then at Bun, who had leaped into my arms. "Are you all right?"

I nodded. "Are you?"

He nodded and pushed Alvin up the path toward the gate, where his car sat alongside Adam's police cruiser.

Adam strode toward us, purpose in every step. "You aren't hurt, are you, Juliette?"

"No, but I was worried there for a while. How did you guys know what was going on?"

"Rob learned Alvin was here from his secretary at the council office. I called the farm and got no answer so I came to the lake. The lake is your favorite spot, isn't it?"

I agreed, hugged Bun tightly to me, and then tucked him into his basket.

"Do you want a ride home? You'll need to come to the station to give a statement," Adam remarked.

"I'd rather ride the bicycle if you don't mind. I'll give my statement after I make sure Bun is okay."

He agreed and opened the rear cruiser door for Alvin. Once Alvin was seated, Adam took off for headquarters.

"Are you sure you want to ride that bike back to your farm? You've had quite a scare, you know, and what's with the rabbit? He acted upon your command."

"He's a smart rabbit. We're best buds, huh, Bun?"

"And I'm brilliant, too."

I ruffled his fur and laughed out loud. Only I could hear him, and as secrets go, it was mine. "Truly, I'd rather ride the bike home. Before I go, tell me who you are?"

"I'm an FBI agent. I've followed the drugs and money for quite a while. I'm certainly not as young as people think, but young enough to pass myself off as a post-graduate student. Too bad about Frank and Della Meeny. For a while, I thought Della might be involved, but the woman was honest—mean, but honest."

"Do you know why Felicia went to the house and why Alvin attacked her?"

"She said it was to pick up photos of the family that her mother wanted. Felicia was in the wrong place at the wrong time. Alvin must have thought he'd killed her. She was fortunate."

"Indeed. I'll see you at the station later on. Does Jack Carver know about you?"

"He didn't know, but I'm sure he will before long. Adam knows."

I walked the bike onto the road and pedaled home, all the while praising Bun for saving me from certain death.

He seemed to hear me, but didn't say a word. Until we got home.

"We make a great duo, don't we? I mean, we've got crime-fighting down to a science. Maybe we should open a detective agency. What do you say?"

"Not in a million years, Bun. And, I know that I won't live that long."

"If you change your mind, I'm on board with the idea. Just think of a sign that says 'The Bun and Jules Detective Agency.'"

That was absolutely out of the question. I'd come closer to death during this investigation than any of the others we'd been involved in before. The farm was my safe haven. Never would I consider such an agency, and I said so.

Bun sighed, then said he'd visit with his rabbit friends and went into the barn while I drove to the police station. Directed to Jack's office by the officer at the front desk, I saw Adam and Rob discussing something that upset Jack. I figured his attitude was due to the discovery of Rob, the FBI agent.

I tapped the door window. All talk halted when Jack beckoned me in.

"Hey, Jack."

"You knew all along, didn't you?" Jack accused.

Indignant, I answered him. "I did not. It wasn't until the event at the farm that I realized Rob was more than he seemed. I confronted him, but he denied it, quite convincingly, too."

Rob smirked and interrupted me. "Not as convincingly as I thought. You knew, somehow."

Jack remarked, "This woman has a sixth sense. I'm telling you, she can figure things out faster than anyone I know. I've mentioned that she should be a detective, but I'm glad she continues to reject the idea."

"All that said, I'm here to give my statement." Kudos were nice, but enough was enough. The idea was ludicrous, to me, at least. I had a farm to run, needed to help

Jessica move into her new home, had Bun to keep up with, and a shop to enlarge.

The men stared through the windows of Jack's office as Denton Clarke, the Eriksons, the college dean, and a few unfamiliar people were taken to the cells in handcuffs.

"What do you think of that?" Jack asked.

"Well, I don't think Denton's sister will want me to bring my rabbits to her daughter's birthday party."

We all laughed, and then sobered before getting down to the business of giving statements. Jack had more proof than he thought possible, which would lead to prison terms for many, especially Alvin.

Done with the investigation and relieved to have survived once again, I turned my thoughts toward home, Bun, and all the rabbits. My life was just the way I liked it.

Don't ever let it be said the universe isn't listening, because it is. Whether it be God, or the universe itself, something out there hears our requests and complies.

Connect with

Us

Visit us online at
KensingtonBooks.com
to read more from your favorite authors, see books
by series, view reading group guides, and more.

for sneak peeks, chances to win books and prize packs,
and to share your thoughts with other readers.

facebook.com/kensingtonpublishing
twitter.com/kensingtonbooks

Tell us what you think!

To share your thoughts, submit a review,
or sign up for our eNewsletters, please visit:
KensingtonBooks.com/TellUs.

Grab These Cozy Mysteries from
Kensington Books

Available Wherever Books Are Sold!

All available as e-books, too!

Visit our website at **www.kensingtonbooks.com**